ACCLAIM FOR *THE SECRET TO HUMMINGBIRD CAKE*

"The book starts out as chick lit but then takes a sharp turn on the genre and gives us something much more . . . a real look at the kind of remarkable female friendships that so many of us experience in real life but few books ever capture. I laughed and I wept, and readers will too. Wow."

—Linda Stasi, Columnist *New York Daily News*, author of *The Sixth Station* as well as six nonfiction books, TV Commentator for NY1, (What A Week)

"A delightful, heartwarming, and heart wrenching story that captures the beauty and essence of living in a small, southern town. A must read for ALL girls, 18 to 80."

—Ladies Southern Lit Society

"McHale's debut novel is such an amazing surprise. Just when you think you've heard this song before, the music changes. It will make you laugh out loud and make you cry and stay with you long after the read is done. All in all, a brilliant raw look at life."

—Melissa Grego, Editor-In-Chief at *Broadcasting & Cable*

"McHale's magnificently penned novel is a story which demonstrates the power of genuine female friendships. The writing is sharp, fresh, and delivered to the reader with finesse and humor . . . a remarkable debut novel that is a must read for all who sincerely believe true friendship is a gift to be treasured."

—MK Torrance, Goodreads Master Reviewer

"Highly recommend this book to bookclubs everywhere. In a world where fake friendship is celebrated, it was most refreshing to read a story that defines what true friendship really is."

—The Dallas Dozen Bookclub

"Finally! A REAL story about REAL friendship! Get the tissues ready . . . for the happy tears and sad ones too."

—Grant Junior League

THE
SECRET
TO
HUMMINGBIRD
CAKE

CELESTE FLETCHER McHALE

THOMAS NELSON
Since 1798

Published in Nashville, Tennessee, by Thomas Nelson. Thomas Nelson is a registered trademark of HarperCollins Christian Publishing, Inc.

Thomas Nelson titles may be purchased in bulk for educational, business, fund-raising, or sales promotional use. For information, please e-mail SpecialMarkets@ThomasNelson.com.

Publisher's Note: This novel is a work of fiction. Names, characters, places, and incidents are either products of the author's imagination or used fictitiously. All characters are fictional, and any similarity to people living or dead is purely coincidental.

Library of Congress Cataloging-in-Publication Data

McHale, Celeste Fletcher, 1961-
 The secret to hummingbird cake / Celeste Fletcher McHale.
 pages cm
 Summary: "Southern charm, hilarity, heart-wrenching emotion, and the remarkable bond of friendship. Carrigan, Ella Rae, and Laine have been friends since kindergarten, since the day Ella Rae beat up a boy who tried to pick on Laine. They all still live in the small town of Bon Dieu Falls, Louisiana, and they've been through everything together, from a State Softball Championship to Carrigan's elopement at seventeen. And Laine is still trying to keep the other two out of trouble.But when cancer threatens to rip the trio apart, their world spins in a way they've never known before. How deep do the bonds of friendship go? Through it all, they just may discover the secret to the divine taste of hummingbird cake--and the secret to a friendship that never ends"-- Provided by publisher.
 ISBN 978-0-7180-3956-1 (paperback)
 1. Friendship--Fiction. I. Title.
 PS3613.C4998S48 2016
 813'.6--dc23
 2015032143

Printed in the United States of America

16 17 18 19 20 21 RRD 6 5 4 3 2 1

For Lynn and Richard, who were my friends . . . and so much more.

Chapter One

I glanced at the grandfather clock. Almost midnight. I padded across the dark hardwood floor of my living room to peer out the window.

Again.

Where *was* he? Just as I reached for the curtain, the phone rang and I nearly jumped out of my skin. Somewhere in the background, I heard my long-gone grandmother asking, "Guilty conscience?"

I'd certainly been nursing one of those lately.

I looked at the caller ID. A man, but not the one I was looking for. The familiar pang of remorse punched me in the belly. I'd brought this on myself, and what was I supposed to do about Cell Phone Romeo now?

"What are you doing?" came a voice behind me.

I jumped. "Good Lord, Laine, don't you ever knock?"

She plopped down on my sofa. "Come on, Carrigan. I'm your best friend. I've been living across the street from you forever. Why start knocking now? And why did you look like a deer in headlights when I walked in?"

I shrugged. No sense in bringing up issues that would send her into one of her classic tizzies. "I don't know, just jumpy, I guess. I tend to get that way when somebody breaks into my house in the middle of the night. What are you doing still up?"

"I had to make a cake for the bake sale tomorrow," she said. "I've been so busy today. I just got the layers in the oven. Your lights were on, so I decided to kill that fifty minutes over here."

My mouth watered. I could taste the creamy white icing and the sweet pineapple. "One of *those* cakes?"

"Yes, one of those cakes."

"I could help you."

"Nice try." She winked.

"Why won't you tell me what's in that cake?" I had to ask the question, even though I knew it would do no good. I'd been trying to get Laine's recipe for years. We all had.

"Because it's not your business, and if I told you, you wouldn't believe me." She sat back and crossed her arms. "Now, give. Why were you so antsy when I came in?"

I avoided her gaze. "No reason."

She picked up my new *Southern Living* magazine and flipped through the pages. "Okay, that's fine," she said. "I'll just read about the geraniums in—" She stopped abruptly as the light bulb went off. I could almost see the glow above her head. It might have been comical had I not known what was going to happen next.

She threw the magazine on the table, and the previously

mentioned tizzy commenced. "It was him, wasn't it? I heard your phone ringing when I was on the porch. It was him!"

The way she said "him" would make an innocent bystander believe the devil himself was calling me. And that assessment might not be too far from the truth.

I winced. "Yes, it was him," I said. "But I didn't answer the phone. I haven't answered his calls all week. It isn't my fault."

"Oh, it never is your fault, is it?" she asked. "This is a bad situation, Carrigan, bad, bad, bad." She began pacing. "I can't believe you got yourself into this."

"Okay, I know it's an . . . uncomfortable situation, but it's been over for weeks. He's just having some trouble letting go. I can handle it." I hoped telling her this would calm her a little. Or maybe a lot.

She stopped pacing and glared at me. "Are you kidding me?"

Clearly I had said the wrong thing. She had no intention of being calm. I braced myself for the scolding and/or lecture.

Laine put her hands on her hips. "Let's just examine that statement, shall we?"

I recognized the content immediately. At least the suspense was over and I knew I'd be dining on the lecture portion of my best bud's verbal buffet tonight.

"You always do this, Carrigan," she said. "You dive off into things and never consider the consequences. You flirt with disaster. You walk right up to the edge of the cliff and teeter there until somebody yanks you back to firm ground. Don't you know that one day you'll go over? This has got to stop! It's time to grow up. No, it's past time to grow up."

I sighed. It wasn't that she was wrong, I just didn't want to hear it. I searched for the pacifier. "I know. You are right. I'll do better, I promise."

"No," she said, "don't you dare do that!"

"Do what?" I tried to sound innocent, but I knew I was busted.

"You know that thing you do when you say what you think I want to hear so I will shut up. I've known you a long time, Carrigan. I know your tricks."

Ouch. There were some distinct disadvantages to having your conscience living directly across the street.

I took a breath and tried to choose my words carefully. "Look," I said. "I know I did a really stupid thing . . . and believe me, I'm not proud of it. But I had my reasons."

"Oh, Carrigan, stop! Jack is not having an affair. And even if he were, it doesn't give you a free ticket to do the same thing. Nobody can make you do anything. Your choices are your own."

She might as well have thrown a lit match into a gas can. "Do you ever get altitude sickness from the moral high ground, Laine? What's the view like from up there? 'Cause we can't all be saints, you know."

I was furious with Laine. She had seen me fret, worry, and agonize over my husband for the past year. At some point all that emotion finally turned into defiance. That shouldn't be difficult for anyone to understand. Especially a best friend. She should want me to be happy, shouldn't she? Isn't that the job description for a best friend—hide the bodies and encourage the bliss?

Our other best friend and my partner in crime, Ella Rae Weeks, didn't care what I did, what I said, or who I said it to. She wanted me to be happy. Period. The end.

Laine, on the other hand, wanted us to get baptized once a week, run a soup kitchen, volunteer at the local day care, and neuter dogs on the kitchen table in our spare time.

Laine was talking again, this time in her subdued voice. "All I meant was, this is not a competition. You forget that sometimes."

Remorse washed over me. I had hurt her, and that was the last thing on earth I'd ever intentionally do. "Sorry."

"It's okay, Carri," she said. "I . . . just want what's best for you."

"I know," I said.

And I did.

CHAPTER TWO

Ella Rae and I met Laine on the playground when we were five years old. She moved to our little town of Bon Dieu Falls, Louisiana, when her daddy got transferred from his job as a state policeman to the troop that served our area. Even at five, a small-town girl in the South has learned to be suspicious of newcomers. You're either born here, married to someone from here, or your grandparents live here. You don't just show up out of the blue.

But the Landrys did. They could've gone to Natchitoches or Alexandria, both fairly large towns within forty-five miles of Bon Dieu Falls. Instead, they moved here. And a dark cloud of suspicion moved with them.

I knew this because I eavesdropped on my teacher talking to another teacher about it. "It's positively strange," she said. The other teacher agreed. These people were not to be trusted. I was intrigued.

So the very first day Laine arrived in our kindergarten class,

Ella Rae and I recruited her to become a part of our posse. I remember the whole thing like it was yesterday. Ella Rae, in a bad paisley dress, with an even worse haircut she'd given herself, voiced some skepticism at first. "My daddy says them people are strange," she said. "What they doing here?"

But that day at recess one of the Thompson boys pushed Laine down and made her break her glasses. Ella Rae ran over to him and popped him with her fist. Laine had been on board with us from that day forward.

Befriending her turned out to be one of our better decisions, and those were sometimes few and far between.

Laine had been the "good girl" of our trio since that very first day. Even when that Thompson boy ran off with a bloody nose, Laine said, "I hope you didn't hurt him."

Ella Rae looked at her like she was crazy. "I was *trying* to hurt him," she said.

I agreed with Ella Rae.

And that pretty much explained the way all three minds had worked in this posse for the past twenty-five years. Isn't it funny how you can remember certain parts of your life that made it better . . . or worse . . . in such vivid detail, no matter how young you were when the memory was made?

"Where is Jack, by the way?" Laine asked.

I snapped back into the present. "Who knows?" I said. "And I know you don't agree, but my guess is . . . he's leaned up against a bar stool somewhere trying to coax a phone number out of a bleached blonde with big hair and bigger . . . assets."

I reached into the refrigerator, came up with a bottle of wine, and waved it in Laine's direction. "Want some?"

"Yuck," she said.

I don't know why I even asked.

"You're wrong, Carrigan," she said. "I don't believe for a minute that Jack is out chasing another woman."

"Then where is he?" When she didn't answer, I said, "I don't know either. But he sure isn't here. Even when he's *here*, he isn't here."

I stood in front of my grandmother's china cabinet and took out one of the crystal wine glasses. Then I put it back and closed the door. Who was I kidding? I fetched a plastic stadium cup from the kitchen and started pouring.

"You think you got enough?" Laine said.

I took a huge swallow and waited a second before I answered. "Nope, I guess not." The taste made me shudder. The truth was, I hated wine. Didn't matter if it was five hundred dollars a bottle or three bucks at the local bait shop, the stuff was equally disgusting to me. But tonight I needed something to take the edge off. I chugged down another huge gulp. It was awful.

"That's not going to help," Laine said.

I made a face and swallowed. "It ain't gonna hurt."

"Tell me that in the morning."

She probably had a point, but that ship had already sailed.

"You know, it's none of my business what you drink or how much you drink—"

"But that's not gonna stop the freight train of your opinion, is it?"

"Aren't we grumpy tonight?" She ignored the dig and kept right on going. "What I was going to say, before you so rudely interrupted, is that we have to be at the ballpark at eight in the morning."

"No," I said. "You have to be at the ball park at eight in the morning. I don't play until one."

"It wouldn't hurt you to show up beforehand," Laine said. "I mean, this is a great cause. You need to show your support."

"I'll be there on time." I tried to shoot her a withering glance, but the wine was already making me fuzzy. "And stop trying to handle me. You know I hate that."

"No one can handle you, Carrigan. I'd sooner try to handle a porcupine."

"Was that a jab at my hair?" I tried to smooth the wild red curls away from my face.

She laughed. "No," she said, "it was a jab at your attitude."

"'Bye, 'bye now." I walked around the bar and grabbed her arm. "You have a cake to see about."

"Are you throwing me out?"

"No, I am making sure you get across the street before the serial killers come out."

"Because that's such a huge problem in Bon Dieu Falls," she said.

"You never know where those Thompson boys are." I opened the door and gave her a gentle nudge.

When I finally got her onto the porch, she turned around and looked at me. "Don't drink the whole bottle."

"I thought what I drank was none of your business," I said. "And besides, this ain't Ella Rae you're talking to."

She rolled her eyes. "Might as well be."

"Go on, go home," I said. "I'll watch you."

She walked down the steps but kept talking over her shoulder. "I am a grown woman, Carrigan. I can walk across the street."

"You got lost in the mall last week, Laine," I said.

"Not my fault," she called back. "They move stores around all the time. You better put that bottle up and go to bed. You need to stop this. It's time to face your problems instead of putting a Band-Aid on them." She never missed a beat.

She said all kinds of other stuff, too, but I turned her off. It was the exact same song and dance she performed after any of my slightly off decisions. I pretty much had the playbook memorized. I watched her walk across the street and into her yard. She waved as she closed the side door to her kitchen. I lay down on my sofa and sipped some more liquid Band-Aid. Laine was right, of course. This wasn't helping. She was probably right about everything she'd said.

But that didn't make me like it. Laine had always adored Jack, even though he'd cheated on me. At least I was relatively sure he'd been unfaithful. Laine took up for him, always insisted that he loved me and encouraged me to hang on and keep trying. But what good was trying if you were the only one making an effort?

She was *my* best friend. She and Ella Rae were the anchors in my now rocky life. Ella Rae never encouraged me to stay with Jack. She didn't care what I did as long as I was happy. Why did Laine insist that I stay? A better question: *How* could Laine insist that I stay?

I drank more wine and laid my head back. Laine frustrated me. She made me mad. And above all, she hurt my feelings. She was choosing Jack over me—there was no question about it. She might have thought she was helping me, but she wasn't. I consoled myself with the fact that she didn't understand because she'd never been in a relationship. Not a long-term one, anyway. She had no idea how twisted and complicated things got years into a marriage. Even if you still loved each other, sometimes that just wasn't enough. And if I were completely honest with myself, I wasn't even sure Jack and I had that left. We seemed like two stars that once burned so bright and brilliant, and now the only thing left was an ash so fine you could only see it when the sun streamed through the windows. I made a face at my own morose thoughts. Well, *that* was depressing

The phone rang again, and my shame meter shot up the charts. No one knew about Cell Phone Romeo except Laine, Ella Rae, and me. For that I was grateful, but I still carried a huge weight of guilt and shame about my indiscretion.

What a stupid word. *Indiscretion.* That's what all the blue bloods, including my family, called an affair. Why didn't they just call it what it was? One huge, idiotic mistake caused by an enormous amount of plain old ordinary hurt. Only there was nothing ordinary about it.

And when I was alone, I allowed myself to feel it. When I thought about the relationship I'd had with Romeo, it made me want to throw up. Because the truth was, I loved Jack—so much that I sometimes physically ached. I still loved him with that wild and crazy passion that had brought us together in the beginning.

And as close as I was to Laine and Ella Rae, I couldn't bring myself to tell them that. As far as they knew, I was ready to divorce him and move on. In reality, nothing could be further from the truth. If I searched for a hundred years, I'd never love another man the way I loved Jack.

But my pride wouldn't let me show it. To anybody. So I found a way to hide it with an attitude, an . . . indiscretion, and a terribly disgusting bottle of—I glanced at the label—Flaming Peach Mist. I was pretty sure the finer homes in the great state of Louisiana weren't serving that same bottle on their hundred-year-old linens. But it was getting the job done in Bon Dieu Falls. And I had the tingly hands to prove it.

Sometimes lately I ripped a page from the Scarlett O'Hara playbook and decided I wouldn't think about unpleasant things today. I'd think about them tomorrow. This was one of those times. I took my wine into the bedroom and glanced at the bedside clock. One a.m. Do you know where your husband is? I took another drink, clicked the remote to an infomercial promising to make me look younger than my thirty years, and stripped. The sheets felt good against my skin. I was asleep in thirty seconds, the concerns of the day drowned in sweet, fermented grapes.

CHAPTER THREE

Ella Rae showed up at the crack of dawn. Actually, it was the crack of noon. It just felt like dawn. Laine had been right, as usual. I shouldn't have finished the Flaming Peach Mist. Yet another fine decision . . . I was becoming quite fluent in idiot.

Ella Rae didn't care what kind of shape I was in. "Get up!" she shouted. She held the empty wine bottle over my head. "I bet this was just delicious."

The sight of the bottle made me want to gag. "Ugh." I turned over and wrapped my head up in my pillow. "I can't play softball today," I said. "I'll die. I'm not going."

She ripped the covers from me. "Oh, yes, you are going," she said. "And put some clothes on. Nobody wants to see . . . all that."

I tugged the cover back over my body. "You've seen me naked maybe a thousand times," I said. "I can't play today. I just can't."

"Seeing all your business when you get in and out of the

tanning bed ain't the same thing," she said. "And nobody dies from a hangover. Go barf if you need to, but hurry up!"

I lay motionless. "Two more minutes."

"Whatever." Then she changed directions completely, a classic Ella Rae trait. "Did Romeo call again last night? Tell me everything."

That made me sit straight up. "Where is Jack?"

"He left as soon as he let me in. Do you think I'm crazy? Asking about Cell Phone Romeo with Jack in the next room?"

So he had come home last night. I glanced over and saw that his side of the bed was rumpled. He had slept here, but I had no idea for how long.

Ella Rae reached into the suitcase she called a purse, pulled out an ancient Rubik's Cube, and began twisting it. "This thing annoys me."

I shook my head. Ella Rae's attention span was three to five seconds long. Shorter if alcohol was involved.

"Thank God Jack is gone," I said. "I thought maybe you'd switched over to Laine's team." I looked around. "Where is Laine?"

"She had to be there at eight this morning, remember? She's keeping score."

"Oh yeah. I think she mentioned that as she was delivering the sermon last night. I love her, God knows I do, but she's so . . . responsible."

Ella Rae laughed. "One of us has to be." She walked to my dresser and began fishing for clothes. She threw a pair of panties at me that hit me in the face. "Get in the shower and hurry. I'll find you something to put on."

I stood up and groaned. The Peach Mist was indeed flaming this morning. Wine had to dispense the absolute worst hangover ever. What was I thinking?

I shook my head. Not the first time I'd asked myself that same question in the last few months.

"Ten minutes, I promise." But as soon as I got in the shower, I stood still in the hot spray. It felt too good to move.

"Hurry up," Ella Rae said and slapped the shower curtain.

"I am hurrying," I said.

"Liar," she said. "You're standing in one spot trying to recover. Now hurry up!"

"Fine." I grabbed the shampoo bottle.

Today's softball tournament was a benefit for a five-year-old boy in our community who had recently been diagnosed with leukemia. His name was Dakota. Sweetest little guy in the world. Ella Rae, Laine, and I had gone to high school with his parents. Good people. Laine had helped put this tournament together. Thankfully, Dakota's prognosis was excellent, but the frequent trips to St. Jude's Children's Hospital in Memphis were taking a financial toll on his family. Most of the expenses of the immediate family were covered by St. Jude's. But where we come from, your immediate family included aunts, uncles, cousins, that one guy who came for the summer five years earlier and never left, and your crazy Great-Aunt Doris who really needed to be in a home but just continued to sit on the front porch under the watchful eye of family and neighbors.

All the proceeds of today's tournament would go directly to Dakota's family to help with their travel expenses. That was one of the perks of living in a small Southern town. Among other things, we came to each other's aid. Bon Dieu Falls, Louisiana, was no different. When one of our own was in trouble, we showed up. We baked, we babysat, and we gave cars, time, and money. Nobody could ever accuse us of being unfeeling or uncaring.

But the flip side of that coin applied as well. Your personal business was also everybody else's. The old adage, "When I don't know what I'm doing, somebody else always does," fit Bon Dieu Falls like a glove.

For a girl like me, that was sometimes quite annoying. Not that I was a wild child. I was no child at all. But I was, well, busy. I was thirty years old, but every time someone asked my age, my immediate thought was "seventeen."

I often wondered why I got stuck there in the first place. Maybe it was because I had married Jack when I was seventeen. Maybe I felt permanently trapped there, holding my breath waiting for my life to begin again. And perhaps the years in between were just really long seconds, and one day I would exhale again and turn thirty.

CHAPTER FOUR

Jack Whitfield III was ten years my senior. His family owned and operated Whitfield Farms, a hugely successful soybean farm and cattle ranch. He was extremely handsome, and his seemingly cool and detached attitude made him all the more attractive. He was considered the catch of the town for years, but no one could seem to make him commit or tie him down for long.

Maybe the reason I succeeded with Jack was because I wasn't trying. At least not in the beginning. But the truth was, Jack had intrigued me long before we ever really talked. The boys my own age bored me. I loved them all as friends, but romantically, they offered me nothing even remotely interesting. I wanted a man, not a boy.

Enter Jack.

And to add fuel to the fire, I was a bit rebellious in my teenage years. Okay, I was a lot rebellious in my teenage years. I just liked to test my limits no matter what I was doing. With grades, ignoring curfews, ignoring expectations. I felt . . .

different. That's about as well as I can explain it. Like the rules didn't really apply to me. Not in an "I am better than you" kind of way, more like in a "that rule is stupid" kind of way.

I had a hard time relating to people who just accepted all their restrictions without question. I had always been able to talk my way out of any situation I found myself in. That itself made me feel out of step with the world around me. While everyone else seemed to struggle to find their voice, words flew out of my mouth at the speed of light. That wasn't always a good thing, but it was pretty much always an effective thing. I never understood what was so difficult about just saying whatever was on your mind. But sometimes folks looked at me like I was an alien, even though I thought it made me determined. I wanted results, and I wanted them immediately. Regardless, I'm not sure my parents found the outspoken trait quite as endearing as Jack Whitfield III had found it. He told me once it was what had made me irresistible to him.

It goes without saying, but I'll say it anyway: Mama and Daddy were less than pleased when I announced I was dating a man ten years my senior, especially one whose womanizing reputation preceded him. They were always cordial when he came to the house to see me or to pick me up. But they didn't like it, not one little bit.

They reminded me often of the age difference between us and the problems that went along with that. They said I liked the idea of a relationship with Jack much more than I liked Jack. Then one night, after yet another round with Daddy, he told me Jack Whitfield III "had a way with women."

That made me laugh, and I said, "I certainly hope so."

My father was furious with that answer, and an argument ensued. Daddy ended the argument by saying he forbade me to see Jack again. He might as well have told me not to breathe. I failed to mention the argument to Jack. Looking back, I am sure he would've done the honorable thing and backed off. But I wasn't about to let somebody else tell me how to live my life. Not even my parents. As much as I loved them, this was *my* life.

For the next couple of weeks, I got pretty slick about hiding my relationship with Jack from them. On the Friday exactly two weeks after I had gotten the I-forbid-you-to-see-him speech from my daddy, Jack and I picked up Ella Rae and Laine, drove to Texas, found a Justice of the Peace, and got married. I had managed to con Jack into believing that my parents, while they weren't happy about it, had consented to the elopement. He questioned me, of course, but I told him they understood what we were doing, but didn't want to be a part of it. I even produced the proper legal document showing my father's signature allowing me to do so.

It was forged, of course, but Jack didn't know that. I know that sounds just awful, but I loved this man, and I knew my parents would too if they just gave him a chance. If I came back married, they'd have no choice but to accept him. And then, I reasoned, we could all live happily ever after.

Jack had wanted to talk to my father face-to-face, but I had convinced him it was unnecessary and unwelcome. "Let's just go," I said. "Don't make it any harder than it has to be. He'll just try to talk us out of it. Don't you want to marry me?"

"Not like this, Carrigan."

It had taken quite a performance, one that surely warranted an Academy Award. But in the end, I won.

Ella Rae had been on board immediately. It took a little coaxing for Laine. At first she had absolutely refused to be a part of it. She had been mortified at the prospect of deceiving Jack and my parents. But then again, Laine felt bad if she gave the dog the cheap biscuits.

Finally she realized if she were the only one of us left in town that weekend, she'd cave in to the questions immediately. So, rather than face the firing squad alone, she reluctantly climbed on board. I'm pretty sure she prayed all the way to Texas. For years afterward, she had apologized to Jack for being part of the deception, but he always smiled and told her the same thing: "Laine, my wife could sell ice to the Eskimos. Let it go."

After a three-minute wedding and a honeymoon the next day at a huge Texas water park, Ella Rae and I felt grown-up and superior and extremely adventurous. We were all quite pleased with ourselves. Except for Laine, who bit her fingernails and wrung her hands for three days.

I have to admit, her paranoia was right on the money. When we got home, there was a big ole small-town mess waiting on all of us. My parents were infuriated and threatened to have Jack arrested because for another week, I was still seventeen. Jack was livid with me for lying to him, and his parents were mortified over all of it. Laine's mother threatened to break off Laine's arm and beat her with it, and Ella

Rae's mother glared at her for thirty straight minutes before she ever said a word.

It was most unpleasant. Every adult in the kitchen of my parents' house was sure I was pregnant, no matter how many times I denied it. Lots of tears. Lots of yelling. Followed by lots of silence. Then more yelling. I can clearly remember my father's clenched jaw being inches away from Jack's face demanding him to explain why he'd agreed to my scheme. But Jack stayed calm and never offered an excuse other than, "I love her, sir. I love her."

That memory still makes me smile.

At the end of a very long night, futility set in. To this day, I feel bad as I recall the resignation on my father's face. He was only trying to do what he thought was best for me. But he could never tell me no. So in the end they relented, although they did insist that we have a small and proper wedding the next weekend in our church.

Jack was pretty unhappy with me for a few days. In fact, he was flat-out furious. I wasn't entirely sure he'd show up at church the next Friday night, but he did. And he looked so good standing at the end of the aisle waiting for me, I almost ran to him.

We settled into our new home on my eighteenth birthday, and life was beautiful. We were young and happy and in control of our lives. Our house was the hangout in town for all our friends, and they were there nearly twenty-four hours a day. Jack adored me, couldn't get enough of me, and catered to my every whim.

He said I made him laugh . . . in the beginning . . .

"Let's *go*, Carrigan!" Ella Rae shouted. "We play in thirty minutes!"

I snapped out of my dream trance and threw on a pair of cutoffs. "I'm ready."

"Get your bat and glove."

"Already in the car," I said. "I anticipated my condition this morning, so I loaded all my stuff last night."

She beamed at me as if I'd won the Nobel Prize for Good Thinking. "Good call!"

I chuckled. Ella Rae woke up in a new world every morning.

The ball park was a three-minute drive from my house. Ella Rae and I usually jogged there and back every morning while Laine rode circles around us on her bike. A ritual we had practiced for years, rain or shine, hot or cold. We had also played softball at this park since we were five years old. Laine had kept the scorebook since she was old enough to figure it out. She wasn't *athletically inclined*, as she liked to put it. Ella Rae and I called it "lazy."

Laine didn't care what we called her. She wasn't about to give up her comfortable chair, the huge purple-and-gold tail-gating tent she sat under, the soft quilt under her feet, or her cutesy flip-flops for cleats, dirt, and sweat on the field. She liked everything to be neat, clean, and shiny. In fact, if we rode in her car after games, she made us sit on towels and take off our shoes. Which explains why her car was spotless and my truck was, well, a hot mess.

As soon as we arrived, I dragged my chair under Laine's tent and hid from the sun.

"And how do you feel this morning?" Laine asked.

I closed my eyes behind my dark sunglasses. "I know you're going to enjoy this," I said. "Go ahead, jab me."

"Oh, I'm not going to jab you," she said. "You slept a total of eight hours and I slept a total of four. I'm too exhausted to jab you."

Ahhh . . . classic Laine. She could have been a travel agent for guilt trips. "I owe you one," I said.

"You owe me about a hundred and twenty, but who's counting?" Finally she broke into a real smile. "It's fine," she said, then lowered her voice. "When did Jack get home?"

"Who knows?"

"It isn't what you think, Carrigan. I'm sure it isn't."

"So you've stated." I put my glove over my face. There was no way I was getting into an argument with Laine this morning. I barely had enough stamina to sit upright in this chair. If she wanted to spar, she was going to have to do it by herself. And what was that stench coming from the canteen? Cotton candy? Pure, hot, sticky sugar? Wine historically gave me liquid courage at night and horrendous nausea the next day. I fought the urge to gag and took a sip of my bottled water.

"Hey, Miss Landry!" I heard a small child say.

"Hey, King!" Laine answered.

Oh crap, a Thompson offspring. Would they never stop reproducing? You couldn't go anywhere in Bon Dieu Falls without tripping over a Thompson. And who names their child "King" anyway? He was stirring greasy nachos with his grubby little fingers. I had to look away.

"Whatcha doin'?" He flung half his cheese mixture onto the quilt.

My gag reflex went from zero to sixty in a second. Those grimy fingers and that greasy cheese coupled with the cotton candy smell from the canteen was about to make me projectile vomit.

"I'm just keeping score," Laine said. "What are you doing?"

"I'm just watching my daddy play ball," he said. He grinned at her as he swiped at the cheese on his chin.

"Okay, Prince, Deuce, Ace," I said, "whatever your name is, shoo! Run away!" I scooted back in my chair.

"'Bye!" he shouted as he ran off.

"Carrigan!" Laine said. "That was so rude! He is a child!"

"Yes," I said. "A Thompson child. Trust me, he's seen and heard worse."

"Hey, y'all!" A saccharine drawl greeted us. I looked up to see bleached hair so bright it nearly blinded me.

Bethany Wilkes. If this didn't finish me off, nothing would.

Her hair was too blonde, her lips were too red, her fingernails were too long, and her boobs were too fake. "Missiles," as my girls and I referred to them. How did you even get your boobies to point like that? Were there special bras for that? Was that actually Victoria's secret?

Besides that, I had never once seen her with a pair of shoes on that I liked. I glanced at her feet. Today was no exception. Were those feathers? I rolled my eyes behind my sunglasses.

Bethany Wilkes wanted Jack so badly she could taste it, and everybody in Bon Dieu Falls knew it, including me.

Especially me.

I wasn't entirely sure she hadn't already had him. The curiosity was killing me. But for now, all I had was speculation, no proof. If I accused her, it would make me seem weak and insecure. If I accused him, it would make it seem like I cared. So I watched and waited all the time for my "gotcha" moment. Until then, I had to force myself to be cordial. I kicked at the nacho cheese on the quilt and smiled broadly at Bethany.

"Hi, Bethany." I used my friendliest voice. "How's it going?"

"It's just going great!" She smiled, revealing her huge and snow-white teeth. "How are you ladies?"

"It's all good." I smiled and looked away. I didn't want to encourage any sort of communication other than niceties.

I could see Laine wiggling in her seat and trying not to laugh, which was her reaction to anything uncomfortable. And I was glad Ella Rae was already in the dugout, because she would have glared and done that snarly thing with her lip, which was *her* reaction to anything uncomfortable.

"How's your new job?" Laine asked. I could've kicked her. Perfect, now we're having a conversation.

"Oh, it's the best job," she said. "I just don't know how they survived until I got there. Between us, those books were a mess!"

What? She worked part-time at a small bakery in the next town. They couldn't possibly sell more than ten cupcakes a day. How bad could the books be? Was somebody missing a quarter? But on the other hand, I sincerely hoped she would eat her way through the summer. She was much thinner than I was, and I only weighed a hundred and twenty pounds.

Did this chick eat at all? Probably all the time. Another reason to be annoyed at her. I wanted to drag her out to the parking lot and beat the crap out of her, but she'd probably even bleed cute.

"Oh? Well, bless your heart. They are lucky to have you, Bethany." I smiled and Laine coughed. "Looks like it's just about game time. It was good to see you." I tried to be lithe so she could see how graceful I was as I pulled my tired body and aching head out of the chair, but I tripped over a wrinkle in the blanket. Great.

"Carrigan—" Bethany grazed my arm with her red claws. "Where is your good-looking husband? I need to talk a little business with him."

About what? Chocolate icing? "I don't know where he got off to." I looked around and as if on cue, he was driving up. I wanted to throat punch him. Or her. Or both. "Today's your lucky day, girl." I pointed toward the parking lot.

She fluttered off all white and poofy and lacy with her ugly sandals on to talk "business" with my husband. What kind of moron wears all white to the ball park? I watched her twist her hips into the parking lot and greet Jack as he opened his truck door. I looked down at my T-shirt, cutoff jeans, and cleats, feeling a little bit like a dirt farmer who had just spoken to a super model. This was quickly shaping up to be a stellar day.

"Hmm . . . ," Laine muttered as I walked away.

"Shut up, Laine." I heard her chuckle behind me.

I spent most of the game playing left field and trying to see what Jack and Bethany were doing without being obvious about it. I told myself I was only making sure Jack wasn't making a spectacle of himself by allowing Bethany to hang all over him. In reality, I was trying to stifle the voice inside me that kept accusing me of being jealous. She's a very irritating voice, by the way. I could usually shut her up by thinking about Cell Phone Romeo, but she was quite a little chatterbox today.

Most of the time Jack, Bethany, and a couple of Jack's friends were standing a few feet from our dugout, talking and laughing. Bethany must have touched Jack's arm fifty times. Couldn't she speak without using her hands? I missed a fly ball while she told an entire story with her arm on his waist. His *waist*. Seriously. How many people talk to somebody with their hand on the other person's stomach? I was furious. I had to hand it to Jack, though. He looked very uncomfortable, and that made me very happy.

Mercifully, we lost the game. It was single elimination, so we were done for the day. As competitive as I am, I never could have tried to lose on purpose, but I absolutely wasn't upset that we had gotten beat. Maybe I could get some much needed rest now.

Jack, Bethany, and their little group were still talking. Ella Rae and I brought our things over to Laine's oasis and dove under the tent.

"Nice game," Laine said and smiled.

"Ha-ha," I said. I sat down and put my glove over my face. "I don't feel well."

"And whose fault is that?" she asked.

"Okay," I said. "I acknowledge that I may have made a couple of poor choices last night."

"Thank you," Laine said.

"You need to slap Bethany Wilkes."

Ella Rae announced this out of nowhere in her "Ella Rae is irritated" voice, which was very loud, almost as loud as her "Ella Rae has been drinking" voice.

"Shut up, Ella Rae!" I said. "And stop looking at them!" I didn't want either Jack or Bethany to think I cared what they were doing or saying.

"I can't believe you're just sitting here!" She didn't lower her voice a single decibel. "I can promise you she'd be wearing that ugly little white shirt around her neck if she was rubbing up against Tommy like that!"

"Tommy wouldn't be over there," I said. "He's a real husband."

"Jack is a real husband too, Carrigan!" Laine said. "You need to take yourself over there and slide *your* arm around his waist!" She turned her attention to Ella Rae. "And will you stop encouraging her to be angry?"

"Are you kidding me?" Ella Rae said. "She'd have to be blind not to be angry. And nobody says *angry*, Laine."

"Yes, they do."

"No, they don't."

"Oh, shut up!" I said. "I'm not angry. Because it doesn't matter. If my hair was on fire and Jack had the only bucket of water in town, I wouldn't go over there. So just stop it. And, Ella Rae, stop looking at them."

"Do you really think we believe you don't care?" Laine said.

"Well, you should," I said, "because I don't."

"I don't care if she cares or not," Ella Rae said. "All I know is she doesn't need to go over there. He needs to come over here. Whether or not she cares is her business."

"You're both crazy, wacko, nuts," Laine said. "He's *your* husband."

"My point exactly," I said, "and this discussion is over. Besides, you need to pay attention to this game. You just missed a run."

She went back to her scorebook, but something told me this conversation wasn't over.

"I am so ready to go home," I said.

"Oh no, you aren't going anywhere," Laine said. "You both drag me all over the place when I want to go home. I participate in whatever moronic scheme either of you has going on, and both of you are staying put today. Till the bitter end."

There was no arguing that logic. I propped up a pillow on top of my bat bag and stole a glance at my husband, Marilyn

Monroe, Jr., and their entourage. I laid my head down and closed my eyes. I might have to be here, but I didn't have to communicate. I put my glove over my face and tried to sleep.

I caught a few cat naps here and there during the day, but there was really no rest for the weary. In a small town, there is no such thing as anonymity. Everybody knows everybody else, and most of them feel compelled to talk to you. About absolutely nothing.

I find this extremely annoying and totally unnecessary. Call me when something important happens, and we can avoid all this "how's the weather" mess. But that's not the way it works. If you don't talk, you get labeled "stuck up," and you spend the next six months having to kiss all the behinds in town.

I've seen it happen. And I can't be kissing anyone's behind. So our conversations that day had ranged from ugly shoes, our new pastor at church, and the Thompsons' choice of baby names, to Sara Greer's gallbladder, and what design Otis had painted on the Bon Dieu Falls water tower that month. Some said a dragonfly, others claimed buzzard, but we all agreed on one thing: How in the world did he keep crawling up that water tower without getting caught or killed?

Otis Moore had been fondly referred to as the town drunk for as far back as I could remember. I had no idea how old he was, but he had looked exactly the same since I was five. He slept in a shed by the Depot most nights, even though he had a ramshackle home and a common law wife. One of the older Thompson kids, Mackerel, I believe was his name (and no, I'm not kidding), told me *town drunk* was not a politically correct term any more. He said Otis Moore was beer challenged. I asked Ella Rae who that child was when he walked away. She glanced over her shoulder, caught a glimpse of him, and said, "Village Idiot."

Such is life in a small town.

Ella Rae was going to have a terrible crick in her neck the next day, because she'd spent most of her time looking sideways at Jack and Bethany Wilkes. I asked her repeatedly to stop the surveillance, but she never did. She never stopped giving reports either. She'd been providing a play-by-play of Jack and Bethany for the last two ball games.

Apparently Jack had tried to walk away several times, but Red Claws kept pulling him back in. I think that annoyed me more than anything. Jack was over six feet tall and two hundred pounds with arms like steel beams. And he couldn't get away from that pasty-faced piece of painted pine straw? What a guy.

I turned over on my stomach and demanded she not tell me another thing.

A little while later, Bethany loosened her grip momentarily, and Jack came and sat down under the tent with us. Bethany stayed put with a swarm of men, but laughed too loud and stared too much at our little compound. *So* seventh grade. I had to turn and face Jack to keep myself from making faces at her. My inner child was aching to jump up and down with my tongue stuck out and sing "nanny nanny boo-boo!"

I tried to fake sleep for a while. I was mad at Jack for

talking to her for so long and furious at myself for caring. But I finally sat up and forced myself to be pleasant. There was one thing I knew for certain about Jack Whitfield III: he loved Ella Rae and he loved Laine, and he'd never do anything to disrespect either of them. That had always kept a soft spot in my heart for him. He wouldn't even argue with me in front of them. If we ever had angry words in their presence, it was because I had started them, but he shut them down.

"Where is Tommy today, Rae?" Jack asked.

"He's fishing again," Ella Rae said. "I don't know why he's fishing again, but he is. We have so much fish in the freezer I can't shut it."

"You should take some to the older folks around town," Laine said.

"What old folks?"

"Any of them," Laine said.

Ella Rae stared at her for a moment. "So just walk up to some old guy on the street and say, 'Here's a fish'?"

"You know," Laine said, "I don't know who the bigger smart ass is, you or Carrigan."

That surprised us and made all of us laugh out loud. Any time Laine used what she called an "unpleasant word," we were shocked.

"Girlfriend!" I said. "You pulled out an unpleasant word!"

"It's because y'all make me crazy!" she said. "It would do both of you girls a world of good if you thought of someone other than yourself every now and then. I know this is hard to believe, but there are other things happening in the world beyond softball and fitness."

"Here we go." I put my glove over my face again.

"I'm serious!" she said. "Ella Rae . . . how old are you?"

Ella Rae made a face at Laine. "About seventeen seconds older than you are."

I laughed. Their birthdays were three days apart.

Laine looked at me, then back at Ella Rae, then back at me and shook her head. "Never mind," she said, "there's no point in this. You both make me crazy, and this discussion is hopeless."

"I am glad we got that settled." Ella Rae pulled a video game from her purse.

Jack chuckled. "If I didn't know better, I'd think y'all hated each other."

"I do hate them," I said.

"Me too," Laine and Ella Rae said in unison.

Jack shook his head. "Females."

The current game was a fast, close one, and I got caught up helping Laine keep the scorebook. Jack was standing close by talking to another rancher from our parish about cattle prices, and Ella Rae was still watching Bethany Wilkes like a hawk. If Ella Rae ever seized on something, neither hell nor high water could keep her from pursuing it. Sometimes that was a good thing, and sometimes it was like trying to talk a jumper off a ledge.

The day dwindled into sunset, and the ball park lights popped on. Bethany, according to Ella Rae, had finally talked all the makeup off her face and left. We then proceeded to have a fifteen-minute conversation about Bethany's lack of using the bathroom. Ella Rae was convinced Bethany was a vampire. "Smooth white skin, perfect body, doesn't pee. And don't even get me started on those teeth. You can't make this up."

Ridiculous, I know, but sometimes you just had to go along with Ella Rae.

Jack had never strayed too far from us after his escape from Red Claws. He had always attended softball tournaments when we were playing, but my mind worked double overtime these days and I was sure he had some ulterior motive. I secretly hoped his presence under the tent with me had thrown a major kink in Bethany's plans. I had caught her looking at us earlier and I briefly laid my head on Jack's shoulder. I wasn't sure who was more surprised—Jack, Ella Rae, Bethany, or me. But I hadn't fooled Laine for a second. She made a disgusted face and mouthed, *You are the devil.* I stuck my tongue out at her behind Jack's back and laughed a little bit too loud.

Luckily, Miss Lucy Grimes had picked that exact moment to spit her chewing tobacco out at one of the Thompson children, and everyone was laughing. Including the Thompson child. Miss Lucy was mean as a snake. Everybody in town knew Miss Lucy didn't have any kids, and Miss Lucy didn't like any kids. Besides, that child was the devil's minion. I'd seen him under the bleachers earlier eating crickets. I don't know how his mama still had hair; I would've pulled mine out long ago.

I was bone tired by the time the last game rolled around. There were only about thirty people left at the park, and most of them were asleep in their cars waiting for their players. When it was just about time to go home, my phone vibrated for what seemed like the one hundredth time. It was Romeo. Again. He'd been blowing up my phone all day, even though I had made it clear to him I couldn't talk. But that hadn't deterred him in the least. Not even the text I sent in big, bold letters that said, DO NOT CALL ME TODAY. PLEASE.

I had even turned off my phone for a while, but when I powered up again I had eight more messages from him. I winced as I read each one. He wasn't going to win the third-grade spelling bee anytime soon. Not that I'm the grammar police exactly, but surely everybody understood the difference between *to*, *too*, and *two*.

"I need two talk two you."

Clearly, this one wasn't a brain surgeon. The only messages I sent back were asking him not to text again, which he obviously either didn't understand or didn't adhere to. So why was I surprised when I saw his car pull up in the parking lot at near midnight?

As only she could, Ella Rae summed up the situation with her usual finesse. "Well, this ain't good."

CHAPTER FIVE

"Jack, will you take Ella Rae home?" Cell Phone Romeo's unexpected appearance threw me into panic, and appearing normal was hard work. "She rode with me, but I'm gonna help Laine pack all her stuff up after the game."

"Sure," Jack said. "Whenever she's ready." If he suspected anything, he hid it well.

Ella Rae caught on immediately. "Look at the time." She glanced at an imaginary watch on her wrist. "I had no idea it was this late! I should've been gone hours ago. Here, Jack, take this for me."

She was talking fast and moving faster, piling anything she could find in his arms—bats, bags, pillows, even the one I was sitting on. Ripped it out from under me so fast my butt bounced on the ground. Jack could barely see over the top of the heap in his arms.

I scanned the parking lot for Romeo. He was still sitting in his car, but staring intently at the little scene developing under the tent. Surely he would stay put until Jack was gone. He couldn't be that stupid.

"Good night, girls." Ella Rae herded Jack toward his truck. "Jack, I just love your truck. I wish you'd sell it to Tommy when you get ready for a new one. I don't know why he wants to buy a Ford. I just love a Chevy. What do you think about a Ford? Not too much, huh?"

"Good night, Laine," Jack called over his shoulder. "I'll see you shortly, Carrigan?"

"Yes, yes," I said. "Soon as we can leave."

"Anyway, I do love a Chevy, and I think I want a gray truck next time. I guess the color really doesn't matter, but I sure do like gray. Do you like gray? Well, you must like gray 'cause you have a gray truck!" Even when they drove away, I could still see Ella Rae's lips moving ninety to nothing. Talk about a wingman.

Laine hadn't said a word during the whole scene except to tell Jack good night. She finally looked at me and said, "You wanna tell me what all that was about?"

I grimaced. "Look in the parking lot to your left."

"Oh my God!" she shouted loud enough that several men nearby whipped their heads around.

I screamed and began dancing around the quilt. "Snake! Snake!"

Big mistake. Every man still standing rushed to our rescue. Laine put her feet up in her chair while they stomped and shook the quilt. And she stared at me the whole time the snake hunt lasted.

There was much discussion among the men about the species

of the snake they'd successfully saved us from. Some said rattle-snake, some said cottonmouth. I thanked them profusely.

"You are one lie away from a fiery hell, Carrigan," Laine said when the snake chasers walked away.

"Still?" I asked, trying to make her laugh. Didn't work.

"Why is that man in the parking lot?" She calmly added another run to her scorebook.

"I don't know. I have texted him fifty times and told him to leave me alone today."

"So you're still assuming he can *read*," she said. "Did you think he was going to abide by that? If you told him not to text but didn't tell him not to come, what did you think he was gonna do? I am not going to help fix this, you hear me? This is your baby to rock, your wagon to pull, your cup of tea."

Great. Laine was multilingual, fluent in cliché, guilt, and Bible. Once she started speaking in cliché, I might never get her to stop. "I am texting him again now," I said. "I have it all under control."

"Let me count the times I have heard *that* statement come from your lips." She scribbled in her scorebook. "I hope you really do have it under control this time, because these are your eggs and your basket."

I made a face. What did that even mean? I started to point out that it made no sense, but I let her have it. "Okay," I said. I pushed the Send button on my phone. "I sent him a message that said to go home, I couldn't talk, and that I would call him tomorrow. You happy?"

"I'm sure it will take him ten minutes to read it," she said.

She began tapping her pencil on the scorebook in her lap. "I hope you also told him to start the car and put it in reverse. I don't think he's bright enough to figure it out."

"Funny," I said.

"What do you always say? I call 'em like I see 'em."

I ignored that. "He's reading it. I can tell."

"It was two sentences, Carrigan," she said. "How long could it take? I hope you aren't planning on having children with this man."

"Did you really just say that?"

"Are you going to keep this . . . thing . . . going with him?"

I ignored that too. "See, he's leaving."

"Good. I hope he never comes back!"

She might as well have thrown a bucket of scalding water on me. "What is your problem?" I said, probably a little louder and harsher than I had intended. "Why don't you want me to be happy?"

Laine locked eyes with me for a second, then shook her head slowly. "Carrigan," she said, her voice softer now. "We've been over and over this. All I have ever wanted was for you to be happy. This man . . . is not going to make you happy. You shove happiness away with both hands, and you can never see what is right in front of you."

"What I *can* see is how *un*happy Jack is making me."

My eyes burned hot with tears, which usually didn't happen unless I was physically wounded, and even then I had to be holding my spleen in my hand. I blinked hard in an effort to keep anyone, especially Laine, from noticing.

Laine opened her mouth again to respond and then promptly shut up. "This isn't the time or the place."

Finally we agreed on something. I began packing our things since the final game was almost over. "I'm gonna take your stuff to your car," I told her.

"Thank you." The words were terse, and she concentrated on the scorebook to keep from looking at me.

I shouldn't have bitten her head off, I guess, but I was so sick of the lectures, the blind loyalty to Jack, and her constant disapproval of the way I handled my marriage. The operative word here being *my*.

Why wasn't she ever on my side? She'd defend me in front of the devil himself, but when it came to Jack she was a brick wall. For one thing, why did she think she was in a position to give me or anybody else relationship advice? She might as well have been lecturing on open-heart surgery, for all she knew about it. If I wanted advice about my love life, I would ask somebody who had one. Not seek advice from a woman who always, always found something wrong with any man she finally agreed to go out with.

I was about one conversation away from telling her just that. But I couldn't do it.

Laine was kind and gentle and loving. I was loud and suspicious and headstrong. In my heart, Laine was my sister, in every sense of the word. The only thing missing was the mutual blood. So I didn't speak to her the same way I spoke to the rest of the world. Even Ella Rae. Ella Rae could take whatever I dished out and give it right back to me.

Laine, on the other hand, was sensitive, and her feelings could get hurt quite easily. I had to handle things differently with her. But I couldn't let this go on much longer. I didn't want our differences about Jack to drive a permanent wedge between us, and my resentment grew every time we had a conversation about it.

I didn't expect her to endorse my poor decisions, whatever they might be. But what I did expect was her loyalty. She would forever have mine.

I didn't want Laine to hold back her feelings—we'd never done that in all the years we'd known each other. I just wanted her to tell me *why*. Why she insisted that my life was so much better in a marriage that had turned into passionless tolerance. But the only response I ever got was, "Jack loves you and you love him. Don't screw this up."

That was no answer. It was an opinion. I needed evidence. Laine couldn't produce it, and Jack wouldn't produce it.

In many ways, Laine's words hurt me more than anything Jack could say or do. My relationships with Laine and Ella Rae were the only constants in my life, save for my family. I expected to be loved unconditionally by her and Ella Rae, just as I was by my blood family.

Besides that, I didn't want to hear logic. I wanted to hear approval or, at least, permission. Ella Rae gave it freely. Laine . . . not a chance.

The tournament finally ended, and we packed the rest of our things and headed to our cars. After a few brief "good nights" to the folks still there, we headed home. I watched her turn into her driveway. She entered the side door and waved.

Jack's truck was home so I knew he was inside. At least he wasn't in confrontation mode tonight. Hopefully. I sometimes grew weary of being "on" all the time. Always braced for the next round. Always ready to spar. Wouldn't I ever just get to relax?

❧

I stood on the porch for a few minutes, peering in the window. Jack was on the sofa asleep.

Not good. This was a new development. No matter how bad things had gotten between us, we'd always slept together—clinging to the edges, maybe, but still in the same bed. My heart sank a little. Maybe spending half the day with Bethany had made me unappealing to him. Dear Lord, where had that thought come from? I had never been insecure before and I didn't care for the way it made me feel. I didn't want to be that wife . . . You know the ones. Always wondering where their man was, who he was talking to, what he was doing. Clingy. Dependent. Anxious. I couldn't be that girl; no way could I be that girl. This marriage had begun turning me into her, and I hated it and I resented it.

I sat down in the porch swing and laid my head on the pillow. I couldn't bring myself to go inside yet. I didn't want to wake up Jack. Didn't want a conversation or a confrontation about sleeping arrangements, Bethany, me, him, any of it. I just wanted to be still for a little while. This certainly wasn't what I had envisioned my life would be like at thirty. What a mess.

My phone suddenly vibrated and I jumped. If it was Romeo again, I was going to kill him myself. But it was Ella Rae, dying to know what had happened after she'd left with Jack. She was texting me from the bathroom closet so Tommy wouldn't hear her. That made me laugh. I knew her husband loved me. Like the rest of us, we'd known each other our entire lives. But I also knew that my indiscretion bothered him. And I knew Ella Rae had told him about Romeo. She told Tommy everything. She even told us she was going to. She was so in love with Tommy. I swear they breathed in unison. And Tommy was just as bad. I don't know how he'd function if she wasn't right beside him. They had started liking each other when we were in the eighth grade and Tommy was a freshman. They'd been together ever since. I had wished a thousand times my own marriage was like theirs. My phone buzzed again. I sent her a thumbs-up icon. I'd call her tomorrow. Finally I slipped my key in the lock and tried to walk in quietly. But the only place I was ever graceful was on the softball field. Just when I thought I was home free, I dropped my bat bag and spilled my purse.

Jack sat up and looked at me. "Hey."

"Hey," I said. "Sorry 'bout that." I began picking up the contents of my purse.

"I wasn't asleep," he said. "Just had my eyes closed. Who won the tournament?"

"St. Paul's Catholic," I said. "I think God was on their side."

"That'll do it."

An awkward silence followed.

"Well, I think I'll go wash the ball field off of me." I headed toward our bedroom.

"Hey, Carrigan—"

I peered around the door and looked at him.

"You looked good out there today." He smiled. "You haven't lost a step."

Something flickered inside me. Was that . . . hope? I smiled back at him. "Thanks."

I hurried to the bathroom and got in the shower. I could've kicked myself for running away after he'd tried to make a little gesture, but I didn't know what to say. And that brief glimmer of hope I felt inside my belly had scared me. I couldn't allow myself to get all soft and giddy just because my husband threw me a crumb from the table. It was too little, and nearly too late.

I stood in one place and let the water pound down on my body. For what seemed like the millionth time in the last year, I tried to think of a reason—any reason—that made Jack pull away from me like he did. Nothing had happened. We were happy. We'd been happy since the day we got married. We almost never argued, and when we did it was about something ridiculous. A football game, a bad call by a referee, my complete lack of domestication. Even then he'd laugh at the burned pot roast or the wrinkled shirt I did my best to iron.

He finally threw up his hands and hired a maid.

We enjoyed each other. We still "courted," held hands, laughed all the time. We had no issues. None. My life had been perfect.

Then I woke up one morning and found a polite stranger in my bed. He was still kind, considerate, gentle, and generous, but the intimacy, both emotionally and physically, had disappeared overnight. At first I thought he was sick. I had asked him for weeks to see the doctor, but he assured me he felt fine. Then I thought maybe he was depressed. But he had none of the classic symptoms. He went to work at the Farm every day. He came home every night. He was cordial, he paid the bills—he gave me everything I needed.

Everything, that is, except himself.

The first few months it had almost driven me crazy. I tried everything I could think of to snap him out of whatever was wrong. When I asked questions, he always said he was fine. When I cooked elaborate meals (with Laine's help, of course) he ate, said thank you, and watched TV. Once I asked if there was someone else—it was the only time I got much of a response. He whipped his head around and said, "Certainly not."

I worked out harder and longer in case it was my body he was tired of. Nothing worked. I was in the best physical shape of my life, but I was an emotional wreck.

Then at some point, I quit. I wasn't even sure when it happened. I was just too tired to try any more, and I threw in the towel.

I would love Jack Whitfield until the day I died. But my self-respect couldn't take the beating any more. I felt lonely and rejected, and regardless of what he told me, I was sure Jack was seeing another woman.

Not to be outdone, enter Cell Phone Romeo. What a huge mistake.

CHAPTER SIX

Summer was definitely upon us in Bon Dieu Falls. It was barely the end of May, but the temperatures had already soared to the upper nineties in the afternoons. The mosquitoes and humidity had made their appearance too. I smelled like mosquito repellent and Dolce and Gabanna all the time. I'd started the annual ritual of keeping my hair in a French braid because fixing it was useless in this steam room folks call Louisiana.

Most self-proclaimed Southern Belles of course stayed inside during the summer. They didn't want to look a mess, and the little bloodsuckers never took a day off. But you missed everything if you were always locked up, and I wasn't about to let a little frizz or a few bites keep me out of the action.

I filed these women away under "weak." Weak women both annoyed and amused me.

School let out for the summer, and I was as excited about that as the students were. Laine was an English teacher at the high school, and I loved it when she was home every day instead of working. It meant she, Ella Rae, and I could spend our days together. Ella Rae was a housewife and I was . . . well, a wife in a house.

Oh, I once had a job in the office at Whitfield Farms; I just didn't attend it regularly. It was a made-up job anyway, entering information on the cattle into the computer. It had been designed by Jack to keep me busy, I am sure. I had agreed to it briefly, but it had gotten really old, really fast. Even though I truly loved the Farm, sitting at a desk all day had made me feel like a caged animal. I think Jack had ultimately hoped I would turn into the domesticated Ella Rae, who kept a spotless house, had supper on the table at six p.m. sharp every night, and had a happy husband.

I guess one out of three wasn't bad. Juanita Winslow kept my house spic and span.

I looked out the window again, checking to see if Laine had made it home from school, but no dice. Where was she? It wasn't like she had anything else to do. I wanted her and Ella Rae to go to Shreveport with me to shop. The yearly Crawfish Boil at Whitfield Farms was that weekend, and I needed a new outfit. I knew Bethany Wilkes would be there in all her glory, and there was no way I was going to let that pasty-faced swizzle stick outshine me again. She would no doubt have her missiles on display and wearing God only knows what on her feet. I had to find something spectacular, although unlike Bethany, I was a fan of wearing my boobies inside my shirt. And I needed Ella Rae and Laine to help because they didn't keep their opinions a secret. In fact, they would gag, laugh, and point if they didn't like something. Good thing I wasn't sensitive. I dialed Laine's number again but still got no answer.

I noticed a missed call on my phone. Romeo. His name wasn't really Romeo, of course. That's just what Ella Rae and I had dubbed him. It was a lot nicer than what Laine called him—Lucifer, Satan, Spawn of the Devil, and on one occasion, "the scuzzified homewrecker that can't spell *ball*"—her precise words.

Anyway, a month had passed since the night he'd shown up in the parking lot. I had only spoken to him once since then and that was to tell him not to call me any more. He finally seemed to be getting the hint.

After our short-lived fling, I had come to the conclusion that sneaking around answering secret phone calls was much more exciting than actually being with him. He was, in fact, an idiot. Every phone call was exactly the same. He told me how beautiful and desirable I was for the first ten minutes, and how much he'd love to have me in his arms. At first I lapped it up like a thirsty Rottweiler, and after that . . . there was absolutely nothing to talk about. The last time I was with him, he spent a good fifteen minutes sharing the story of his high school toenail fungus.

Toenail fungus. I kid you not.

Truthfully, I loved hearing him go on and on about how much he wanted me, how beautiful I was, how we were meant to be together. It was fun to be chased again. It made my recently plummeting self-esteem race up the charts. But then one day he said God had made our paths cross . . . that God had brought us together.

That was it. In that moment I felt as if God had a damp dish towel and slapped me across the face with it. I was no Bible scholar, but I was completely sure God wasn't sitting on his throne with his notepad and pencil, smiling and saying, "Let's get Carrigan Whitfield involved in a completely inappropriate relationship with a man she barely knows."

I wasn't about to drag God into this toxic, twisted little indiscretion. Or be manipulated by someone who believed that God was in the business of endorsing infidelity, and that the Taj Mahal was just a hole at the local putt-putt golf establishment.

He could step right on out of my life and take his toenail fungus with him.

When I told Laine I had ended it, she was elated—for lack of a better word that conjures up images of moonwalking down the street from euphoria. She gave me the whole obligatory speech about not doing anything stupid like this any more, and how I could now concentrate on my marriage and maybe think about starting a family.

Where did she come up with this stuff? Had she not been around for the last year? I started to remind her that sex had to be a part of that scenario, but instead I just let her talk. I shook my head in all the right places and hung it in very real embarrassment in others. I don't think she enjoyed my shame, but I think she was very glad I felt it.

What I really wanted wasn't Cell Phone Romeo, but the life

I used to have with Jack. It was a sobering thought. I had no idea how to get back what we'd lost. I wasn't going to throw myself at a man who no longer wanted me. I was going to keep my pride intact, even if it killed me in the process.

Laine finally popped in the door.

"Where have you been?" I said. "I've been calling you for thirty minutes."

"Ugh, school." She headed straight for my sofa and fell face-first into a pillow. "I am exhausted."

"From what?" I said. "You were there forty-five seconds!"

"I'm still tired," she said. "I was up half the night." She rolled over and put her arm over her forehead.

That was odd. Laine was a ten o'clock girl most nights. "Why?"

"*The Way We Were* was on."

"Sister gal," I said, "you need to step out of la-la land and find you a man. You can have your own real-life romance. But you can't start today. Today I need you to go home, change clothes, and splash some water on your face. We're going to Shreveport for new clothes. Woo-hoo!"

"No," she said, "not today."

"Yes, today," I said. "There are only three shopping days left till the Crawfish Boil. I'm under incredible pressure. There is no telling what the Vampire Bethany will have on, and I have to look stunning."

"Noooooo." She buried her head in the pillow again.

"Now, go on, scoot!" I tugged at her arm until she sat up. "I'm not about to look like I just jumped off the cover of

Popular Mechanics while Bethany Wilkes looks like she's been rolling around on the red carpet."

"You are crazy," Laine said. "Jack does not want Bethany Wilkes. And I do not want to go to Shreveport."

"Too bad," I said. "We're all going. Ella Rae is on her way. We'll pick you up shortly."

"Crap." She dragged herself off the sofa in dramatic Laine fashion and walked to the door muttering her favorite phrases. "I can't believe y'all are making me go. I never get to stay home. It's always something. I've been to a thousand places I never even wanted to go. I have to go shopping and I want to stay home . . ."

"See you in a few!" I called after her as she closed the door.

Laine could whine and moan all she wanted, but the truth was, if Ella Rae and I were going somewhere or doing something, she wanted to be there too. She might hate the activity, but she was going. She'd scream at us while we skinny-dipped in the creek. She'd frog hunt with us and keep her eyes closed. She ran yoyos in the river with us, so petrified of alligators she couldn't move, and sat in Tiger Stadium with cotton in her ears. But she always showed up.

I watched out the window as she walked home, saw her mouth moving, and knew she was still grumbling. It reminded me of a night years ago, the night of my twenty-first birthday. The memory always made me laugh out loud. It was probably the one night she really wished she'd stayed home.

Jack and the girls threw me a big birthday bash at the country club in Natchitoches. All our friends were there and the party was a blast. But just before midnight, and after I'd had a little bit too much to drink, Lexi Carter had shown up, uninvited and unwelcome. Jack had been dating Lexi right before he and I had gotten together. Actually, Jack had dated just about everybody in town except Laine and Ella Rae before we got together, so the fact that he'd dated her wasn't what bothered me. I couldn't very well stay mad at half the women I knew.

But he'd stayed with Lexi longer than he stayed with most girls. In fact, everyone in town assumed he would marry her, me included. The thing that really made me want to spit nails was a letter she'd written to Jack just after he and I got married. The letter had expressed her undying love and affection for him, and she'd promised to wait for him until he was over his infatuation with me. The last line of that letter was burned into my mind like a tattoo. "Call me when your little girl gets done playing house."

I was infuriated. Worse than infuriated. I couldn't say her name without wanting to spit. Jack had assured me over and over again there was nothing left between them, that he'd never really loved her at all. He told me he didn't want secrets between us and that's why he gave me the letter in the first place.

Eventually I believed him. Nobody could fake a love like we had going on during the first few years of our marriage. We were solid. But seeing her at my birthday party had been like pouring gasoline on a smoldering fire. Jack and I had been married a little over three years by then, but the memory of that letter had never faded. Looking back, I might have let it go had she just made a brief appearance, said hello to me, and left the same way she came in. But as the evening wore on, she inched her way closer to Jack. Meanwhile, I had been sipping whiskey all night trying to feel like a grown-up. Not a good combination of events.

"I'm going to talk to her," I finally told Laine and Ella Rae.

Ella Rae, always my biggest cheerleader, had been chomping at the bit for a confrontation all night. "Yeah, you're going to talk to her," she said. "And I'm gonna talk to her too."

"You're not going to do any such thing!" Laine caught Ella Rae's hand. "You are going to act like a lady, Carrigan, and you are going to shut up, Ella Rae!"

"Who you talking to?" Ella Rae said. She also tried to feel like a grown-up on this night.

Laine put her arm around Ella Rae and tried to explain to her why ladies didn't confront people and how she was going to make ladies out of both of us one day. I knew that discussion could last for a month, and I took the opportunity to escape. By the time they realized I was gone, I was standing right in front of Lexi Carter.

Jack must've seen it coming because he was by my side in an instant. "How's my birthday girl?" He slid an arm around my waist.

I shoved his hand. "Get off me, Jack," I said.

"Why are you here?" I asked her. I felt Laine's hand on one arm and Ella Rae's on the other. Didn't take them long to show up. Lexi smiled at me, and if I hadn't been furious and my adrenaline wasn't pumping at a hundred miles per hour, the red lipstick on her caps would've been hilarious. "Now, Carri," she said. "Haven't we buried the hatchet, sweetheart?"

Two problems with that answer, actually. One, she'd called me Carri, which was reserved only for those closest to me. And two, she'd been condescending. Sweetheart? Seriously? She might as well have thrown a drink in my face. I was tipsy, I was mad, and I was twenty-one. In other words, the self-created drama was intense, all-consuming, and ridiculous. But at the time, I felt more than justified.

"I tell you what we can bury, Lexi," I said. "We can bury the hatchet in your—"

Jack had caught me around the waist again and was trying to pull me away. Laine walked over to Lexi and was telling her something I couldn't hear. Whatever it was, it didn't appear to make a difference.

"If Carri wants me to leave, she can ask me to leave," Lexi said to Laine. Then she looked at me.

I assumed that was an invitation to insult her. I obliged. "I want you to leave. You weren't invited, I don't want you here, and good-bye."

There . . . that oughta cover it. Jack released his hold a little.

"What's wrong, Carri?" She smiled and looked Jack up and down. "You afraid of a little competition?"

I felt Jack's arm stiffen, but I handled it like a champ. "I might be," I said. "If I saw any."

"Lexi," Jack said, "get out of here. Now!"

"Still can't control her, Jack?" Lexi said. "This is what happens when you get involved with a child."

I didn't have time to react, and neither did Jack. All I heard was Ella Rae's protest, "Oh, *hell*, no she didn't," and the pop of a fist connecting with a jaw. Only Lexi ducked, and Ella Rae landed an impressive right hook square on Laine's cheek.

"Mmmmmm! Mmmmmm!" Laine danced around holding her cheek.

"Oops! Oh no! Oh, Laine, I'm so sorry!" Ella Rae said. She tried to assess the damage, but Laine wouldn't have it. She wouldn't let Ella Rae or me anywhere near her. She just danced around and held her face and stomped her foot.

Jack took over in an instant. "Lexi, I told you once to get out, now leave. Tommy, please take Carrigan with you and Ella Rae. I'm taking Laine home."

Jack ushered Laine out the door while the rest of us stood there a little sheepishly. Tommy handled that situation in his laid-back, country boy way. "Come on, y'all. It ain't a party till somebody gets a black eye. Nice jab, baby." He patted Ella Rae on her backside. The crowd rippled a little nervous laughter, and the music started again.

I thanked everyone at the party as fast as I could, and we left ten minutes behind Jack and Laine. When we got to her house, she refused to talk to Ella Rae or me. In fact, she wouldn't even look in our direction. Jack had put a bag of frozen peas on her eye, and she was already in her robe on the sofa.

Ella Rae tried to adjust the pillow behind her and knocked a vase off the end table instead. I snickered a little and Ella Rae laughed out loud. Laine never moved and never spoke. She just pointed at the door with her peas stuck to her face. We tucked our tails and left, bursting into spontaneous laughter as we closed the door. She yelled at us from inside, "I can still hear you!" Which actually made it funnier.

It took Laine an entire week to speak to us at all. And you couldn't really call it speaking. She ranted. She raved. She lectured. All Ella Rae and I could do was take it. Ella Rae had given Laine her first shiner, and I had started the whole mess. Not to mention that Laine was always mortified of being a part of any sort of scandal. What was she supposed to tell her students? Miss Landry was in a drunken brawl at the country club?

That had made Ella Rae and me laugh and really started some fallout. She told us it was time to put away childish things. I was pretty sure the preacher had said the same thing from the pulpit Sunday, but if Laine wanted to preach, who was I to stop her? She lectured for at least thirty minutes before Ella Rae or I got a word in. It was hard to look at her too. I had never had a black eye like that, and I had played some type of sport my entire life. I wanted to tell her how impressed I was, and then thought I should just leave that alone. But anytime she turned her back Ella Rae would whisper, "Did you see her eye? I didn't know I could do that!" Ella Rae really did feel awful about hitting her, but she was like me. We'd both had knee surgeries, broken fingers, busted lips, stitches, you name it. All this commotion over a black eye seemed ridiculous. But this was Laine we were talking about, and she was a girlie girl.

By the time the fight story had circulated Bon Dieu Falls a time or two, I had broken Lexi's arm, cracked two of her ribs, and rearranged her face enough that she needed plastic surgery. My parents even came to my house to question me about it. So many rumors, and I never even got to touch her. Ahhh . . . life in a small town.

⚜

Lexi left the parish shortly after that. I never knew exactly where she went, but I heard she moved to New Orleans. Then a few months ago I saw her again. I drove up to the post office one morning and there she was. I sat in my car and watched as she got into hers.

Why was she here? Had she moved back? I called Ella Rae immediately. She had heard nothing about Lexi Carter. I texted Laine at school. She didn't know anything either. I called Jack at the Farm next. I played it casual, asked how his day was going. Finally I mentioned I had seen Lexi and asked him if he knew she was in town.

"Yeah, somebody told me she had moved back," he said.

It didn't take me long to put two and two together. That night I felt a distance between us. Eventually I asked him if he'd been seeing her. Of course he denied it. And of course I didn't believe him.

Sometimes I followed him. I went through his wallet, his

phone, his truck, his receipts. And every time I did it, I loathed myself. I'd always despised women who did stuff like that, and then I became one. I never found any evidence, but there was *something* wrong at my house, and I was crushed.

Then she'd disappeared just as quickly as she'd shown up. I was elated, hoping against hope her absence would bring Jack back to me. But he was still withdrawn and reserved, even more so now. Strangely enough, it was only when we were alone. Out there, I was still the love of his life. I supposed he needed to keep up appearances—after all, we had to keep that Whitfield name shiny.

And that made me sadder than anything. Hurt me with the truth, but don't comfort me with a lie.

The sound of Ella Rae's screeching tires yanked me from my trip down memory lane. I shook my head. The girl knew two speeds, wide open and dead stop. I grabbed my purse and headed out the door.

CHAPTER SEVEN

The morning of the Crawfish Boil broke bright and beautiful. I was going to the Farm early, and the girls were going with me. Jack had left around six that morning and kissed my forehead while I faked sleep. Where had this come from? And what did it mean?

He was becoming a little more affectionate lately and it annoyed, pleased, and confused me. Why now, when I had clearly crossed a line in the marriage? Why now, when I had all but given up?

I swung my legs over the side of the bed and wondered, not for the first time, how my life had gotten this complicated. I was thirty years old and married to the love of my life. It shouldn't be this way.

But should or not, it was. And even if I felt ready to quit, I had to keep going. For the sake of my marriage. For the sake of my sanity.

At least my new outfit was perfect. *We'll see who wins this round, Count Bethany.*

❧

When we arrived around ten, the Farm was already buzzing with life. The party didn't officially start until four that afternoon, but that never stopped anybody from showing up early. It was always like this. People started arriving before noon and left after midnight.

And I knew these people, really knew them. I knew Bobby Ray Curtis would get drunk and hit on me tonight but not mean a thing by it. In the big city, they called that sexual harassment. In Bon Dieu Falls we called it, "Bobby Ray Curtis got drunk and hit on me last night."

I knew Jeannie McMillian would get mad at her husband sometime this afternoon and stay mad at him until they left tonight. I knew Jamie Washington would hug me so tight my ribs would almost crack. Then he'd tell me he how he still remembered when we were in first grade and I slapped him for using my purple crayon. We rolled on the floor and fought till our teacher broke us up. And he'd laugh the entire time he told me.

Just thinking about it made me smile. People could say what they wanted to about small towns, but I could call just about anybody I knew, black or white, and they would show up if I needed them. Any time of the day or night. These were *my* people. The black ones, the white ones, the old ones, the young ones. You couldn't drag me out of this town.

I made the rounds like a good Whitfield and talked to my in-laws, my parents, and many guests before catching up with

Ella Rae and Laine. I found them under the largest oak tree in the yard. Several of our friends had gathered there and were in the middle of a pretty hot game of horseshoes. I squeezed between the girls in the tree swing, only to pop right back up when I saw a familiar face.

"There you are!" Charlotte Freeman reached out to hug me. "I've been looking for you all morning! Where have you been?"

Charlotte was a couple of years older than Ella Rae, Laine, and me, but we had spent a lot of time with her in high school. She had gone off to LSU and married a foreign boy—he was from Mississippi—but they came from Vicksburg every year to the Crawfish Boil. She had proven time and time again to be a true and trusted friend, and I was genuinely glad to see her. In fact, after my girls, Charlotte and a couple of my softball teammates were about the only other females I really trusted.

"I've been keeping a low profile." I laughed.

She raised one eyebrow. "I find that hard to believe! But you look fantastic! And so tiny!"

"I'm starving myself," I said. "I haven't had anything that tasted good in two months."

"Because?"

I rolled my eyes. "Bethany Wilkes, the porcelain princess."

"Oh, please!" Charlotte said. "I have heels higher than her standards. Is she still sniffing around? And is she still having shoe issues?"

"Worse than ever," I said, "on both counts."

"I don't know why in the world you would ever give her a second thought." Charlotte made a face as though the thought left a bad taste in her mouth. "Jack doesn't want Bethany Wilkes."

"And you base this psychic knowledge on what?"

"On the fact that you're ten times prettier, smarter, and funnier than she is," Charlotte said. "Not to mention the fact that the man married *you*. And he married you while facing a firing squad, I might add."

I shook my head. "I just don't know what to think any more, Charlotte," I said. "I wish I knew how to crawl inside his head and see what he's thinking. But it doesn't really matter any more. I just don't think it's going to work out. I . . . I . . . crossed a line." I looked at her to see if she understood the obvious.

She did. Right away. "Oh, honey, you didn't." She grabbed my hand.

Looking at the sadness on her face, I finally understood the gravity of the mistake I had made. I felt a brand-new ripple of guilt. "I just . . . I don't know. It seemed like the thing to do at the time."

"What a completely stupid reason," Charlotte said.

That, at least, made me smile a little.

"Is this a full-blown affair or just a fling?"

"Just a fling," I said, "and it didn't mean anything. I know that sounds cliché, but it's true. And it's over. It's been over for months."

"Does Jack know?"

"*No!*"

She looked around. "Honey, you gotta get a hold of yourself. These things happen. And I believe you when you say it's over, but Jack is a smart man. You just be careful."

That got my attention. Suddenly I was not only guilty, I was scared. What if Jack knew?

Charlotte pursed her lips in thought. "Look, Carri," she said. "I'm glad your fling is over, and I'm not judging you for having one. But I have to tell you, I don't think Jack is seeing someone else. I never have."

I didn't want to believe that Jack had been unfaithful to me. But how could I deny it? One day we were happy. The next day he was cold. And it just happened to occur when Lexi Carter rolled back into town. True, I'd never had any solid evidence that Jack was cheating on me. But I had a feeling. Some nagging, annoying wariness I couldn't shake or make sense of.

Besides, what else could it be? I sometimes wished he'd just go ahead and ask me for a divorce and get it over with. As much as it would hurt me, anything had to be better than this purgatory.

"I'm quite sure you've talked Ella Rae into believing Jack is cheating on you," Charlotte said, "but she only believes it because you do. She's your loyal disciple, you know that. If you said you saw Elvis in the garden at the cemetery, Ella Rae would say, 'Yeah, and he was singing "Hound Dog."' But fifty bucks says you haven't sold Laine on the idea."

"Oh, you are right about that," I agreed. Laine could see

a video of him with another woman and swear in court it was fake.

We both looked at Laine, still in the tree swing watching Tommy give Jimmy Dreison a solid whipping at horseshoes. Ella Rae was cheering while Laine looked on smiling.

"And speaking of Laine, what have y'all done to her?" Charlotte asked.

"What do you mean?"

"She looks terrible," Charlotte said. "Like she hasn't slept in a week."

I hadn't noticed it until now, but Laine really did look tired. Maybe she'd had a romantic comedy marathon last night. I'd had to suffer through one or two of those with her before. Or maybe it was that church project she had going on. I knew she'd been working day and night on a project for Bible School, which was coming up next week. Laine was there every time the doors of First Baptist were open. Ella Rae and I were mostly Sunday-morning Christians.

"You know Laine," I said. "She's working on something for Bible School and it has to be perfect. She probably really hasn't slept in a week."

"Maybe so," Charlotte said, "but she sure looks like she could use some rest."

I gazed at Laine. She just looked like she needed some sleep and maybe a session or two in the tanning bed. She was white as Casper the Ghost, but she always was. She wouldn't even go in the same room as the tanning bed and wore SPF twelve thousand anytime she stepped out on the porch. She didn't look any worse than if we'd made her pull an all-nighter. Still, I made a mental note to ask her later if she felt all right.

The horseshoe match got loud, and Charlotte and I joined the cheering. Sure enough, Tommy kept his town champion title, and Ella Rae gave him a big kiss.

There were a dozen different activities going on under the massive oaks at Whitfield Farms. The older folks enjoyed Bourré games, dominoes, and spades in the shade-covered backyard, while the younger crowd gathered in front to play volleyball. A petting zoo had been set up at the barn for the little ones, and you could hear them squealing with delight as they hugged baby goats and touched noses with the calves. Most every tween in town was either in the pool or around it.

The ranch hands had built a wooden dance floor under the oaks, and I laughed to myself at the various Baptists who were cutting a rug. Wasn't all that supposed to lead to something else? I once asked Reverend Martin if he knew the difference between Catholics and Baptists. He said he did not.

"Catholics speak to each other in the liquor store," I said.

He was not amused.

The party was in full swing by four p.m., and I had officially been on my best behavior all day. I hadn't had anything stronger than water and had even turned down the sissified mint julep Jack's mother had offered me earlier. No use in tempting fate.

Bethany had arrived, fashionably late, missiles on full alert, and looking like a million bucks. Except for those wooden salad bowls on her feet. I wondered if she ever noticed me staring at her feet. I knew from the instant irritation I felt looking at her, I'd be on straight water the rest of the day. My twenty-first birthday had taught me a lesson about mixing alcohol and one of Jack's girlfriends. Besides, I liked to think I was a little smarter than I was nine years ago. Recent events of course contradicted that self-proclaimed nobility.

Thankfully, Jack was so busy talking about football, cattle, soybeans, and politics—pretty much the only four things men in Louisiana talked about—he'd never even noticed Bethany. I knew because I had watched him. All day. It was exhausting but necessary when half the women in town would give their great-grandmother's china to be in my shoes.

I had seen very little of Ella Rae and Laine all day. I had eaten crawfish with them earlier, but since my last name was Whitfield, I was part of the hostess regime. Ella Rae had spent most of the day playing volleyball. Poor thing was as competitive as I was. We sometimes stayed up all night long playing Yahtzee because neither of us would quit if we were behind. The domino games were worse than that.

Laine was under one of the big white tents entertaining everybody's kids with face painting and games. Children thought she was the original Mother Goose. I wished she would have a baby of her own, and I encouraged the idea at every opportunity. "I'm not married!" she said. "I don't even have a boyfriend!"

I pointed out, several times, that neither a husband nor a boyfriend was a requirement to get a baby. If she was uncomfortable with a one-night stand, then she could go the turkey baster route.

I thought she was going to pass out discussing it. She'd made me promise to go to church the next Sunday just for suggesting she have a "baster baby out of wedlock." Needless to say, she was neither amused nor interested. But she begged Ella Rae and me to have a baby so she could take care of it. Ella Rae wasn't about to give birth to anything that kept her off a softball field or a tennis court, and the last thing I needed to add to the messed-up mix at my house was a baby. Besides, I didn't hold anybody's kid until their heads had stopped flopping around. Strange little creatures.

The Crawfish Boil was, once again, a huge success. It had really been a good day. I had been so excited to see several friends who no longer lived here but always came down to attend the Boil, especially Charlotte. We talked on the phone once or twice a month, but there was no substitute for actually seeing a friend. Even her Mississippi husband had begun to grow on me a little. They left promising to meet us at LSU in the fall for a football tailgate.

I couldn't stop thinking about that conversation with Charlotte. I desperately wanted to believe that Jack hadn't cheated on me, but how could I let myself? She was right about one thing, though—I knew my husband better than anyone. And I knew something was wrong and had been for a long time.

It *had* to be about another woman. How could it be anything else? But if it were, why wouldn't he just ask me for a divorce and be done with it? I'd signed a prenuptial agreement, something he hadn't wanted but I had insisted upon. He wasn't going to lose a dime, not that he cared much about money.

I was grasping at straws. It always happened when I thought about it too much. *Come on, Scarlett, help a sister out. Get this out of my mind for a while. Let me think about it tomorrow.* But my Southern sister was nowhere in sight and the battle in my mind raged on. I tried to be logical about it, to eliminate my emotions and make a decision based on my head and not my heart. That lasted about ten seconds.

Then I looked at it from Jack's side of the fence. He could walk away from me right now and pretend like the last eleven years had never happened. I'd give him a divorce. Without a fight. So why wouldn't he go ahead and ask? I would pack my bags with my head high, and even if my heart were in pieces, no one else would ever know it. If he was fooling around, I didn't want to stay with him.

I wasn't going to be anybody's second choice. I sure wasn't going to end up just like Nancy Wheeler, whose husband's affairs were so common that the man was virtually scandal proof. I swear, if he drove up through the middle of town with two hookers and a circus clown, nobody would even blink an eye. We'd probably all think, *Oh, poor Nancy,* then go back to our regularly scheduled program. I didn't want to be the next Nancy Wheeler. I'd rather have my information right between the eyes, thank you very much.

Whatever was going on with Jack, one thing was true. He'd been a saint today. In fact, he'd been the Jack I married. Very loving, very focused, and very present. Every time I got anywhere near him today, he held my hand, put his arm around me, or introduced me to someone.

But it was just a show for today's audience. And it made me want to scream.

CHAPTER EIGHT

July was hotter than any I could remember. It also found the girls and me busier than any other summer. Ella Rae's mother had just gone through knee replacement surgery, and Ella Rae had gone to Shreveport to help her until she could get back on her feet. Laine had accepted a position teaching summer school and she tutored high school kids four nights a week. We'd hardly seen each other at all since the Crawfish Boil because I was at the Farm with Jack. His parents had gone on a monthlong cruise, and Jack had to be there to deal with the day-to-day operations.

Things might have been strained between us, but I wasn't going to add fuel to the fire by staying in town without him. Speculation about the state of our marriage ran rampant and was pretty much split down the middle in Bon Dieu Falls. Half the town was betting on divorce, and the other half said we'd always stay together.

It never failed to stun me when somebody shared that

kind of gossip with me. How was I supposed to respond to that? It took me a very long time to realize I didn't have to say anything at all. There was no sense in running around town putting out fires or sweeping up speculation. Charlotte had put that in perspective for me: "Honey, if they aren't sleeping in your bed or paying your bills, whatever you do is none of their business."

It had taken years for Diane Whitfield to talk Jack Whitfield Jr., into taking this Mediterranean cruise. He always found every excuse in the world not to go, but after forty years of marriage, he'd run out of ammunition. I had never seen Mrs. Diane so excited or Jack's daddy more apprehensive.

Poppa Jack, as we called Jack's father, had spent at least an hour going over the same things he'd explained the day before. As if my husband didn't already know how to run the Farm. I asked Jack once if it annoyed him when his daddy gave him the same instructions over and over. But he simply smiled. "Just who he is," he said.

And that's who Jack was too. Nothing much bothered him. I loved Poppa Jack, but I'd have been in his face about it, saying something like, "Who do you think took care of this place while you recovered from heart surgery five years ago?" Still, I kept my mouth shut.

Jack was a great deal like his father in other ways. They were both fairly quiet and reserved. But when they spoke, it was significant. They were polite and reflective, but there was never any doubt about who was in charge if either of them were in the room. It always left me in awe. It wasn't just their physical presence, although they were both big men, over six feet tall. It was more of an aura that followed them, an attitude, the way they carried themselves, that was both natural and mystic. Seeing them handle different situations over the years had left me in amazement on more than one occasion.

Mrs. Diane had asked me to ride her horse, Gilda, every day while she was away. She had been quite the accomplished rider in her younger days and had won competitions all over the Southeast. The library was filled with her trophies and ribbons, but when she'd married Poppa Jack, she'd given it all up to help him run this farm and raise their only son.

I often wondered if she ever resented giving up everything and moving from Tennessee. I asked her once if she felt like she'd missed out on anything. "No," she said. "It was a wonderful time in my life, but I am exactly where I want to be." I adored her, almost as much as I adored my own mother. Mrs. Diane had welcomed me into this family with open arms and an open mind, even though I had married her only child when I was just seventeen years old. Looking back, I knew they surely had concerns over that. But they had never voiced them to me or to Jack, as far as I knew. All I had found here was love and acceptance. They had treated me like their own from the second I had stepped foot into this house. In fact, when I was seeing Romeo, it was the thought of his parents, not Jack, that produced the most guilt.

The Farm was only fifteen minutes out of Bon Dieu Falls, but when I was here, it felt like a different and all-inclusive world. I liked being here. I liked lazing in the big wicker swing on the massive porch that wrapped around the house. I liked listening to the hired hands tell Jack about their day. I liked helping Mamie in the kitchen, although I am pretty sure Mamie didn't like it too much. I was pretty useless in a kitchen situation. She'd asked me to peel potatoes for her and I did. After I gave her the bowl, she said, "Humph"—or something like it—and, "Now peel your peelings." But she did let me lick the spoons every now and then if she was baking.

Mamie had been with the Whitfields since they'd moved in and even lived on the Farm in a little house Poppa Jack had built for her. She'd known Mrs. Diane when they were both still in Tennessee, and from what I could gather, she'd run away from an abusive relationship. Nobody ever talked about that too much, not even Jack. I don't think he knew much more than I did, anyway. All I knew was she wasn't interested in a man and she loved this family like it was her own. Jack thought she hung the moon and the stars.

I loved it here, but I missed Laine and Ella Rae. I talked and texted with them every day, and I had repeatedly asked Laine to come out to the Farm for supper, but she was always too busy. She lived for that job. I guessed all teachers must. You would have to for the things you had to put up with. I knew I wouldn't last fifteen minutes. The first time one of those kids popped off at me, I'd have gone to jail. But Laine always defended them, saying you never knew what things were like inside their homes, or they were just trying to find their way, or they were sometimes really good kids that got dealt a bad hand. Laine's mother, Jeannette Landry, had just retired from the teaching profession recently, and I knew she'd been the same kind of educator Laine was. That apple sure hadn't fallen far from the tree.

I was lounging in the wicker swing when Ella Rae called. "Somebody's going to die tonight," she said. "I'm either going to smother that woman with a pillow or slit my own wrists."

I couldn't help laughing. "What's your mother done now?" I said.

"What hasn't she done? She's after me all the time. Last night, out of sheer self-defense, I washed down one of those p.m. sleep aids with a shot of whiskey. I woke up this morning being sprayed in the face with a plant mister."

"And you're supposed to stay with her for six weeks?"

"Yeah, but I don't see how that's happening." Ella Rae paused. "I don't know, Carrigan. I suspect I'm not cut out to be a nurse."

I laughed so hard my sides ached. Ella Rae had many good qualities and I loved her down in my soul, but a nurse she was not. In fact, I think I'd prefer the angel of death to Ella Rae.

I missed my friends. But I really did love being here. It was peaceful and serene, two things that weren't usually high on my priority list, but I was learning to embrace them both. Something about this place drew me closer to Jack, though, and I had to be really careful about that. This was, after all, where it had all started. Right here at the Whitfields' Crawfish Boil when I was sixteen years old.

❧

The memory came back to me on a wave of passion and sadness.

I knew who he was, of course. Everybody did. But I'd never actually talked to him. He was twenty-six years old, ancient by my standards. He was good-looking and charming and, trust me, he didn't disappoint. But I was ready and running on all eight cylinders that night. When I saw him walking in our direction, I told Ella Rae and Laine, "Let me handle this," and they did. Mainly because they had drool running down their chins.

He leaned up against the tree we were sitting under. "I believe I have stumbled upon two of the best softball players in the state and the newly elected president of the Louisiana Beta Club. Congratulations on the State Championship, ladies, and on your election, Miss Landry."

Laine and Ella Rae wiggled around like praised puppies and honestly, I was pretty shell-shocked myself. This man was exceptionally handsome up close and in person. Those blue eyes alone were enough to make a girl stupid. Thankfully, I recovered quickly enough to say, "Why, Mr. Whitfield, you sure have done your homework."

"You can call me Jack, darlin'."

"Oh, it's sweet of you to offer," I said, "but my daddy taught me to respect my elders."

He chuckled and crossed his arms. "A blonde, a brunette, and a redhead to boot? How lucky can a country boy get?" All that and dimples too. I thought Ella Rae and Laine were going to melt into a puddle. I wasn't feeling too stable either, and my heart was pounding. But I wasn't going to fall at his feet like everybody else seemed to. Even if I had to jump in a cow trough to cool myself off.

"A country boy?" I asked, "You've been off to college in Baton Rouge and traveled all over the place. You still consider yourself a country boy?"

"Oh, I consider myself many things, darlin'." He winked. "Sorta like a Jack-of-all-trades."

Ella Rae and Laine giggled like they were ten years old at their big sister's slumber party.

"Do you have any idea how cheesy that was?" I said.

"Was it now?"

I could see Lexi Carter standing on the balcony of the house watching this little scene with a scowl on her face. I turned to Jack and gestured with my eyes. "While we all appreciate this oh-so-original banter, I don't think your girlfriend is loving it."

"Hmm . . . ," he said. But he didn't bother turning around. Instead, he leaned toward me until his face was inches from mine. If he'd gotten any closer, he would've been able to hear my heart pounding. "Tell me something, Miss Carrigan Suzanne French. Are you always this sweet?"

I sucked in my breath, willing my voice to stay even. How did he know my entire name? And besides that . . . when he used it, I wanted to wiggle like a puppy. But I found my self-control and swung for the fence. "Don't that just beat all?" I said. "I was sweet yesterday and you missed it."

He pulled away from me and smiled. "Just my luck," he said. "You girls staying around awhile?"

"Probably not," I said.

"Where you headed later?" he asked.

I smiled the smile I reserved for my daddy when I really wanted something before I answered. "You know, I think we're headed over to the National Federation of None of Your Business. By the way, we're children. You could get arrested for this."

He laughed in earnest, then leaned in close to me again and smiled just enough that I saw those dimples up close. "Ms. French," he said, "I am acutely aware of just how dangerous it is for me to be around you."

There went my heart again. "We sure appreciate your hospitality," I said. "But I'm afraid we need to run now. Good night, Mr. Whitfield."

Mercifully, the zombie girls followed me as I walked away. It was *killing* me not to turn around to see if he was still looking, but I knew it would ruin our exit. However, I could hear his quiet laughter behind us, and that pleased me, indeed.

Before I had this conversation with Jack, I hadn't really cared if he paid much attention to me or not. I had other stuff going on—sports to play and general fun to be had. At sixteen, I was living for college and an escape from the suffocating confines of Bon Dieu Falls, Louisiana. I wasn't interested in a relationship. I had always assumed I would fall in love with some baseball player at LSU and we would produce little athletes and live happily ever after.

Still, I could understand why women were so captivated by Jack, especially after the encounter at the Crawfish Boil. A girl would have to be dead not to appreciate that. Something about him made me deliciously uneasy. The attraction made no sense whatsoever, but that's what made the feeling so intense.

And it wasn't just women who were fascinated by him. Men appreciated him too. He was extremely attractive, extremely wealthy, and oblivious to either of those facts. He was just as at home at a softball game in Bon Dieu Falls as he was at the Governor's Mansion in Baton Rouge. If the hands on the Farm were fixing fence, he wasn't in the truck watching. He and Poppa Jack were fixing fence with them. He could drink beer with the good ole boys on Saturday night, then move mountains in the State Legislature come Monday morning. He was perfect.

Only nobody is perfect.

So I became obsessed with finding the chink in his armor. And I started looking for it. For months I paid closer attention when he was around. I had to be as inconspicuous as I could, though, lest he was watching me watch him. It was exhausting, but bear in mind, I was seventeen and on a mission. You can accomplish quite a bit when you are young and determined. Then one night, near the end of summer, I thought I had discovered the flaw that would keep him from perfection. What I had actually done, though, was seal my fate with the man.

There was a boat landing on Red River where everybody from age sixteen to thirty congregated if there was nothing else going on in town. (After age thirty, we talked about you if you were still loitering at the landing, and you were immediately filed under "Creepy" if you showed up.) We were all on friendly terms with the cops, and they would usually turn a blind eye if we were hanging around in parking lots talking and listening to music and drinking a little beer. But sometimes, if there was a new cop in town, we fled to the boat landing for fear he'd try to flex his muscles. Besides, we weren't troublemakers, just kids and young adults having a get-together. Bon Dieu Falls wasn't exactly a mecca in the entertainment department. We had to make our own fun instead of buying it. The landing was right on the parish line, and the war had waged for years about which police department had the responsibility of patrolling it. So nobody did. It was a perfect gathering place.

There were probably forty or fifty people there that night, and there was a pretty good party going on. We never got too rowdy, just built a bonfire, listened to music, and generally escaped our parents. The beer flowed freely, but another thing about small towns is you know who will turn idiot when the tap is turned on. And you know how far they will go.

For instance, we all knew that Junior Morris was going to strip at some point that night. He was about one hundred pounds overweight, as strong as a bull, and virtually unstoppable when he began whooping and unbuckling his overalls. And when he started the striptease, he'd be about ten minutes away from passing out. His buddies would throw a blanket over him, load him in the back of his pickup, and drive him home. That's about as out of hand as it ever got. And nobody was impressed with Junior's striptease, but that never stopped him from performing it.

On this particular night, I knew everybody, except for a couple of guys who'd driven up on Harley Davidsons. We all eyed them, but they were talking to Eddie Rivers and Johnny Mac, two boys we went to school with, so they seemed harmless, and the party continued. The night was young and Junior still had his clothes on. I was relaxing in the front seat of Tommy's truck with Laine, listening to an Eagles CD.

Sometime around nine, I saw Jack and Lexi Carter drive up in his pickup. Lots of people came down here regularly, but I'd only seen Jack here once, looking for a young guy who worked for him. I sat up immediately to get a better view.

I watched Lexi get out, making an unpleasant face and wiping at a speck of dirt on shorts that looked like white panties. Good Lord. Was I jealous? At the time, I knew very little about Lexi Carter, just that she had gone to high school at Grayson, our parish rival, she was a hygienist for some dentist in Alexandria, and she dated Jack Whitfield III.

She and Jack started talking to a group of people near where they'd parked. I hopped out of the truck and leaned up against Hunter Tillman's tailgate and observed from afar. Lexi kept her hand on Jack's arm even when she was talking to somebody else, which I found childish and stupid. Jack didn't seem to notice it much at first, but when he did, he pulled away from her, which I found pleasant and encouraging.

"What are you staring at?" Ella Rae said.

"Nothing." I looked away from Jack and Lexi.

"Bull," Laine said from inside the truck. "She's staring at Jack Whitfield."

"I am not!" I said. "I'm just bored, that's all."

Laine continued flipping through radio stations. "Whatever."

"Y'all wanna go climb the fire tower?" Tommy said.

Laine groaned. "Please, not again."

"That's only fun the first fifty times," I said.

"Y'all wanna get drunk and climb the fire tower?" Ella Rae said.

"You're already drunk," Laine said, "and besides, Carri doesn't want to leave here 'cause she's enjoying the view too much."

I made a face. "I'm not the one that peed my pants the last time he talked to us."

Ella Rae laughed too loud and too long, the way she always did when she was drinking. But it was contagious, and Tommy and I laughed too.

"I did not 'pee my pants,' as you so eloquently put it," Laine said. "But you have to admit it. The man *is* good-looking."

"He's all right," I said. But my heart quickened when he looked our way. I turned hastily toward Tommy before Jack could meet my gaze and found myself staring at a face I didn't know.

"Is your name Carrigan?" he asked.

Wow. Don't light a match, I thought. Pure grain alcohol breath. "Who wants to know?"

"I'm Garrett," he said, "and I like what I see."

When did we lurch back to the Neanderthals? "Is that right?" I kept my tone cordial but not friendly. "Well, Garrett, I'm flattered, but not interested."

"Don't be like that, baby." He leaned up against the tailgate. "I got a fine Harley over there that says you are interested. I'd love to take you for a ride."

"Horrified of motorcycles," I lied. "Sorry."

"Not a pretty little spitfire like you." He took a step closer. "I thought redheads liked an adventure."

I took a step back. "Really," I said, "I appreciate the offer, but I'm just not interested."

"Come on." He winked at me. "Just one little ride. Ladies like to ride on my . . . bike." He cackled drunkenly at his unfunny joke. I could usually handle guys and their unwanted advances, but this fella was making me a little bit uncomfortable. I looked at Tommy, who'd already begun to assess the situation and was helping Ella Rae off his shoulders.

"Look, man," Tommy said. "She already told you she ain't interested."

"Who are you?" Garrett asked. "Her husband?"

Tommy put his hand on my shoulder. "What's it to you, bud?"

"Back off, man." Garrett shoved Tommy's hand. It was clearly the wrong move. Tommy reached and grabbed him by the collar.

"We having a problem over here?" a voice said behind me. Without turning around, I knew it was Jack.

"No problem." Garrett straightened his shirt as Tommy shoved him backward. "How you doin', Jack?"

"It's all good, Garrett." Jack's voice was steady and even. "You been hitting the whiskey pretty hard tonight. Why don't you go on home?"

"Just trying to talk to the lady," Garrett said. "Not looking for trouble."

"Did the lady wanna talk to you?" Jack asked.

Garrett laughed. "I think she's playing hard to get."

"Not likely," Jack said. "She's pretty outspoken. Go on, Garrett. Get out of here." He kept his tone light, but there was no doubt that Jack Whitfield III meant what he was saying.

I had been watching all this with a growing admiration, but things were about to take a sharp detour south.

Garrett turned on me, and his demeanor changed before my eyes. "She's a stuck-up tramp." He turned to Jack. "And this is none of your business, rich boy."

Jack put his hand on Garrett's shoulder. "You know, Garrett," he said, "you are absolutely right. This is none of my business." He walked back toward his truck.

What? Was he serious? He was going to ride in like a knight on a white horse, then just leave me here with this drunk? Of all the cowardly moves I had ever seen, this one took the cake.

This was what was wrong with Jack Whitfield III. He was all hat and no cattle. Well, at least, thank God, I finally knew he wasn't perfect. I was so infuriated I hardly noticed it when Whiskey Breath began talking to me again.

"Whatcha say, baby? How 'bout that ride?"

"Get away from me." I flung Garrett's hand off my arm. My anger at Jack fueled my rage. I didn't care how this idiot reacted. I'd fight him myself.

I heard Ella Rae's laugh, then Tommy's whoop, then Laine's "Oh my!" about the same time I heard metal crunching and glass breaking. I whipped around to see Jack's four-wheel drive pickup on top of Garrett's Harley Davidson. He'd driven over the top of it, and not just once. After the first time, he backed up and drove over it again, sufficiently crushing it.

Garrett was momentarily frozen, then broke into a run toward his demolished pile of metal. He was screaming obscenities I had never even heard before, and I was an athlete. In the midst of this melee, I remember thinking, *Do those words really go together?* The girls, Tommy, and I ran over with everybody else to see the mangled pile of what used to be a Harley, shattered beyond recognition. I was utterly stunned. If you hadn't known that twisted mound of metal had once been a motorcycle, you never could have identified it now. I slowly looked at Jack who had gotten out of his truck and was scratching his head.

He looked over at Greg Grimes, who ran the auto shop in town. "My clutch has been sticking for a week, Greg," he said. "I guess I need to bring her in and let you take a look."

Garrett unleashed another barrage of obscenities guaranteed to make a sailor blush and ran to his now warped motorcycle. "I will kill you for this!"

Jack leaned against his truck and smiled slightly. "Be careful, Garrett," he said.

Garrett kicked at the remains of his bike, then took off in Jack's direction. "Let's go, me and you! Right here!"

Jack slowly began rolling up his sleeves. "I'm ready when you are."

Garrett's buddy was dragging him back by the arm. "Hey, man," he said, "I don't think this is a good idea!"

Garrett made a weak effort to throw his friend's arm off of him, but it was becoming pretty clear he didn't want to tangle with Jack. Half the men there had already moved behind Jack and were ready to defend him, including Tommy.

"Get out of here, Garrett," Jack said.

Garrett got on the back of his friend's Harley, screaming over the roar of the engine. "This ain't over, man! I'm coming for you, Jack! It ain't over!"

"Send me the bill," Jack said.

Garrett and his partner rode into the night with Garrett still screaming and cursing. I held my ears as the Harley roared out of sight.

Jack walked over to where I was standing while everyone else gathered around the pile of Harley. "Are you all right?" he asked.

I gazed up at him. "Mm-hmm," I managed.

He smiled, the sweetest and most tender smile. I don't think I will ever forget it. He leaned a little closer. "Can I call you tomorrow?" Had Jack Whitfield just asked me if he could call me tomorrow?

"Uh . . . well. I . . . ," I stammered and caught a glimpse of Lexi Carter staring at us from beside Jack's truck with her hands on her hips. I may have been a lot of things, but I was no homewrecker. I looked back up at him. "Are you and Lexi still together?" I asked.

"Not for long," he answered. "I've been waiting a long time for you to grow up, Carrigan. I don't think I can wait any longer."

✿

I must've been lost in the memory, because suddenly there Jack was on the porch, standing beside the swing. "You must be thinking about football," he said. "It usually gives you that misty-eyed look."

He was teasing me. That hadn't happened lately. I glanced up and smiled a little, but kept my feelings in check. "Hey," I said. "I didn't hear you."

"I came in on stealth," he said. "Move over." He sat down in the swing beside me.

I bit my lip. Dear Lord, he looked good, all sweaty and dirty and tan. I scooted back into the seat.

"So what were you dreaming of?"

I weighed the question and decided to pull the trigger. What difference did it make at this point? I might as well tell him the truth. "Actually, I was thinking about the first time you ever really talked to me." I pointed toward the tree down by the driveway. "I was standing right down there."

"I remember." He grinned. "You had on white shorts, an LSU jersey, and a pair of running shoes."

"You can remember what I was wearing?"

He shrugged. "It was a big day for me."

"Really?" I asked. "How so?"

"It was the first time I talked to my future wife," he said. "And I knew it then."

His admission gave me the warm fuzzies, but it was point-less to let that sentence affect me. No sense in getting all swoony about it. We sat in silence for a few minutes, watching the sunset over the river. Then, out of nowhere, he turned to me. "I do love you, Carrigan."

"What?"

He pulled me closer. "I said I love you. Come here, girl." He wrapped his arm around me.

I reluctantly leaned back into the crook of his arm as we rocked gently in the swing. We sat there in silence for a little while before he spoke. "Carrigan," he said, "I know things have been . . . strained between us. I know you need . . . an explanation." He paused, and I guessed he was waiting for me to speak. When I didn't, he continued, "If I ask you to do something for me, will you?"

A torrent of emotions ran through my mind. So I clung to the one that had always served me best. Humor. "It doesn't involve whips, chains, or leather, does it?"

He chuckled. "No."

"Okay," I said, "I'm game."

He held me closer to him. "Come out to the old barn tomorrow. I've got to do a few repairs on it, and I thought if you were gonna exercise Gilda anyway, you could ride out there. We'll talk. About everything."

The decision was made in about two seconds. "Okay." I had about a million questions, but I left them unspoken. I was afraid if I asked them, the mood would be broken and I'd never be able to get it back. Sometimes you just need to keep your mouth shut. And strangely enough, I did.

We sat in the swing in silence, his arms wrapped around

me. Honestly, I didn't know how to process any of this. I didn't know what Jack was thinking, what it meant, or how to proceed from here. But tonight I didn't want to worry about what-ifs or maybes or anything else that would cast a shadow over this night. I didn't want the battle that raged inside me between my pride and my love for this man to rear its ugly head again.

Maybe that made me as weak as all the women I made fun of. But I didn't care. Tonight I wanted to be Jack's wife again. I wanted to be seventeen and watch my knight in shining armor fight the bad guys and whisk me away on the back of a fiery steed. Being next to him felt good. It felt right.

It felt like coming home.

Later that night when we went to bed, for the first time in a long time, he held me close to him all night. No sex, no talking, just lying wrapped up in his arms the way we used to sleep before the indifference and distrust had somehow crept into our marriage. I fell into the most peaceful sleep I'd had in months. I didn't know then, but it was also the last peaceful sleep I would have for a long, long time.

The next morning I woke up and found a note on the pillow beside me. "Have one of the boys saddle Gilda and meet me as soon as you can. Jack." I jumped in the shower and was ready to go in thirty minutes. I grabbed an apple from the kitchen and headed out the door with Mamie begging me to let her fix my breakfast.

"I'll probably be back before lunch," I told her. "The apple will be fine."

She cackled and shook her head. "I don't think you gonna make it back for lunch, Miss Carri." I didn't ask her what she meant. I just flew out to the barn, had Chester saddle Gilda, and took off. The old barn was at least a mile and a half deep into the property, and I would first have to cross a soybean field, a creek, and a hayfield to get there. I rode across this gorgeous, well-managed land aware of how much I loved this place. Jack's place. And mine.

Jack had already been working for a while when I got there. He walked out of the barn, shirtless, in faded jeans and boots, all tanned and muscled and sweaty. There was a picnic basket under a cedar tree and a blanket next to it. No wonder Mamie didn't expect me for lunch. I'd be lucky to get back for Christmas.

Jack took the reins from me and I slid off Gilda into his arms. All those worries and questions that ran through my mind were suddenly gone. Just like that. Nothing mattered to me except this moment. Maybe some other day I'd drown myself in concerns about what he had or hadn't done, but today was mine. Ours.

Mamie had packed fried chicken and fruit for lunch. We never touched the food, but the blanket got a pretty good workout. Making love on a blanket in the July sun? Then again in the barn when a summer thunderstorm caught us unawares?

Last week I had wanted to claw his eyes out of his head, and today I would've given him my soul if he'd asked for it. My husband was back. The gentle, attentive lover. Whispering tender words in my ear, making me feel like the only woman on earth. This was what I had missed. Not the sex, although it was as incredible as it had ever been. It was the intimacy. The closeness. The familiarity. God, how I had missed him.

We rode back slowly that evening, stopping now and then to steal a kiss, squeeze a hand. Neither of us wanted the day to end. But it was getting dark and we had to get back. When we'd made it almost home, he stopped his horse and grabbed the reins of mine. "We never got to talk today."

I squeezed his hand. "It's okay, Jack," I said. "We'll talk."

"Before I tell you anything, I just want you to know I have always loved you," he said. "Even if you didn't think I did."

Tears sprang to my eyes. Suddenly I no longer cared what he'd done or who he'd done it with. Just like that, it didn't matter any more. We had both made mistakes. Whatever his were, they certainly couldn't be any worse than mine. But we were still standing, we were still here, and we still had a chance. Isn't that all anybody could really ask for?

In that instant I didn't care if everybody in Bon Dieu Falls thought I was a fool. This was *my* Jack. What could another woman do to touch what was between the two of us? I was immediately filled with regret and disgust for my part of the mess we had made. I was just about to tell him how sorry I was and how I loved him, and beg him for forgiveness, when I heard a shrill and panicked voice. Ella Rae?

"Carrigan! Carrigan!" Ella Rae was shouting my name.

I slid off the horse and ran toward her. Why was she here? What had happened? When I reached her she was trembling all over. I'd never seen her like this. She was rambling about her cell phone and no reception and calling me. And she was sobbing.

"What is it?" I heard my own voice shaking, horrified of what she was about to tell me. "Ella Rae! Is it Tommy?"

She shook her head and bent to grab her knees as if to catch her breath. Jack was beside her instantly, holding her up, soothing her. "What is it, Rae?" he said. "Can you tell me?"

She grabbed his hand and finally looked up, her face wet with tears. She took a deep breath and looked into my eyes. "It's Laine," she said, "and it's bad."

CHAPTER NINE

I knew the man was talking, I could see his lips moving. But the roaring in my ears prevented me from understanding a word he said. I caught broken sentences once in a while, a few words strung together, but it made no sense to me. Like a cell phone with awful reception.

I stared at him, willing myself to *hear* him. Still . . . broken phrases. "Often asymptomatic . . . terminal . . . maybe a year . . ." What was he talking about? Had I lost my ability to process English? I stared at him again. My hands were shaky and cold and clammy. And as much as I tried, a coherent thought would not come. But mostly I was furious, and it was all I could do to remain in my chair.

Ella Rae and I sat in the conference room on the third floor of Shreveport Medical Center with Laine's mother, Jeannette, and her brother, Michael. There was a man sitting at the head of the conference table, a doctor, telling us Laine had been diagnosed with stage four ovarian cancer.

But surely that wasn't what he had said. He said the cancer had spread. He said she had a year left, maybe eighteen months with treatment. He said they could make her comfortable but didn't sound too convincing about it.

I looked at Mrs. Jeannette. Stunned. I looked at Michael. Stoic. I looked at Ella Rae, who had cried so much her eyes were nearly swollen shut. She was clinging to my hand as if it were a life raft. I wanted to cry, too, but the tears wouldn't come. I knew they should, and I felt guilty because they wouldn't. But my eyes remained dry.

The room was stifling, and the walls kept creeping in until it was becoming smaller and smaller. It smelled like hand sanitizer and carpet cleaner. I changed positions in my chair again, tugged at my collar, tried to breathe. "Do any of you have any questions for me?" the doctor said.

I stared at him again, his little wire-rimmed glasses and bald head. What was his name? He had told us his name, but for the life of me, I couldn't remember it.

I looked around. Nobody said a word. They just sat there. Staring. Seriously? I had a million questions.

"I'm sorry," I said. "Doctor . . . I can't remember your name . . ."

"Rougeau."

"Yes, Doctor Rougeau." I fidgeted, wringing my hands until they hurt. I tapped my foot. "I'm not sure I understand what you're saying. I mean, I get that she's ill, and it's serious, but it's treatable, right?"

He cleared his throat and glanced at his desk before

looking up at me. "As I said, I am not optimistic. But stranger things have happened."

I blinked. Finally. "What does that even mean?" I asked.

He took a deep breath. "Your friend is very sick. Stage four means—"

"Look," I said, "I know what stage four means. My grandfather died of lung cancer. I'm not an idiot. But this is a young, healthy woman. She's thirty years old." The more reasons I came up with for why Laine couldn't possibly have cancer, the louder I got. "She was riding a bicycle for miles two months ago. There is no way she can have stage four cancer!"

He looked at me sympathetically, but he didn't budge. "I'm so sorry."

"She doesn't smoke." I continued as if he hadn't spoken, as if I could change the outcome if I just kept talking. "She doesn't drink more than a thimble full of fuzzy navel once a month. She takes care of herself. She can't have cancer."

Doctor Rougeau nodded. "Sometimes . . . and we don't always know why . . . people get sick. I wish I had an explanation to give you. I just don't. We'll make her as comfortable as we can."

White-hot anger flew all over my body. "That's it? Are you kidding me? You can make her comfortable? This is crap." Ella Rae grabbed my hand.

"Carrigan, don't!"

In the background I heard Mrs. Jeannette apologize to Doctor Rougeau. "She and Laine are very close, and Carrigan can be a bit . . . headstrong."

"Come *on*, Ella Rae," I said. I couldn't stand it one more second. It had become impossible to breathe and even more impossible to listen to the conversation. I hated the doctor for talking, and I hated everybody else for staying silent. I dragged Ella Rae down the hall so fast we were almost jogging.

Ella Rae stumbled to keep up. "Carri, please!" she said. "Stop! Please!"

I stopped and turned on her. "What?"

"What are we gonna do?"

Tears were spilling down her cheeks. It hurt me to look at her. I closed my eyes and clenched my jaw so tightly it popped. I knew I should hug her, comfort her, but I couldn't. In my mind, if I acknowledged her pain, this whole nightmare would become real. So I shoved her into the ladies' room. "Straighten your face up," I said. "I don't want her to see you like this. And hurry up."

I stood in the hall waiting for her and forced myself to take deep breaths. I knew I had been close to hyperventilating sitting in that conference room, and I wasn't sure it had passed yet. I couldn't pull that mess in front of Laine. I felt bad for being so hateful to Ella Rae when I shoved her in the bathroom. But she had to get it together. I clamped my jaws down again, determined. If I was going to have to be the strength of this little group, then fine, I could do it. I had to do it. If everybody else was willing to give up on her, that was their business. But I wasn't going to. I wasn't going to let Ella Rae give up and I surely wasn't letting Laine give up on herself.

Ella Rae stepped out of the bathroom but began to cry again as soon as she looked at me. "I can't do this, Carrigan."

"Yes, you can." I tried to make my voice a little gentler. "You have to." I pointed down the hall toward the conference room we'd just left. "They've already buried her. You hear me?" I felt my own voice break with the words. "But she's not gonna die. She just isn't. Now, come on."

Ella Rae, bless her, did all she could to put on a brave face as we headed down the hall. But it was a thinly veiled front, and I knew she could fall apart any moment. In some way, I wished I could join her.

Laine was asleep when we walked into her room, the remaining effects of a sedative still hanging on. Ella Rae sat on a chair beside the bed and cried softly. There was no sense in telling her to stop. She couldn't and I knew that.

Asleep, Laine looked frail, and it was clear she was sick and suffering. How could Ella Rae and I have missed this? She was white as the sheet she was lying on. There were dark circles under her eyes, even more pronounced because her face was thin and pale.

I had seen her only three weeks ago. How could this have happened already? Somewhere in the back of my mind, I remembered Charlotte saying Laine looked tired at the Crawfish Boil back in May. My mother had mentioned it to me at church a couple of weeks later. Laine herself had complained about being tired a time or two, but she always said she was tired.

Why hadn't I seen this? Was I so wrapped up in my own petty crap that I allowed a third of my lifetime trio to wither away in front of my eyes? Was I so shallow and superficial, so caught up in me, my wants, my needs, my indiscretion, that I couldn't see the truth? I had lugged her all over the place when she wanted to stay home. I kept her out half the night when she didn't want to stay out. I worried her all the time with my marriage, Romeo, and my preposterous, insane, self-created drama.

Everything was a joke to Ella Rae and me. Everything we did was for entertainment purposes only. Not Laine. She took life seriously, her job, the kids she taught, everything. She took my marriage more seriously than I did. I swallowed at the bile rising in my throat. I couldn't stand my own skin and wanted to claw at the thoughts inside my head.

Laine began to move her legs around, and after a few moments she opened her eyes. She looked at me and smiled slightly, then at Ella Rae. "I'm so sorry."

Ella Rae laid her head on Laine's chest and completely crumbled. They both began to sob. I was frozen, unable to react verbally or physically. It was one of the truest moments of my life. I wanted to sob along with them, but the tears in my throat were as thick as the July humidity. That in itself was an anguish I couldn't describe or ignore.

Surely there was something else when tears weren't enough, some other outlet for these emotions I had never experienced. I felt numb and inadequate. I couldn't talk, and evidently couldn't move. I just stared at them, crying quietly now and clinging to each other.

Then Laine reached her hand out to me. I zombied over and sat on the side of the bed, trying to find my voice.

Finally I managed to squeak out one weak sentence. "It's gonna be okay."

"Of course it is," Laine said. But the second our eyes met, I knew neither of us believed it.

She gently pushed Ella Rae away from her. "You got my gown soaking wet, Rae," she said.

"Laine! I'm so sorry!"

Laine shook her head. "I was joking . . ."

Ella Rae and I looked at her and neither of us laughed.

"Come on," she said. She sat up straighter in the bed. "I know this is bad. But, please, don't either of you get all weird on me."

I looked at Ella Rae, who was staring at her hands.

"Please," Laine said, more forcefully this time. "I can take it from anybody but the two of you."

"Okay," Ella Rae and I said in unison.

"Look, I know this is . . . shocking for you both," Laine said. "But I've had some time to digest it." She folded her hands in her lap and looked back and forth from Ella Rae to me. "And I need to say something to you both. Today. Right now, while it's just us and before Mother and Michael come back in here. There are some things I need you to do for me, okay?"

"Okay," I said. The conversation was making me terribly anxious. "Listen, we'll do *anything* you want us to do, but this isn't . . . you know . . . Nobody's giving up here . . ."

She smiled a little and grabbed my hand. "Just listen to me, okay?" She took a deep breath. "First of all . . . never turn weird on me again. I'm still me. I'm just . . . sick. If I can't count on the two of you, I don't know . . ." Her voice trailed off.

"Of course you can count on us," I said. "For anything."

Laine nodded, obviously relieved. "I need to know the two of you will always, always tell me the truth no matter how bad the truth is. I'm not sure Mother and Michael will. They want to protect me. And I know y'all do, too, but promise me."

We nodded.

"And one more thing." Her lips trembled. "I need you both to stay with me, no matter how hard it gets. Can you do that for me?" A tear fell from her cheek onto my hand. Ella Rae began crying again, and I felt as if I had been punched in the gut.

"Of course." I choked out the words.

Laine gathered her composure and cleared her throat. "I . . . understand what the prognosis is. I understand the cancer is in stage four and it is a rapidly growing type." She paused and looked at me. "I know you won't like what I'm about to say, Carrigan, but this is my decision and I've made it. I am at peace with it." She took a deep breath before she spoke again. "I have chosen not to take chemo. I don't want them injecting me with poison that won't prolong my life by much but will make me sick for the remainder of it."

I finally found my voice. "Are you crazy?" I snatched my hand from hers and stood up. "Of course you're taking the chemo!"

She put her hand in the air. "It's not negotiable, Carrigan," she said, "and it's not your decision."

I sucked in my breath to speak again, but she shook her head. "Don't. Please."

I pressed my lips together. I would let it go for now, but not for long. If this cancer was as aggressive as Doctor Rougeau said it was, there was no time to waste. I wanted to wheel her over to the chemo store right now. She was absolutely taking it, whether she knew it or not. I would somehow convince her to do it. I had to.

"I am sorry," she apologized again, "sorry for putting you both through this."

I shook my head. "Don't say that," I told her.

Ella Rae couldn't respond.

Laine smiled. "I'm glad y'all are here," she said. "Makes it more bearable." She closed her eyes. "I can't shake this pill they gave me. I'm gonna catch another nap, I think. You'll be here when I wake up?"

"Where else would we be?" I said.

Ella Rae held Laine's hand and laid her head on the bed next to her. *I might never get her to leave that chair,* I thought. After a while, they were both asleep.

I sat on the windowsill and watched them for a very long time. I finally looked out the glass across the courtyard to the other wing. I wondered whose lives had just changed on the other side. Who'd just had the rug pulled out from under them over there? What doctor had just said, in a matter-of-fact voice, to some other unsuspecting group of loved ones, that death was on the horizon and you better get used to it 'cause you sure couldn't stop it? I had lost loved ones in my life, my grandparents, uncles, aunts. I had loved them and grieved for them when they passed. But the young buried the old—that was just the way the world was supposed to work.

This wasn't right. It wasn't normal. It was unnatural. This was Laine. A healthy, vibrant, thirty-year-old woman. Nobody had ovarian cancer at thirty. It was absurd! It had to be some kind of mistake. It just had to be.

I was mad. No, I was worse than mad, I was furious. So furious I couldn't cry. I was mad at the doctor. How dare he speak to me like I was a child? We'll make her comfortable? Sometimes these things just happen? That wasn't good enough.

I was mad at Laine too for refusing the chemo. Why on earth would she say that? Did she want to die? Nobody wants to die. Of course she was going to take the chemo, if I had to administer it myself. I was mad at Ella Rae and myself for letting our friend waste away before our very eyes. The guilt I felt was an albatross around my neck, a burden that I didn't foresee lifting anytime soon. And I hoped everyone involved had the good sense not to speak to me about God. I was mad at him most of all.

I felt a hand on my shoulder and jumped.

"Hey, baby," Jack said, kissing my forehead.

I was so glad to see him I could have crawled inside his shirt. "What are you doing here?" I asked. "Who's at the Farm?"

"Some things are more important." He squeezed my hand. He looked over at Laine, still asleep and lightly snoring. "How is she?"

I didn't answer. His unexpected presence was such a relief. The tears I couldn't cry earlier were threatening now. But I couldn't cry in here, not in front Laine or Ella Rae either. Somebody had to be strong, I reminded myself. I couldn't afford the luxury of falling apart, although the temptation was gathering momentum at the speed of light.

"It's okay." He pulled me closer. "You don't have to answer."

I pulled away from him and faced the window again. His tenderness would make me soft, and I couldn't afford to be soft right now. I bit my lip so hard I thought it would bleed, but gathered my composure and said, "It's fine. I'm good. I am."

I am sure he knew what I said was complete and total crap, but at least he didn't call me on it. "I know you'll be here with her until she goes home, so I have checked into the Hilton down the street."

I turned around then and put my hands on his arms. His daddy would have a stroke if he knew Jack was going to be gone from the Farm that long. "Jack, you can't," I said. "You need to be at the Farm. We'll be . . . okay here."

I didn't know what this journey would bring. Or how long we'd be on it. The truth is, I hated hospitals, but the only thing that horrified me more was the idea of leaving Laine in one.

"Carrigan . . . I'll be down the street until we all go home. I know what you're thinking, but Daddy would endorse this." He exhaled. "I know this is hard for you. It is for me too." He looked at Laine. "She is . . . special. I'm staying."

I swallowed the lump and hugged him as tightly as I could. He loved Laine. Of course this was difficult for him. He was such a good man. How had I ever questioned who he was? Even if he'd made mistakes, so had I. But he'd always been there for me when the rubber met the road. Even at the lowest point in our lives, he'd always had my back. I shoved the guilt and regret from my mind. This was no time to, yet again, wallow in my disorder. I closed my eyes and lingered in his embrace.

"Cut that mess out." Laine's voice was soft, but I could hear the smile in her tone.

Jack walked over to the bed and took her hand. "What do you need?" he asked. Straightforward, no-nonsense Jack . . . always cut to the chase.

Laine shrugged slightly and pondered for a moment. "I think I just need the people who love me to love me, indeed."

"Done." He kissed her hand and held it against his face a moment, then abruptly left the room.

"What did I just witness when I woke up?" Laine asked as the door closed, her eyes twinkling.

I smiled. "Hell freezing over?"

"Start from the beginning."

Mrs. Jeannette and Michael walked in, and our conversation ended.

Ella Rae stood up and Laine's mother took her chair beside the bed. Michael stood behind her. These were two of the finest people I knew. Mrs. Jeannette had taught school for over thirty years and had just recently retired. It was easy to see where Laine's dedication to the profession and her love for the job had come from. I think she would've taught forever, but her health wasn't up to par. She'd struggled with rheumatoid arthritis for years and it had become quite a battle recently. In fact, Laine had toyed with the idea of moving in with her to help her with day-to-day needs, but Mrs. Jeannette had nixed the idea. Independence was very important to her. Laine's father had died suddenly of a heart attack several years before, when Laine was still in college. She'd wanted to move home then, too, but Mrs. Jeannette wouldn't hear of it. Michael lived here in Shreveport, but he was married with four kids, and the twins were still in diapers. I wondered fleetingly what would happen now.

Jack came back into the room, shook hands with Michael, and hugged Mrs. Jeannette. He asked her if he could see her in the hall. She took his hand as he led her out.

Laine shot me a questioning look.

I shrugged.

"Carrigan," Michael said, "it's been ages since I have seen you. You look well."

"Thank you," I said. "So do you. How are Belinda and all twelve of your kids?" I laughed at my own joke.

"It seems like twelve at bedtime, I assure you. But they're all doing fine."

"They call me about once a week," Laine said, "but they all talk at one time and I never understand a word they say."

"I haven't understood a single sentence uttered in that house for years," Michael said.

"Wait until they all become teenagers," Laine said, "and good luck with that."

An uncomfortable silence followed that statement, each of us thinking of the future and what it might mean.

The subject quickly turned to the weather, the humidity and lack of rain. Why is it, in Louisiana anyway, when a conversation becomes strained or lags, the chatter turns to weather? Even in the closest circles.

Mrs. Jeannette entered the room again, followed closely by Jack. I could tell that she had been crying and was clinging to Jack's hand. She thanked him before she sat back down beside Laine. I had no idea what their conversation had been about, but she looked grateful and relieved.

I had been yearning to ask a question, but wanted to wait until Mrs. Jeannette and Michael were both in the room, and now was my opportunity.

"Laine," I said and sat down on the edge of her bed, "why don't we get another opinion? You know, just to be sure. I mean, doctors make mistakes all the time. They're as human as we are. This diagnosis just can't be right."

Even the thought of a second opinion had given me something to hope for. Actually, it had felt like manna pouring from heaven and gave me some sliver of control in an out-of-control situation. Of course we needed a second opinion. You didn't just get news like this and swallow it without a fight. The only thing Doctor Rougeau had left me with was despair and terror. He wasn't the be all, end all of the doctor community. There were hundreds of others we could ask. We'd go to Zimbabwe if we had to. The thought of a second opinion gave me confidence and hope and direction.

Laine didn't answer and began smoothing the sheets on the bed with her hands. She looked at her mother and then at Michael. They both looked at the floor.

"What is it?" I said. The silence continued. "Tell me."

Laine took my hand in hers. "I need you to listen to me, Carrigan, you and Ella Rae both. *Really* listen, because you never do. And don't say anything till I'm done, you hear me?"

I frowned, but agreed. Ella Rae nodded her head as well.

She took a deep breath, looked at Ella Rae, who had never in her life been this silent, then looked back at me. "I have known I was sick for a while—"

"What do you mean you've known?"

She threw her hand up. "*Listen* to me."

A thousand questions were running through my mind, but I kept quiet. For once.

"I already have a second opinion, and a third. I don't want another one." She paused. "This is what I've been given, and this is what we'll deal with."

The room stayed still save for Ella Rae's quiet weeping.

I could feel the explosion rising inside me. "*What?*" I shouted the question, and had no reservations about it. What kind of irrational, idiotic announcement had she just made? Was she kidding me?

"Carrigan," Laine said, unsurprised at my reaction. "I knew you weren't gonna like the answer, but I need you to accept this . . . You . . . you have to help me accept this."

Accept this? Was she out of her mind? I wanted to punch her in the mouth and I know how that sounds, but it was the truth.

"Are you crazy? Are you all crazy?" I said, looking at them all. I was sure they'd slipped Laine and the rest of these people some sort of mind-altering drug. I turned my attention back to Laine. "And you! Are you just gonna . . . quit? And what do you mean you have three opinions? How long have you been sick? Why didn't you tell us? Who else knew? Why didn't you say anything?" I looked at Ella Rae, hoping for someone to take my anger out on. "Ella Rae, you better hope you didn't know anything about this!"

Ella Rae, still crying, finally spoke. "I didn't, I swear."

"Where did the other two opinions come from?" I yelled. "Jekyll and Hyde? Rougeau's partners? This is crap, Laine."

I paced in front of the bed and fumed with anger.

Mrs. Jeannette, ever the lady, began to look really uncomfortable, but I didn't care. I needed her to back me up or get out of the room. I needed anybody to back me up, but they all sat like statues, watching me. Except Jack, who began to walk toward me, but I put out my hand to stop him.

"He's a good doctor, Carrigan," Laine said. "I trust him."

My mind began grasping at straws then, for something that could make a difference, change the outcome, and give me just one more glimmer of optimism. I finally seized a thought through the chaos in my brain. "Okay," I said, "okay, if you trust him, then take the treatment. We'll help you if it makes you sick. You know we will. They don't know if it'll fix you or not. Miracles happen every day. So just take the treatment."

"Carrigan, please . . ."

I saw the tears in her eyes and I knew I should shut up. I *knew* I should. But I couldn't and I didn't. "Laine, you can't just *quit*! You have to fight! You can do this, I know you can. We will help you, I swear! But you have to fight."

"Carrigan," Mrs. Jeannette said, "we all know you love her, but this isn't helping. You need to—"

I was furious now, furious and frustrated and helpless—the worst combination of emotions imaginable for me. They made me unpredictable, irrational, and sometimes hateful.

"I need to what?" I said. "Dig her grave? Is that what y'all want?" I gestured wildly at the hospital room. "Let's just call the funeral home!"

"Carrigan!" Ella Rae said. "Stop it!"

"Why?" I said. "I just said what everybody else is thinking, didn't I?" I looked at Laine. "So, fine! If you wanna die, do it! We're all here and there's no time like the present. I'm ready! Do it! Do it, I *dare* you! Just die now."

The tears that had threatened all day had finally started to spill, and my words were coming out in a torrent of sobs. I was powerless to stop them, even though I knew they were hateful, mean, and cruel. But I wanted her to be mad at me. I wanted her to get her spirit back. I wanted her to fight. I didn't care if she never spoke to me again as long as she stayed alive.

Jack was at my side in an instant, this time not allowing me to push him away. "Carri

gan," he said, "come on, baby, let's go outside."

Laine cut him off. "Let her talk, Jack. I know what she's doing . . . She needs to get it out . . ."

Her perception pierced my soul. Who else knew me like that? Who else knew it was either say it or explode? Her permission broke my heart and my anger gave way to panic. My heart pounded and my hands were shaking. "Please, Laine," I said. I would've gotten on my knees if I thought it would have helped. "*Please* take the chemo."

She shook her head gently. "I love you, Carrigan," she said, "but it won't help me. I don't want to be sicker than I have to be . . . I'm sorry . . . but the answer is no."

I ran blindly out of the room, bumping into Michael and almost turning over a metal cart in the hallway. I ran down the hall, past the elevators and down the stairs until I reached the ground floor. I ran until I found the garden I had stared down at from Laine's room. And then I cried. I cried like I hadn't cried since I was a child. Deep, mournful sobs that racked my body and came from the pit of my soul. I cried until I fell on my knees into the yellow roses whose beauty belied the hopelessness in the day. I was dimly aware of Jack's hands holding my hair back while I gagged and retched and tried to catch my breath. He whispered soothing and comforting words in my ear, but they barely registered. The only voice I heard was the one in my head telling me Laine was going to die.

⚜

Much later, I sat still on the cold, stone bench in that same garden, my head on Jack's shoulder and my eyes swollen from crying. The sun was setting in the western sky, birds were singing, people walked by laughing, going on with their lives. Didn't they know Laine was dying? How could life just go on?

I knew, of course, that it wasn't their fault, but I hated them just the same. This had blindsided me. It was like a sucker punch, you know, when you weren't looking and some-body or something coldcocked you? It had happened to me on the softball field once years before. I was standing on second base, not paying attention, and got hit in the head by a line drive I never saw coming. I woke up in the hospital. This was the exact same feeling. Once again, I wasn't paying attention, I got hit by a line drive, and I woke up in the hospital. Only this time it had happened to my heart rather than my head.

CHAPTER TEN

"I had forgotten how pretty this place is." Laine looked around from her vantage point in the big wicker swing on the porch at Whitfield Farm. "So many times when I've been here, it was for a party or a get-together, with people everywhere. But when it's still like this . . . it's gorgeous."

She was right. This was a beautiful place. Huge oak trees, well over a hundred years old, dotted the landscape in every direction. Jack's mother was a master gardener, and her rose garden was the envy of every woman in Bon Dieu Falls. The yard and flower beds were pristine and beautiful, not because hired hands kept them that way, but because she did. Lush, green fields where cattle and horses grazed lay just beyond the wooden fence. Soon the leaves would be turning and the mums would be blooming. Time seemed to fly by these days. None of us had ever been so intensely aware of that.

Two months had passed since that awful day when we learned of Laine's cancer, and we had settled in nicely here at Jack's parents' home. Laine had stayed in the hospital for exactly a week. The doctors had run all the tests she would allow, cauterized the original tumor in her ovary to keep it from bleeding any more, and given her pain medication, although she insisted she didn't need it.

Since Mrs. Jeannette was unable to care for Laine the way she needed, Jack had asked if Laine might stay here at the Farm with us during her illness. He'd asked her to move in as well, but she declined. She came every day, and we'd even convinced her to spend a night here and there. But she couldn't bring herself to impose on us like that, she said.

We had tried in vain to assure her there would be no imposition. The house was huge with plenty of room, plantation style, with wraparound porches, balconies, and all those things you see in a Southern novel. It had been in the Whitfield family for generations.

Poppa Jack and Mrs. Diane were wholeheartedly in agreement with the arrangement. Anybody would be hard-pressed to find two finer people than my father-in-law and mother-in-law.

Jack hired a full-time nurse, something else Laine insisted she didn't need. But it sure made the rest of us feel better. The nurse, Debra Pierson, was an RN. She came highly recommended from a family Poppa Jack knew who had retained her services during a similar situation. Debra was in her late forties, had never been married, and had no children. She was friendly and cordial, but definitely no-nonsense. She kept a close eye on Laine, and she ate meals with us, but after she was done with both, she disappeared into her room. I'm not sure she understood the whole living arrangement we had going on at Whitfield Farms, but at least she had the good sense not to question it.

Mamie, however, was having a ball. She loved to "cook large," as she put it. Mamie was *Webster's* definition of nurturer. She asked Laine every morning what she wanted for supper and every night it appeared. Laine ate like a bird, but I didn't think that was a cancer thing. She'd never had a huge appetite. Maybe that was all wishful thinking, but I watched her like a hawk just the same. I made sure her favorite things on earth, orange popsicles and salt water taffy, were always in the house.

Laine wasn't gaining weight, but at least she hadn't lost any. I, on the other hand, had picked up seven unwanted pounds and Ella Rae had gained five. The fried chicken in this house should have been on the front of every cookbook that came out of the southern United States. I don't know what made it so different, but I was sure glad Laine asked for it on a regular basis. I told Laine all the time if Bethany Wilkes took Jack away from me, it was going to be her fault. But she scoffed at that, assuring me Jack wouldn't leave me for a supermodel. Lately I had finally become convinced she was right

While Laine was still in the hospital, my mother packed my things and I came straight to the Farm. I hadn't left the property since. Ella Rae was with us too. Tommy was working in a Texas oilfield and I didn't have to ask her twice. Most of our days were spent on one of the porches at the Farm or riding around the place on an ATV. Time had become precious to all of us. We squeezed every second from every day and hated to go to bed at night.

On this particular day, we were sitting on the front porch sipping lemonade and watching Jack and the hands repair the roof on the stables.

"Don't you get nervous when he's on the roof walking around?" Ella Rae hid her eyes with her hands. "I'm nervous for you."

"Jack is like a cat," I said. I watched him, admiring the way his tanned chest glistened in the sun.

Laine cackled. "I never thought I'd see it, but you are lusting after your husband!"

I made a face. "Lusting?" I said. "Are we in the nineteen fifties? I was merely appreciating my choice of mates."

"It sounded like you were appreciating him last night," Ella Rae said.

"Seriously," Laine said.

"What?" I tried to hide my embarrassment. We had been making up for lost time, but I hadn't realized everybody in the house knew it.

They both began laughing. I was mortified. I would talk about any subject in the world with these women, but I drew the line at sex. Even during my brief tryst with Cell Phone Romeo, my friends might have known it was happening, but they didn't know details. Bottom line was, if I wasn't having a sexual relationship with you, then I wasn't going to talk about sex with you. It was my version of being a lady, although that was one thing I'd never really been accused of being.

"Do you think Poppa Jack and Mrs. Diane heard us too?"

"How could they help it?" Ella Rae said. "It sounded like y'all were swinging on the chandeliers!"

"Oh no," I groaned and slid down in the wicker swing.

"Did I hear you praying last night too?" Laine asked. "I kept hearing someone calling out to God."

They rolled all over themselves laughing, and I took a swing at Ella Rae. "Y'all are both lying!" I said, realizing I had waltzed into that one. Still, I was horrified because I had just given myself away.

Laine patted my hand. "It's okay, Carri," she said. "You're married to him. You get to do anything you want to do with him."

"Y'all know payback is gonna be bad, don't you?" I said.

"Ain't nobody worried with you," Ella Rae said.

I looked back at Jack driving nails into the roof of the stable. Things were good between us again. Normal. Natural. Even though we had yet to finish the conversation we started the day we found out about Laine's illness. It had become pretty much irrelevant to me. The insanity of the last year was just that—insanity. I rarely wondered about Jack's leave of absence. What mattered to me now was Laine. Every day was about her. It had to be. There would come a day when Jack and I could completely mend our fences. But I didn't have time for that now. I'd have to think about that later . . . *Thank you again for that pearl of wisdom, Scarlett.*

What I did remember, with white-hot shame, was Romeo. My indiscretion with him was all about revenge, but that didn't make it okay. I desperately needed to confess it to Jack.

The guilt was terrible when I allowed it to be. I had a pretty good method of handling my various baggage filled with guilt over my actions and despair for Laine's illness. I only permitted myself to think about disagreeable things when I was completely alone. Which wasn't often. I suspected that wasn't emotionally healthy, but I'd deal with that later too.

At first, I had decided to confess to Jack. I wanted to bare my soul, to make a clean slate, a clean slate, indeed. Ella Rae had advised against it. In fact, she railed against it. She ranted and raved and cited a hundred different reasons why it was the "stupidest idea you've ever had, and face it, you've had a few." No argument there, but still I wasn't convinced. I wanted some sort of penance.

In the end, it was Laine who talked sense into me. "I understand the need," she said. "Maybe it will purge your guilt, but it'll only hurt Jack. You say it doesn't matter to you any more what he did or didn't do. What makes you think it matters to him? It was nearly a year ago, Carrigan. Let it go."

That had clicked for me. What good would it do, really?

Laine then advised me to go to God with my guilt, and release it. I nodded in agreement, but I wasn't interested in talking to God. About anything. She trusted him completely, without reservation, and he was the maestro of her circumstances, wasn't he? I had nothing to say to God.

"What's on the menu tonight, Laine?" Ella Rae asked.

"It's a surprise," she answered.

"Is it Hummingbird Cake?" I asked. "Please say you made a Hummingbird Cake."

"No, it is not Hummingbird Cake," Laine said. "But I promise to make one soon."

"Then tell us what's in it."

"Nothing special. Just a regular cake."

"You know that's a lie," I said. "It tastes different from everybody else's Hummingbird Cake. Is it . . . some exotic ingredient? Do you have to order it?"

"Is it a gross ingredient and you don't want to tell us?" Ella Rae said.

Laine raised one eyebrow. "It's chicken feet, Ella Rae."

"Forget it," I said. "She'll take it to her grave."

"Literally," Laine said.

I had probably said that very sentence fifty times in the past about Laine and the Hummingbird Cake. But tonight I felt as if I had said some horrible, awful thing that no human should ever utter out loud. And I was mortified. "Oh my God, Laine . . . ," I said, "I didn't mean . . ."

"You know how many times I've heard that before, Carrigan?" she said. "Forget it. I know what you meant. And just so you know . . . you are correct. I am taking it to my grave." She patted my hand. "Really. Forget it. Now, who wants to guess what's for supper?"

Tommy perked up. "Frog legs?"

Ella Rae poked him in the ribs. "Shrimp and grits."

Laine looked at me and slightly nodded. I knew she wanted me to lighten my mood, to dismiss my comment. I tried to oblige. "I hope it's not fried chicken again." I patted my backside. "My wardrobe can't afford it."

Ella Rae pinched a make-believe roll on her stomach. "Mine either!"

Laine winked at me and mouthed, *Thank you.* She amazed me. Always taking care of everyone else. Still.

Later that night, we all sat around the dining room table while Mamie put the finishing touches on supper.

"I'm just saying," Laine said, "in most circles, this meal is considered dinner."

"The hell you say." Tommy frowned. "What do they call dinner?"

"Lunch."

"I don't understand folks sometimes." Tommy shook his head.

Tommy had gotten a week off and had driven out to the Farm to surprise Ella Rae. She had squealed with delight when she saw him. I felt like doing that when Jack was on the roof today. Maybe my marriage wasn't so unlike Ella Rae and Tommy's after all. Well, except for the odd little detour we'd taken.

I was so hungry I could have eaten the plates off the table, but Mamie was taking her own sweet time tonight. She didn't allow anyone in the kitchen for supper preparation. I think the only reason she let Mrs. Diane in was because she owned the place. Any of us could hang around for breakfast or lunch, but when it came to supper, she fancied herself as Picasso, only with a spatula instead of a brush. I was very excited when the French doors that led to the kitchen swung open and Mamie appeared with a platter. I just knew it was fried chicken and my mouth was already watering. But when she set the platter down, it was full of sunny-side up eggs. Mrs. Diane followed with platters of bacon, sausage, grits, and biscuits. I was immediately disappointed, but this was Laine's favorite meal, right after fried chicken.

When the platter came my way, Jack tipped it and slid two of the eggs onto my plate. I watched them for a minute, and my stomach lurched. I bolted from my chair and into the nearest bathroom just beyond the kitchen. Jack was close on my heels.

He knelt down beside me. "Are you all right?"

"Ugh . . . ," I said. "Those eggs—did you see how they were shaking?"

"Shaking? I didn't notice a shake."

"Hand me a washcloth, will you?" I asked.

He wet the cloth and gave it to me. The cool, wet cloth did the trick, and the nausea passed as quickly as it had appeared. "That was weird."

Ella Rae peered around the bathroom door. "When was your last period?"

"What?" I said. "How long have you been standing there?"

"Long enough to realize what you idiots can't figure out." Ella Rae grinned. "When was your last period?"

I looked up at Jack, who was staring down at me. The look on his face matched mine. Pure and absolute astonishment.

"Uh . . . I think, probably, let's see."

"This is not a difficult question, Carri," Ella Rae said.

"Really," Laine said.

"Who else is out there?"

"Just us," Ella Rae said. "Now, think. Look, Laine, her boobies are huge."

"What?" I looked down at my chest. Wow . . . where had those come from?

Jack was looking at my chest, then back at my face. He wore a little lopsided grin. "Well?" I thought back. I knew it had been after the Crawfish Boil, then before Laine had been in the hospital, so that meant . . . I hadn't had a period since June. This was the first week in September.

I looked at Jack again and whispered, "June."

Ella Rae let out a huge "Woo-hoo!" that brought the rest of the house running.

Picture this . . . I'm sitting on the floor of the bathroom, hands hugging the toilet seat. Jack is sitting on the edge of the tub beside me. Ella Rae is doing what later becomes known as the "Baby Dance," and Laine is pumping her fist in the air as if the Tigers just converted a fourth and five, not that she'd know what that meant. Then my mother-in-law, father-in-law, Mrs. Jeannette, Tommy, and Mamie all joined in.

That night we did what Louisiana folks do best. We had a party at the drop of a hat. Laine called my mother, who called a few of our friends, and we celebrated Baby Whitfield. Or I should say "they" celebrated Baby Whitfield. Jack and I mostly stood around in shock. Although he was in better shape than I was, that was for sure. At least he was talking.

Looking back, I'm sure I was in shock. In one of those weird cocoons when you're so freaked out that everything seems a little surreal. And everybody sounded like Charlie Brown's teacher. I grasped for every straw I could think of. Maybe it was something else, right? I'd certainly been under a lot of stress lately. Couldn't that cause your little friend not to show up? I mean, I couldn't be pregnant. I just couldn't be. I could barely take care of myself. How in the world would I take care of a baby?

I went over and over the last couple of months in my mind. I had gotten off my pills in May and was going to take the birth control shots. I was in no hurry to get back to Shreveport to my gynecologist. There was no point since Jack and I were barely speaking. We went to stay at the Farm when Mrs. Diane and Poppa Jack left on their cruise. And then we had that picnic . . . quite a picnic, apparently. When Laine got sick, I never thought about it again.

Ella Rae and Tommy dashed into town to buy a home pregnancy test, but there was no need to take it. I knew it was true. I started remembering little things I passed off the last few weeks as insignificant. Too much was going on here without whining about a nagging backache, or the horrible smell of coffee in the mornings, or the constant and irrational craving for peaches. I assumed we were all adjusting to the new normal. Besides, I had always hated the smell of coffee. It had just never made me want to projectile vomit until lately.

I stepped out onto the patio and quietly closed the door behind me. I wanted to be alone for a few minutes, to let this information sink in. And I needed to decide how I really felt about it. The truth was, this couldn't have happened at a worse time. I didn't want to terminate the pregnancy—that was absolutely out of the question. I wanted Jack's baby. I hadn't known I did until now, but I did. Still, I didn't want any attention taken off of Laine. I could be pregnant anytime. She was going to . . . die.

That thought punched me in the gut like it always did. I sat down on the metal patio bench and looked out into the field. The next few months should be about her, and only her. She deserved that. It's why she was here. It's why we were all here. I was stealing the show again, just like I always had. Laine had always been in the background no matter what I was doing, either cheering me on or screaming at the top of her lungs for me to stop. It seemed unfair now that I couldn't even give her center stage when she was about to exit the show.

"Hey," Laine said.

I looked up and saw her standing in the patio door. "Hey."

She walked over and sat down beside me. "Are you okay?" The tears that had eluded me for most of my life now flowed like a faucet, at least once a day, even if I tried to hide them. But there was no hiding tonight.

"Carri, what's the matter?" Concern filled her voice. "You are happy about this, aren't you? The baby, I mean?"

"Of course I am . . ." I started to blubber a little. "It's just . . ."

"What?"

How could I tell her I wanted her to star in her own death show and being pregnant would steal her thunder? I couldn't. So I just cried instead.

She grabbed my hand. "Carrigan!" she said. "This baby—it *is* Jack's, isn't it?"

That jolted me back into reality and I snatched my hand from hers. "Are you kidding me?"

"Well, you know, there was Romeo, and I wasn't sure . . ."

I glared at her. "Of course it's Jack's baby, you idiot!"

"Okay, my bad. I was just making sure. It's not always easy to keep up with you. So, what is it? Tell me."

"Laine, I . . ." I tried to make the words come out, but stammered. "This is a really bad time for . . . What I mean is . . ."

She caught on quickly. "Ahhhh, I see," she said. "You think this would be a crappy time for you to be pregnant while I am . . . ill."

"Yes."

She stood up and stared down at me. "Are you out of your ever-loving mind?"

"What do you mean?"

"What better time could there be?" She towered over me, both hands on her hips. "It's . . . it's . . . life restoring itself." She gestured around us. "It happens on this farm every day with plants and animals. It's the natural order of things. It is a *blessing*, Carrigan. Trust me."

I stared at her. She had amazed me the way she'd accepted her death sentence. She spoke about her death like it was matter of fact and wanted everyone else to speak about it the same way. Well, I couldn't just talk about it like it was a weather report or a football score. And I didn't want to, even though I knew it would make the days easier for her and for me too, if I could. I hadn't wanted her to accept it either. I wanted her to go out in a fighting blaze of glory. But it was already way too late for that. It was almost like she embraced the idea of it. I hated that part of her. Hated it. So I filed it. And I went along with it because if I didn't, it would upset her.

She knelt in front of me. "Carrigan," she said, "I couldn't be happier about this. I *love* you. I have always wanted this for you. For you and Jack. Don't you see? It gives me a reason to . . . hang on." Tears sprang to her eyes. "This is going to be an amazing time. Please don't try to downplay it or restrain your happiness or act like it isn't a big deal. It's a huge deal. This has made me feel better in the last hour than I have physically and emotionally in months."

I weighed her words. I wanted to be happy and excited and all those things you were supposed to be when you find out you're pregnant. I wanted to celebrate. But I felt so guilty about it. She was the one who deserved a happily ever after, but I was the one who got it. How could somebody rejoice and mourn at the same time?

She sat down beside me and put her arm around my shoulder. "This baby is like a gift for me," she said. "Don't you understand that? And I know what you're thinking." She paused. "Look at me."

I turned my face to hers.

"I will see this baby," she vowed. "I promise you I will."

I hugged her so hard I was afraid I had hurt her. "Thank you."

Ella Rae popped her head out of the patio door and produced a pregnancy test. "Time to pee on a stick!" Great. Just what I always wanted. Fifty people standing outside a bathroom waiting for me to produce a urine sample.

I looked at Laine and held my hand out to pull her up from the bench. "Let's go find a potty."

She smiled. "At least we aren't at the boat landing looking for one."

CHAPTER ELEVEN

The following weeks were filled with excitement and preparation for the baby. You would've thought I was giving birth to royalty the way everybody treated me. Mamie now checked every morning with Laine and, me too, to see what we wanted to eat the rest of the day. She also made sure we both cleaned our plates. But she kept eggs off my menu.

Luckily, I craved fresh fruit and pancakes. I was forced to sneak orange popsicles because she thought I was getting too much sugar. I made Jack buy some and put them in the freezer in the barn where they kept the animal meds. But I think he counted them as well. Mamie even had him on board with the sugar thing.

Finally I went to the doctor. Correction: Jack, Ella Rae, Laine, and I went to the doctor. "April third," Doctor Davis said. "That's your due date."

I looked at Laine, and she reached over and squeezed my hand. I was sure everyone in the room understood that gesture. I was torn between wishing the days would pass fast so the baby would get here and Laine could enjoy him or her, and wishing they'd slow down so we'd have more time.

Jack's mother was the chairperson of the baby room committee at the Farm. Jack said she was driving him insane. He and Ella Rae had painted the room four different times; each time she would come in and say, "Too pale" or "Too bright," and they'd have to start over. When I asked him what color it was, he shook his head and said, "Yellow. It's yellow."

Nobody would let Laine or me remotely near the paint fumes, and we spent most mornings on the front porch sipping Mamie's smoothie concoctions and talking. My favorite was the coconut pineapple that tasted like a piña colada without the rum. It was delicious.

The morning before Thanksgiving, I asked Laine, "Do you remember one night years ago, we were frog hunting in the creek behind Ella Rae's house?"

"Do I remember? How could I forget? I'm still carrying the scar where you tried to kill me."

"Listen, that knife slipped out of my hand while you were shrieking about an alligator. That whole cut thing wasn't my fault."

"Whatever," she said. "Funny how I never get injured unless you or Ella Rae are around."

"Ha-ha," I said.

"What made you think about that night?"

I slurped the rest of my drink and put the glass on the wicker table. "You told me that night you had a secret, something you'd never told Ella Rae or me. I've asked you to tell me that secret almost as often as I've asked you about the secret ingredient for your Hummingbird Cake. And you always said you'd tell me someday." I paused for effect and looked at her. "We 'bout there yet?"

"I wondered when you were gonna bring that up." She stirred the last of her drink with her straw. "You know," she said, "I think we have arrived at that day."

I sat up in my chair on full alert and mindlessly rubbed my baby bump. "Then do tell," I said. "And look, this better be good. I've waited on it for years."

"I think you'll find it . . . interesting," she promised.

"I'm ready," I said. I was truly excited to hear this deep, dark secret she'd been keeping for years. Of course, she was probably about to tell me she'd cheated on a test in fifth grade or stuck her tongue out at her mother when she was nine or some other offense she believed would send her to hell. Regardless, I was eager to hear the confession. Laine looked tired this morning, and although she'd never admit it, I could tell she was in some pain lately. I questioned Debra about it, but didn't get very far. She was fiercely protective of Laine's privacy and had repeatedly told me when I asked questions that it was something I should ask Laine. I supposed that's what nurses were supposed to do, but the only response I ever got from Laine was, "I'm fine."

"This may shock you a little bit," Laine said.

"Really?" I made a face. "Yes, because I am so sweet and innocent, your terrible deed, whatever it was, is gonna make me swoon."

She laughed a little bit, then took a deep breath. "Do you remember Mitch Montgomery?" The name sounded familiar, but I couldn't place him.

"Maybe," I said. "Why do I know that name?"

"He went to high school with us," she said, "but only for our junior and senior year."

I thought back and then it hit me. "Lots of curly black hair? Tall? Quiet guy?"

"Yep, that's him."

"What about him?"

"He was in college at ULM the same time I was," she said. "I had seen him on campus a few times, but he'd cut his hair short and I wasn't sure it was him, so I never spoke to him. Then one day I saw him off campus at a coffee shop." She paused. "So we had dinner together that night and . . . break-fast the next morning."

I stared at her. "So?"

"We had *breakfast* the next morning."

"People eat, Laine," I said. "What, was it like the best breakfast you've ever had? I mean . . ." And then it dawned on me. She had *breakfast* with him the next morning. "You slept with Mitch Montgomery?"

"Thank you," she said. "You want to yell a little louder? I'm sure everybody in the barn wants to know. And there's probably a guy on a tractor in the next parish who didn't quite catch it."

"I'm sorry," I said. "But, Laine . . . I mean, you're . . . you never . . . You're a virgin."

"No, you and Ella Rae always said I was. I just never confirmed or denied."

My mind was racing. The fact that she'd had sex with Mitch Montgomery wasn't a big deal to me, but the fact that she'd never told us was huge. "Why didn't you tell us? What happened? Where is he? Was it just a one-night thing or did you have a relationship with him? Tell me everything! Were you in love with him?"

"Seriously, Carrigan?" Laine asked. "Which question do you want me to answer first?"

"Can I tell Ella Rae?"

"Of course," she said. "But don't scream it."

"Ella Rae!" I yelled. "Come out here! And bring a popsicle!"

"You have always been so loud," Laine accused, holding her ears, "and I think being preggers just makes you worse!"

Ella Rae appeared a few moments later, splattered in yellow, with a popsicle in one hand and a paintbrush in the other. "What is it?" she asked.

"Sit down," I said. "Laine, tell her."

Laine opened her mouth, but I changed my mind and cut her off.

"Never mind, let me," I said.

She waved a hand. "Be my guest."

"Laine had sex with Mitch Montgomery."

Ella Rae frowned. "Today?"

My delight in sharing the secret was immediately deflated. "Yes, Ella Rae," I said. "While you were painting and I was in the rocking chair, Mitch Montgomery drove up, and they had sex in the porch swing."

Ella Rae made a face. "What are you talking about?"

Laine started laughing. "Ella Rae," she said, "when I was in college at ULM, I had a . . . fling with Mitch Montgomery."

Ella Rae rolled her eyes. "Whatever. You're a virgin," she said, "and who the hell is Mitch Montgomery?"

"I am *not* a virgin."

That was even funnier, and now all three of us were laughing, even if Ella Rae had no idea why.

"Okay, okay," Ella Rae finally said after we'd composed ourselves. "Somebody tell me what's going on."

Laine repeated the story, and Ella Rae listened intently. When she was finished talking, Ella Rae asked the same twenty questions I did.

"You two are the exact same person sometimes!" Laine said. "Okay, it happened my senior year. It lasted six months and it was wonderful. Yes, I was in love with him, and yes, I believe he was in love with me. And I didn't tell either of you because . . . I knew from the beginning it wouldn't last."

We were hanging on every word she said. In some circles, a college fling wouldn't be that big a deal, but in Laine's case the news was enormous. How could she have kept this kind of secret all these years? She'd graduated from ULM nearly eight years ago.

"Why did you know it wouldn't last?" I asked. "He didn't want to move back to Bon Dieu Falls?"

Ella Rae jumped in. "He wanted to move to the city and become an actor?"

Laine got quiet again.

"What happened, Laine?" I said.

She took a deep breath. "Mitch had gotten married his freshman year at ULM. He met a girl, started dating her, she got pregnant, and they got married."

She paused when she saw our expressions. Ella Rae and I were both stunned. Our Laine involved with a married man? "They were separated," she said. "In fact, they had already filed the divorce papers, and that happened before I entered the picture."

"Wow," I said. "I knew there had to be an explanation. Not that I would judge you. I mean, things just happen sometimes. No one knows that more than I do."

"For real," Ella Rae said.

"Shut up, Ella Rae."

Ella Rae rolled her eyes. "I was just trying to help."

I ignored her and turned back to Laine. "So why didn't it work out?"

She shook her head, "I knew, in the end, he would choose his son over me." Her eyes brimmed with tears. "I've never blamed him for that. It's what he should have done. We kept in touch for a year or so after they got back together, but I just never felt right about it. You know, a man living with his wife and child and professing his undying love. It just felt so . . . wrong. I eventually told him not to contact me any more."

"I'm so sorry, Laine," I said. "You deserved so much more."

She shrugged. "It's fine. Water under the bridge, and I don't regret it. Not a second of it. You both always wondered why I wouldn't date anybody more than once or twice. Well, Mitch was the reason. Nobody else ever measured up, I guess. Maybe it was wrong, but I loved him."

"It wasn't wrong," Ella Rae said. "He was almost divorced. They weren't together, and you didn't pull them apart."

Laine nodded. "I know."

A brief silence followed before Ella Rae asked the question that was uppermost in my mind. "Do you want to see him again? I mean, you know, since . . ."

"Since I'm dying anyway, and what difference would it make now?"

"Ugh." I hated the death reference. "I don't think that's what—"

"Oh, come on, y'all," Laine said. "You both promised me from the beginning we'd call a spade a spade. Don't back out on me now."

I shook my head. "Fine, so . . . do you want us to find him? Tell him? Do you wanna speak to him again?"

She looked out across the field. "I admit I have thought about it. Just to tell him good-bye, you know? And to make sure his life has been happy." She looked back at us. "But what good would it do now? It's done. There's no changing it.

Maybe it would just mess him up, and I would never do that to him."

"Why? Why would you want to spare *his* feelings?" Ella Rae said.

"Ain't that the truth," I said. If Mitch Montgomery were in front of me right now, I'd beat him to a bloody pulp. He left her and she was still trying to protect him? "What do *you* want, Laine?"

"Don't, please don't do that," she said. "Don't be mad at him. It wasn't his fault."

Neither of us commented. She could take up for him all she wanted to, but the fact remained she loved him and he left her. She'd been young and naïve. He was married. He had known the score. Laine was the innocent in this. But if she wanted to defend him, I'd keep my mouth shut.

"Sorry," I said.

"Me too," Ella Rae said. "But I don't mean it."

Laine laughed. "I love you both for supporting me, but it's okay, really. I learned how to live with it a long time ago."

"But tell us if you want to talk to him, Laine," Ella Rae said. "Really. We'll find him. Promise?"

"I promise," she said. "And listen, now is a good time to say something to both of you too." She sat up straight and looked back and forth between us. "And just listen to me, okay? I really want to say this. I know how much you hate sappy stuff, Carrigan, but you're just gonna have to deal with it."

I braced myself as Laine began to speak.

"I wouldn't trade a second of this friendship, do you hear

me?" she said. "Not a night when you were both too tipsy to drive and I had to. Not being yanked out to a creek at midnight so y'all could skinny-dip. Not a time when I had to stand between you and somebody you wanted to punch, Ella Rae, and not even the night you punched me. I wouldn't trade a single thing about my life, and that means Mitch too. He may have been the only man I have ever loved, but the two of you were the real loves of my life. The ones I could always count on to beat up a bully in first grade, or come to my rescue, or watch me walk to my house in the dark, or help me look for a lost dog for three days.

"I was never lonely and I was never afraid I wouldn't have somebody to do something with. I went on your honeymoon, for heaven's sake, Carrigan! Some people go their entire lives without a friend like that, and I've had two. I have been so blessed. And I am blessed now. My heart is filled with gratitude. Look at all this." She gestured at the beauty all around us. "Who gets to go out like this? Y'all did this for me. I love you both so much."

Ella Rae had begun crying after the first sentence and reached for Laine's hand. "I love you too. I wish you didn't have to go."

"Me too." She smiled and wiped her tears. "But I don't make the rules."

I felt the tears stinging my eyes too, but willed them not to fall. Then she mentioned the Rule Maker, and my hurt turned to anger. If I live to be one hundred, I will never understand the logic behind Laine's illness. If God wanted me to talk to him, he needed to answer some questions first, and so far, he'd been silent. So that made two of us.

"Enough," Laine said. "I don't want to waste days on tears. Let's see the baby bump today."

I was glad to get off the subject and raised my T-shirt.

Laine shook my belly slightly. "Asleep?" she asked.

"All morning," I confirmed. "Probably so he can wiggle all night."

"She," Laine said.

I smiled. I didn't have a feeling either way, and Jack and I had decided not to find out.

"You know that's Henry the Eighth," Ella Rae said. "Or Jack the Fourth, whatever." She and Jack had been convinced from the start the baby was a boy.

Jack walked up the steps then and reached down to pat my belly. "Jackson Madison Whitfield the Fourth," he said. "What's my boy been doing today?"

We became engrossed in the daily argument over the sex of my child, and the Mitch Montgomery conversation was forgotten. Later that night, while I listened to Jack's even breathing in bed beside me, I slipped out of bed, sat in the window seat, and thought about it again. Laine's confession had stunned me. And my heart ached for her. Not just because of the circumstances, but because she never shared the burden with us.

Things had always been easier for me because of Ella Rae and Laine. Whether it was choosing an outfit or some problem I couldn't solve, they had always been my sounding boards and my touchstone. They kept me grounded, and even when they didn't agree with me, or downright told me I was an idiot, I could always take my problems to them. I couldn't imagine my life without either of them, although the day was approaching when I'd have to.

"Hey, baby." Jack's voice was heavy with sleep. "You okay?"

"I'm fine." I went back to bed, laid my head on his chest, and closed my eyes. But sleep didn't come for a very long time.

CHAPTER TWELVE

On the first day of December I woke to muffled but clearly panicked voices. I grabbed my robe and rushed downstairs to see Jack carrying Laine in his arms out the front door. Debra had her nursing bag in hand as she ran after them and called back to me, "Laine is hemorrhaging. We're headed to the ER."

My knees felt like jelly, but I ran back upstairs and woke up Ella Rae.

"Get up, Rae. Laine is bleeding."

Immediately she was wide-awake and horror stricken. "What?"

"Get dressed," I said. I ran to my own room to do the same. The God I didn't talk to heard plenty from me on this morning, but it was the same terrified plea over and over and over. *Please don't take her yet, please don't take her yet.*

Within ten minutes Ella Rae and I were downstairs and ready to leave. Poppa Jack was waiting with his SUV running. My heart was full of love for Poppa Jack at that moment. He didn't say a word, just took my hand, helped me into the front seat, and patted my shoulder. Then he made sure Ella Rae was secure in the back. And off we went to Shreveport at blazing speed.

Ella Rae and I said very little during the ninety-minute drive. Each of us texted and called Jack and Debra every five minutes, but we never got an answer. Poppa Jack reminded us that Jack was probably driving faster than normal and unable to respond, and Debra was surely tending to Laine. He was silent for most of the trip too. But at one point he looked at me and said, "She'll be all right. She's a fighter in her own way."

I had never heard anyone call Laine a fighter. Quite the opposite. She was a peacemaker. A fighter? She wouldn't even take the chemo. I wondered what in the world would've made him say that. Poppa Jack was wrong, and I was scared to death of what we'd find waiting for us at the other end of this trip because Laine *wasn't* a fighter.

Poppa Jack dropped us at the ER door and we ran inside. Jack was waiting for us.

"They took her back as soon as we got here," he said. "Laine said she wasn't in much pain. Frankly, I'm not sure that was true. Debra said it started as soon as she got up this morning and it was a significant hemorrhage. I don't know anything more than that."

Ella Rae cried. I got mad. In other words, things were as normal as you could expect them to be in this situation.

For the next hour, I paced back and forth, trying to see

between the crack in the doors, hoping to catch a glimpse inside the dungeon. She was back there somewhere, and I was in a state of high alert. But as long as I couldn't see anyone in scrubs rushing or shoving carts around, or hear anybody yelling "code blue"—whatever that meant—I could convince myself she was okay. So I watched through that little sliver of daylight for nearly thirty minutes before Jack made me sit down. And I only complied because he said the stress wasn't good for the baby.

No one would answer any questions, and the sixteen-year-old gum-popping receptionist was about one more bubble from having Ella Rae snatch her out of her chair and send her back there to fetch some information. She was miraculously saved when an ER nurse came out and said, "Carrigan Whitfield? Ella Weeks? You can come in now."

We nearly ran over each other getting to the door.

"She's in room 8, to your left," the nurse said.

We walked into the small room and found her sitting up in the bed.

"Hey, y'all." She smiled.

I could've slapped her. Then hugged her. Then slapped her again.

"You scared us to death," I said.

"What happened?" Ella Rae said.

"The tumor started bleeding," Laine said. "They've stopped it now, but I need a little procedure to have it cauterized. It's not a big deal." She looked more pale than usual, but her voice was strong and she was in good spirits.

"Of course it's a big deal, Laine," I said.

"No, really it isn't," she said. "They will do the surgery, give me a couple of pints of new blood, and send me home. I'll be good as new. I've called Mama. Mrs. Diane called her right after we left this morning, then went to pick her up. They'll be here shortly. It's okay. Y'all go home."

Neither Ella Rae nor I had an answer for that.

Laine gave me a puzzled look. "What's the matter?"

"What's the matter?" I said. "Really?"

"We thought you were dying," Ella Rae said.

"I am," Laine said.

"Stop it!" I said. "I hate it when you do that. Be serious."

"Carrigan, everything about this place, this situation, this whole thing, is serious. It's why I don't want to be. This is no place for you right now. It isn't good for the baby. You need to go home. Ella Rae, you too. I need to spend some time with Mama. I'll be home in a couple of days. I promise."

"Why are you rushing us out of here?"

"Because you don't need to be here," she said. "You could get the Swahili flu around this place. Now wash your hands and get out of here."

"You promise that's all the doctor said?" Ella Rae asked.

"I promise," Laine said. "I would tell you if it were anything else. My oncologist was in the hospital making rounds this morning, so they paged him and he was the one who told me what was happening. I promise. He says I'll feel better after this little procedure. It truly isn't a big deal. I'd just like to spend this time with Mama. Alone."

"Do you need anything?" Ella Rae said.

"Food, clothes, anything?" I said.

"No," Laine answered. "I'll be in this lovely designer gown with my backside showing for a couple of days. Debra had the presence of mind to grab my robe when we left. I doubt I'll go dancing on the way home. So I'm all set. Go home. Do something for the next couple of days that doesn't revolve around me. It'll be good for both of you."

We left reluctantly, with Laine shooing us out the door. Poppa Jack stayed to ride home with Mrs. Diane, and Debra rode back with Jack. Ella Rae and I left in Poppa Jack's SUV.

"That scared me, Carrigan," she said.

"It scared me too."

"I can't believe she made us leave," Ella Rae said. "But I get that she wants her mama."

"I get it too. Doesn't mean I didn't want to stay, though."

I know," Ella Rae said.

"I wish Mrs. Jeannette would just come stay at the house. There's plenty of room."

"She's just a lady like that, Carrigan. Doesn't want to impose. You and I are imposers."

I laughed. "You and I are a great many things."

"Carrigan . . . your shirt is moving back and forth by itself. Is that Henry the Eighth doing all that?"

I laughed again. "It is. Wanna feel it?"

"No . . . Kinda . . . I'm not sure."

"You're thirty years old. You've never felt a baby move?"

"Okay, I don't just walk up to any random pregnant chick and put my hand on her stomach."

"Just give me your hand."

"No!"

"Hurry while it's still turning flips."

"Is it weird?"

"Is that why you won't ever touch my belly? You think it's weird?"

"Look . . . I just don't have that whole 'Wow . . . you're glowing . . . I'm enchanted' maternal thing going on."

"No? You're kidding me." I don't think anybody had suspected Ella Rae of a maternal streak.

"Ha-ha. I mean, I'm happy for you if you're happy. I just don't see me doing it. Ever."

"Never say never, Rae. And give me your hand."

She finally put her hand on my belly, and after a few seconds the baby put on a show.

Ella Rae's hand flew over her mouth. "Are you kidding me? That is so cool! It's like a big lizard rolling around in there! I bet it's all slimy and slick."

I threw her hand off me. "A lizard?"

"No, let me feel!"

"No," I said, "you are not calling my baby a lizard. Now play with the radio and keep your hands off me. I'm driving."

"That was seriously different," she said. "When we get home, I think I'll watch *Jurassic Park*."

A classic Ella Rae moment.

※

Laine rallied after the transfusion and actually looked and felt better than she had in weeks. Christmas was a happy time at the Farm for everyone, but I couldn't seem to dredge up the spirit. I tried not to let it permeate everything, but in my heart of hearts, I knew this was Laine's last December. I was moody and weepy most of the month, but managed to sell it as hormone wars. At least I sold it to everybody but Jack.

"I don't know why you think you have to be brave even when we're alone," he told me in bed on Christmas Eve. That was all it took. I cried myself to sleep on his shoulder and woke up Christmas morning determined to have a good day.

And it was. The house was full to the brim with family—Jack's, mine, Ella Rae's, and Laine's. It was a joyful day, full of laughter and love. Laine gave Ella Rae and me each a picture that she'd had enlarged and framed—a snapshot of the three of us sitting on the old stone bridge at Willow Creek.

Tommy had snapped that picture of us with the new camera Ella Rae had given him for his birthday. He loved to take pictures of wildlife and said Ella Rae and I were the perfect example of that, and Laine was a doe caught in headlights. That was still a running joke.

The bridge had long been out of use and was covered in moss and ferns. Laine was pointing to something in the water, and Ella Rae was looking at it, smiling. I had my head thrown back laughing. It was a beautiful, unplanned shot that caught the spirit of us all.

❧

For New Year's Eve, Jack planned a fireworks show at the Farm. One of his buddies owned a demolition company, and another one owned a fireworks company. I knew Sean O'Reilly, the explosives friend. Years ago he blew up a beaver dam on the creek behind the old barn, and blew off his little finger in the process. Jack assured me there would be no holes in the earth this time and that Sean had gotten much better at what he did now.

He was right. The show was spectacular.

The Farm had become the gathering place for close friends and family as the months had gone by. New Year's Eve brought a huge crowd. While Ella Rae had once been reluctant to rub my belly, it never fazed anyone else. Thirty people touched my stomach that night. I had become accustomed to it, but I don't think Jack ever cared for it. Around ten o'clock, he came and stood behind me and laced his fingers across my stomach.

I laughed. "Are you jealous?"

"I'm not," he said. "I'd just rather not watch everybody in town lay their hands on you."

"So you are jealous."

"Probably," he said. "Anyway, problem solved."

The stroke of midnight came and we toasted with champagne, and for me, apple juice. This pregnancy had been relatively easy on me, except for the nausea early on. But for a girl who used to party until the wee hours, when ten p.m. came, I was ready to go to bed. So midnight was a stretch for me. I said good night to the crowd and climbed the stairs to our bedroom. Jack walked up with me and asked me if I wanted him to stay.

"No, not at all," I said. "Go mingle with the peeps. I'll be asleep as soon as my head hits the pillow."

He nuzzled my neck. "What if I want to love on my wife when I come to bed?"

"You do whatever you gotta do, buddy." I put my hands on either side of his face. "Just don't wake me up."

"Ouch." He winced and held his chest. "You got me." He popped me on the backside with his palm and slipped out the door.

I had just turned the light off when the bedroom door opened again. I didn't bother to turn over. "Give it up, Jack Whitfield. No sex tonight."

Laine giggled. "Come on, just one time."

I flipped on the light to find Laine and Ella Rae standing in my bedroom, each holding a bottle of champagne and covered in confetti and streamers. "What are y'all doing?"

"What are *you* doing?" Laine said.

I sat up in bed and threw back the covers. "Ella Rae! Did you let her get drunk? You know she's not supposed to drink while she's taking pain pills!"

"Will you chill out?" Ella Rae said. "She's only had, like, I don't know, a half a bottle." Ella Rae looked at her own bottle. "And I've only had, like, two. It ain't that big a deal."

"Half a bottle? She can't drink a shot glass of alcohol, Rae, you know that! Sit down, Laine," I said. "Are you okay?"

She plopped down in the overstuffed chair and rolled her eyes. "You need to get over yourself, Missy. And by the way, I did have my medication and I did wash it down with champagne and it was goooooood!"

Ella Rae jumped into my bed and stuffed the pillows behind her. "Here's what," she said. "Laine got a little drunk . . ."

"I told you not to say drunk." Laine put a finger to her lips.

"I mean tipsy," Ella Rae said. "Laine got a little tipsy . . . so she could explain death to us."

"Not that either, idiot." Laine snatched the bottle away from her. "You drank it all?"

"Ahhh." Ella Rae pulled a bottle from the pocket of her coat. "But I came prepared."

"Thank God!" Laine rubbed her hands together while Ella Rae struggled with the cork.

Laine and Ella Rae drinking while I was pregnant and trying to sleep? This had surely been a season of firsts. I watched Ella Rae fumble with the cork for a full thirty seconds before I said, "Give it here. You're going to put somebody's eye out." I twisted the wire and popped the cork. "Here you go."

"I'm sorry you can't have any," Ella Rae said.

"I'm good," I said. "Now what are we here to discuss?"

They looked at each other, clueless.

"My funeral," Laine said. "I want to plan my funeral."

I stared at her. "You want to plan your funeral . . . tipsy?"

She cocked her head. "Can you think of a better time?"

I thought about that for a second. I had to give her this

one. I reached into the drawer of my nightstand for a pen and notebook. "Okay." I looked back at her. "Knock yourself out."

She leaned back in the chair, swirling the champagne in the bottle. "Okay, first of all, I don't want this big, weepy, drawn-out cry fest. I mean, it's so . . . ridiculous."

I continued to stare at her.

She looked at me. "Write it down."

"Okay." I began writing. "No big, weepy, cry fest."

"No wailing or moaning," she continued. "I mean . . . really. No wailing or moaning."

"No wailing or moaning," I repeated.

"Hey, you've had that bottle for ten minutes," Ella Rae said. "Give it back."

"I've had it for like . . . ten seconds."

I snatched the bottle from Laine and passed it to Ella Rae.

Laine pouted a moment but continued, "There should be music, but not sad music."

"Music." I wrote it down. "Not sad."

"Well, maybe a little sad. I'll be dead and all."

The little dagger in my heart twisted.

"Help me think of a good song."

"I know!" Ella Rae began singing, "I'm going home gonna load my shotgun, wait by the door and light a cigarette, he wants a fight, well now he's got one, he ain't seen me crazy yet."

"Don't even pay attention to her," I said.

"What?" Ella Rae said. "What'd I do?"

"I think maybe something by—I don't know," Laine said. "You decide."

I drew little circles on the paper in an effort to push this whole conversation from my mind.

"And I need you to deliver the . . . you know, the, well . . . the eulo . . ."

"The eulogy?"

"Yes, the eulogy."

"Yes! Bingo. Yahtzee. Booyah. Touchdown!" Ella Rae said.

I slammed the notebook shut. "No," I said. "I can't do it."

Laine waved me off. "Of course you can," she said. "Just tell them who I am . . . was. What's the big deal? It'll be easy."

"You've lost your mind, Laine." I threw the notebook back in the drawer and slammed it shut.

Ella Rae laughed. "Ouch," she said. "Sister gal didn't like the request."

Laine laughed with her. "Well, I'd do it myself, but I'll be the dead one. So there's that."

"She's gotcha there, Carri," Ella Rae said.

"Ella Rae, shut up. You aren't helping."

"Wasn't trying to," she said. "Duh."

Laine was crazy. I couldn't stand in front of a church full of people and tell them who she was. Not without the aforementioned wailing and weeping. She should know better than to ask me. It was wrong. So wrong.

"Laine," I said, "maybe we should talk about this when we're—you know, maybe . . ."

"Do you think there's any more of this champagne downstairs?" Ella Rae peered into the empty bottle.

"Ella Rae, please."

"Fine." She crossed her arms. "I'll wait for you to go back to sleep, if that baby lizard will let you. You sure have been grouchy lately. I don't know when you stopped being fun. Wait . . ." She pointed to the sky, indicating a light bulb moment. "It was when you got knocked up."

"Hormones," Laine said. She turned back to me. "Listen, it ain't that big a deal. All you have to do is stand there and talk for ten minutes about all the wonderful traits I used to have, still have, you know what I mean. Whaddaya think, buddy?"

"I think maybe we should discuss this tomorrow."

She looked at Ella Rae who was apparently counting something on the ceiling and snickered. Then she turned sober as a judge. "Please say you'll do this for me. Nobody wants to talk about it . . . me either. But I need to know you'll do this last thing for me."

Everything in me was screaming, *No!* I'd rather have my eyes pecked out by rabid crows. But how could I deny her? She was right, of course. It would be the last thing I could ever do for her. I was constantly looking for ways to make her comfortable. Not just physically but emotionally as well, and she never took me up on anything. I couldn't tell her no now. And how could I really trust anyone else to do it? I would pick their words apart, because unless it was Ella Rae or me, there was no way to do her justice. I closed my eyes and heard myself saying, "Yes."

She smiled and stood up. "Come on, Ella Rae," she said. "We got what we came for."

"Finally," Ella Rae said. "Can we ditch this stick-in-the-mud and go back to the party?"

Laine winked at me. "Thank you." She squeezed my hand. "It means more to me than you know."

I faked a smile at her as the door closed behind them, then flung myself back against the bed. I would dread this promise from now until Laine was no longer with us. How was I ever supposed to make anybody in that church understand who Laine Landry is? Was, rather. And what was I supposed to say? Here lies a chick who was so loyal she compromised her standards a thousand times to accommodate my lack of them? TMI, probably.

How about, here lies a chick who loved McDonald's French fries but hated their burgers? Or loved Burger King burgers and hated their fries? Or had a heart for the underdog and a moral compass that would rival Mother Teresa?

How could I ever explain how her words could cut me to the quick but always came from a place in her heart that wanted the very best for me? How could I communicate to anybody in ten minutes or ten hours, or ten days even, what I had lost? What the world had lost? I would never be able to make anyone understand. Not even if I wrote a book about it.

There were no tears that night, just an increasing alarm that the days were flying by and they were taking Laine's life with them.

Much later, when Jack came to bed, I clung to him. The weight of what the future would hold felt like a ton of bricks on my shoulders. I had avoided thinking about Laine's death, and I absolutely never thought about her funeral. When the notions pushed their way into my mind, I had always pushed back. But the day was coming, and I was helpless to stop it. No matter how much I tried, no matter how much I fought, this was a battle I wasn't going to win. There would be a funeral, and even the guest of honor had embraced it.

CHAPTER THIRTEEN

By the time late March rolled around I was miserable, for many reasons. Laine was slipping; I could see it happening every day. The changes weren't dramatic, but even small things alarmed me. The circles under her eyes seemed darker, her appetite wasn't good, and she'd lost some weight. Maybe only five pounds or so, but it was noticeable. Her demeanor, however, hadn't changed. She was still her cheerful self and quite excited about the arrival of the baby.

I, on the other hand, had gained twenty-two pounds and felt like a beached whale. Everyone, including my doctor, said my weight was perfect. But I felt like a cow and was sure I resembled one. I wondered all the time how other women did this four and five and six times. When I sat cross-legged in the bathtub I felt like a Buddha statue.

Being pregnant had been fun for exactly seven months. After that, it had just pretty much sucked. My boobies felt like rocks, I had to pee every thirty seconds, and if anyone looked at me sideways I cried. When I compared my pregnancy to what Laine was going through, I realized how incredibly shallow and whiny I was being, but I couldn't seem to help myself.

I was sitting on a bar stool in the kitchen when Jack came in and kissed my forehead. "Good morning, beautiful," he said.

"Whatever," I said. I made a face. When he didn't respond, I pressed. "Do I disgust you?"

He picked up one of Mamie's famous cinnamon rolls, still warm and thick with icing, and took a big bite. My mouth watered watching him eat. Just the smell of those rolls could pack five pounds on a person. I didn't dare eat one. Besides, I might as well bypass my mouth and tape them directly on my butt and thighs. That's where they'd end up anyway. I peeled an orange.

"You are more beautiful to me than you have ever been," Jack said.

Laine sipped orange juice and nibbled a piece of dry toast. "Don't even bother, Jack," she said. "She won't believe a word you say."

"You didn't have to get a winch truck to pull you out of bed this morning." I squinted my eyes at her. "There are mirrors in this house. I can see myself, you know."

"Carri, you are the perfect size," Laine said. "Even Doctor Davis says so. You look cute in your clothes, not all puffy and swollen. But I do wish you would wear something other than these sad-looking, faded overalls every day." She tugged on the strap.

"I can't help it," I said. "They're the only thing that feel good."

She was right, though. I wore them daily, and I was now two weeks into zero makeup at all. My hair was in a clip on top of my head, and I could see red curls springing every direction. I probably should at least brush my hair. I turned to Jack again. "Really, do I disgust you?"

He smiled and patted my cheek. "I love you, sweet girl. See you at eleven." And out the door he went.

"See?" I said to Laine. "He can't even look at me for long."

"Get over yourself," she said. "We're almost there." She shoved her plate of toast and fruit away from her, even though she'd barely touched it.

"You didn't eat anything, Laine," I said. "Are you feeling all right?"

She shrugged a little. "Most days," she answered.

That wasn't the answer I was looking for but most probably all I was going to get. I always wanted more, but those boundary lines had been drawn a long time ago. I tried not to cross them, but once in a while I did anyway. Sometime around Christmas I had asked her if she still thought nixing the chemo had been the route to take and she'd gotten a little defensive with me.

"Look, Carrigan. It was my choice to make. And as soon as I made it, I had inner peace instead of that awful turmoil I had gone through for days. I didn't take the treatment because I didn't want my last days on earth to be spent sick and bald and throwing up. I wanted to spend it appreciating and loving the people who had been in my life. It may have bought me a little more time, but at what cost? I want to feel strong until this disease I didn't choose strips me of that. Not because a poison I *did* choose did it for me. I can't speak for other people, but for me it was a no-brainer. I know you love me and I know this hurts you. But please, don't question my decisions any more. If there's something you need to know, I promise I will tell you."

What do you say to that? She wanted to fight the monster on her terms, and I grudgingly had to admire that. It was easy for me to say I'd have taken the treatment. I wasn't the one with the death sentence hanging over my head. From that day forward, I'd been careful to let her set the tone. Even if it drove me insane, and it always, always did, Laine changed the subject back to me. "So, as cute as you look in your little overalls, will you please change clothes before we go to the doctor's office?"

"Fine." I threw up my hands. "If you and Ella Rae can find me something to wear, I'll put it on."

An hour later, I had been pronounced fit to leave the house. I had to give them props. I did look a lot better. I didn't like how these clothes clung to me, but they were stylish and cute and I felt pretty, and that did wonders for my attitude. I'd turned into such a girlie girl lately. When Jack came in, he whistled at me and I blushed like a little girl. Ugh, these freaking hormones. How embarrassing.

Jack had begun making the "OB run," as Ella Rae called it, with us when I started having to go weekly. When I was only going to the OB-GYN monthly, just the girls and I went. We shopped, had lunch, and made a day of it. But the closer my time got, the more Jack hovered. We had watched a Lamaze film in our bedroom a few nights earlier, and I thought he was going to change his mind about the delivery room. "I don't think I can watch this, Carrigan."

"What?" I said. "What do you mean?"

"I mean, maybe you should just let them put you to sleep and take the baby out." He looked a little pale.

"Jack," I said, "you watch cows have babies all the time. What is wrong with you?"

"It's not having the baby," he said. "Do you hear her? I don't think I can listen to you do that."

I winced. I hadn't been too thrilled about the screaming either, and it was awfully sweet of him to be so concerned, but if he thought he was going to leave me in the delivery room, he was out of his mind. "I won't scream like that."

"You say that now," he said. "She probably said it too."

I laughed. My sweet Jack, who was tough as nails, didn't want to see me in pain. "I love you."

"I bet you won't be saying that then." He pointed at the TV.

"Oh, I will too," I said. I planted a kiss on his cheek. "It won't be that bad." I didn't believe a word of that, but it had seemed to pacify him. Slightly.

"Let's roll, Team Whitfield," Laine called. "Places to go and people to see."

My entourage was waiting in the driveway when I came down the porch steps. Jack jumped out of the driver's seat and held my hand while I got in the SUV. I took the hand he extended. "I hate this," I said. He just smiled. Truthfully, I really had enjoyed being pregnant up until the past month. I felt awkward and clumsy now. Two things I had never felt in my life. I couldn't jog at all any more either. I kept feeling like I needed to hold my hands under my belly. I was ready for this baby to see the outside world. I highly commend and admire women who love being pregnant and want to have a baby every year . . . but I ain't one of them.

My OB-GYN, Doctor Ike Davis, was also Laine's and Ella Rae's regular doctor. He was a sweet, jolly, older man with kind eyes and a heart of gold. He had a deer camp close to Bon Dieu Falls and was a college friend of Poppa Jack and my daddy. He often came to the annual Crawfish Boil as well. I knew he'd felt awful about Laine. She had gone for her regular checkup barely a year before she'd been diagnosed with ovarian cancer. The checkup had revealed nothing abnormal. Laine knew that a routine pap smear wouldn't detect ovarian cancer, and after her diagnosis, she assured Doctor Davis she understood that. He called the Farm every week or two to check on her and had even stopped by a couple of times. I knew her illness had broken his heart, and on some level he felt some misguided responsibility. But Laine had never blamed him. Laine never blamed anybody.

"Here are all my favorite patients!" Doctor Davis said when he entered the exam room. He hugged each of us and shook hands with Jack. "How are you feeling, dear?" he asked Laine.

She playfully hit him on the shoulder. "Like pitching for the Saints."

He looked at me puzzled.

"She thinks they play baseball," I explained.

He laughed. "Sometimes I wish they did." He smiled. "And how are you feeling, dear?"

"Like a busted can of biscuits," I said.

Doctor Davis laughed. "First time I've heard that one," he said. "But your chart looks great. You've only gained twenty-three pounds. And your blood pressure is perfect. I'm proud of you."

"Whoop-de-do," I said.

Laine gave him a pleading look. "Please deliver this baby so her attitude will get better."

"You been giving everybody a hard time?" Doctor Davis said.

"I have no idea what she means."

"Huh," Ella Rae said.

"Jack?" Doctor Davis said.

"Been a perfect angel," he answered.

"Ass-kisser," Ella Rae said.

We all got a good laugh at that, including Doctor Davis.

"I need to utilize your pregnant-wife skills with some other husbands, Jack," he said. "Now, let's take a look, shall we?"

I looked at Ella Rae, Laine, and Jack, all glued in their same places. "Come on, y'all," I said, "at least look out the window till I get the sheet wrapped around me."

Ella Rae looked exasperated. "Is there anybody in this room who hasn't seen you naked?" she asked.

Everybody looked at each other and then all looked back at me.

It's one thing to go to the girl doctor by yourself, you know? It's uncomfortable, and it's always cold and always humiliating. But imagine if you had the doctor, his nurse, and three other people in the room with you. See what I mean?

"How can you ask me to leave when I'll never witness anything like this again?" Laine said.

"Really?" I glared at her. "Did you just play the death card so you could stay in here?"

She smiled smugly. "I did." Of course Ella Rae wasn't about to leave if Laine was staying. Jack argued he put the baby there in the first place and he certainly wasn't going anywhere. So I lost the round and everybody stayed. I could have gone out to the highways and byways and compelled the widows and the strangers to come in, I guess. I could've gathered people off the street. Doctor Davis's rules seemed to fly out the window when we arrived.

At least Jack had the good sense to turn his back during the actual exam. But I'm pretty sure the other two would've taken pictures if Doctor Davis would have let them.

When the exam was completed, Laine jumped right in. "Well?"

"Well," Doctor Davis said, "anytime now."

I struggled to sit up and reached for Jack's hand. "What do you mean, anytime? I'm not due till next week."

"Babies have a way of showing up whenever they want to." He smiled. "You're three centimeters dilated. You could stay there for hours or for days. Call me when you go into labor or when your water breaks. You have my cell number and home number, right?"

I nodded. It just got real in here.

Ella Rae was dancing up and down in place and Laine was grinning from ear to ear. Jack was silent and squeezing my hand so hard it hurt.

"Jack." I wriggled my hand around. "Ouch!"

"I'm sorry, baby." He picked up my hand and kissed it. "Better?"

I made a face at him. "What am I, five years old?"

"Next time I see you, we'll fetch a baby, okay?" Doctor Davis said.

"Okay," I said. "Thank you."

"Can I see you outside a minute, Doc?" Jack asked.

"Sure, Jack." He slid open the door. "Laine, you be sure and call me if you need anything."

Doctor Davis and Jack disappeared into the hallway, and Laine and Ella Rae both started squealing and asking questions.

"Are you scared? Are you freaked out? Does it hurt? Can you feel it? What's it like?" They fired off round after round so fast I couldn't tell who asked what question. But I could tell them, for sure, the answer to each one was an emphatic, *Yes!*

"I just wasn't expecting him to say . . . you know, I mean, I thought I had a week or two . . . Yes, I am freaked out."

"It's okay." Laine handed me my pants. "We'll be here, I promise."

My heart was filled with gratitude because Laine would

be here to see my baby, to hold it, love it. On the other hand, I was so terrified I found it hard to complete a sentence. I wasn't afraid of having the baby, but I was suddenly quite intensely aware that I would be its mother. What did I know about a baby? They had bobbleheads and they made puppy sounds. That was the extent of my knowledge on the subject.

What had I been thinking? I couldn't be anybody's mother. I had just learned how to be a wife fifteen minutes ago. I'd been living in la-la land for the past seven months. As long as the baby was inside me, I was mother of the year. But it was coming out now, and they were going to deposit it in my lap. I had to take it home with me. Its little life was in my hands. It would look to me for food and safety and guidance. I was an idiot! And my hands were shaking like leaves.

"I'm good." I faked a smile and slipped on my pants. "It's all good."

"Great," Laine said, "'cause I am starving. Let's eat."

Music to my ears. She ate like a bird now and any declaration of hunger sent us all scrambling to fetch food for her. The announcement also temporarily distracted me from worrying about dropping my baby the first time I held it or forgetting where I put it. Jack was waiting for us in the parking lot and we drove over to our favorite Mexican place, Simpaticos. We were seated at the table before I even thought to ask Jack why he'd spoken to Doctor Davis.

"What was that all about?" I asked.

"Nothing."

"Something," I corrected.

"I was just asking about anesthesia," he said. "Nothing special."

"What? Are you serious?"

"Look, Carri," he said, "that film we watched was bad. It was bad."

The girls and I began laughing.

"I don't want to take anything, Jack," I said. "That's why we watched the Lamaze DVDs."

"We'll see." He took another drink of his beer. "I'm just making a backup plan."

I shook my head. That was my Jack. Always a backup plan, no matter what the circumstances.

Ella Rae gave Laine the eagle eye. "You don't have to lick the bowl, Laine. They'll bring you some more."

"Shut up, Rae." Laine scraped the bottom of her salsa with a chip. "You complain if I don't eat and you complain if I do."

Ella Rae flagged down our server. "Excuse me," she said. "Could we have some more chips and salsa? Thank you." She turned to Laine. "Slow down, Porky, help is on the way."

"They're just so good today," Laine said, licking her fingers, and pointed at my salsa bowl. "Can I have yours?" I slid my salsa over to her. "Knock yourself out, girl," I said.

"I feel great today," Laine said. "Like I could run a marathon."

Ella Rae snorted. "Please. You wouldn't run thirty feet when you didn't have cancer."

In some social circles a statement like that would undoubtedly be rude, even cruel. But in our circle, it was hilarious. Laine laughed so hard I thought she'd choke on her chips.

Jack shook his head. "You three have the most unusual relationship."

"Yes, we do," Laine said. Just then the fresh chips and salsa arrived. "Ahhhh, finally."

"So," Ella Rae said, "let's talk baby names. And I want answers this time, not any of that 'we haven't decided' crap. It's bad enough you won't tell us what flavor it is."

"I don't know what flavor it is." I smiled and looked at Jack. "But Jack knows."

"What?" Ella Rae and Laine said in shocked unison.

"When did you find out?" Laine crammed her mouth full at the same time she tried to ask the question.

Jack smiled but remained silent.

"This is wrong," Ella Rae said. "Why does he get to know and we don't?"

"You know, Rae," I said, "I don't know why my *Baby Daddy* should know and you shouldn't. He wanted to know, so he called and Doctor Davis told him."

"That's so unfair," Laine said. "Wait . . . I see a light." She grabbed her chest and rolled her eyes back in her head. "This could be it. I feel myself slipping . . ." She looked back at Jack. "That didn't work, did it?"

"Not even close."

"Please tell me you don't know, Carrigan," Laine said to me.

"I don't. I swear," I said. "And don't do that fake dying any more. I don't like it. He won't even tell me what it is. I guess I could ask, but we're this close now, I'll just wait."

"What's happened to you?" Ella Rae asked. "Who are you? The whole time you've been preggers, you've either been mad as an old wet hen or chilled out like a glaucoma patient in California. I never know what I'm gonna find in the mornings."

I laughed. "Have I been that bad?"

Nobody answered.

I laughed harder now. "Sorry, I thought I'd been a picture perfect pregnant person."

Ella Rae contorted her face and put on her best whiny pouty voice. "It's hot. It's cold. I want a popsicle. I hate popsicles. I'm sleepy. I can't sleep."

"I'm hungry. I'm nauseated. It's too bright. It's too dark. I want pizza. I hate pizza," Laine added.

I was cracking up and so was Jack. "Stop," I said. "I get it."

"I'm never getting pregnant," Ella Rae said. "It makes you a nut case."

"That ain't why," I said. "You can't leave alcohol alone for nine straight months."

"That is a lie!" she said.

"We all good here?" our server asked, appearing at the table.

"One more margarita," Ella Rae said.

"See!" I shouted.

"Nothing says 'I mean business' like a shopping cart at the liquor store, Rae," Laine said. "I was mortified."

"It was for a party," Ella Rae defended.

"A party of one," I said.

"Okay." Ella Rae stopped laughing long enough to pretend

to be offended. "Is this some kind of intervention? Because I gotta tell y'all, I'm not fixing to be intervened. Besides, drinking rum before ten a.m. doesn't make you an alcoholic; it makes you a pirate."

Laine spewed iced tea through her nose, and I had to hold my belly under the baby, I was laughing so hard. Jack said nothing, just shook his head. The truth was Ella Rae didn't drink nearly as much as we teased her about it. And she absolutely didn't drink before ten a.m. But when she did drink, she was loud. That had earned her the reputation. She just never bothered denying it. Ella Rae was one of those people who never worried with what other folks said about her. She only cared about the opinion of her family and what she called her "inner circle." I had always admired her for that.

"Girl, stop," Laine said. "You're killing me."

Laine felt good, and she wasn't faking it. I could always tell when she faked it. But there wasn't an imitation smile or reaction in her today. It was all authentic. She didn't look great, but she felt great, and I'd take that any day. It made me feel like the whole world was perfect. We'd laughed so much the past hour and a half, I hadn't even thought about the cancer or what a terrible mother I was going to be. I looked around the table at everyone, so happy and relaxed, and wished I could bottle it, save it, preserve it.

"Enough," Laine said, wiping the tea from the table. "Let's go buy something for the baby. Of course, if we knew if it was a boy or a girl, it would help the selection process tremendously." She looked at Jack.

He grinned. "Not a chance."

"You are mean as a snake, Jack Whitfield," Ella Rae said.

I stood up to go. Immediately a whoosh of warmth ran down my legs. I stood still, looking at the puddle I was now standing in.

"My water just broke," I said.

Leave it to Ella Rae to sum up a situation: "Well, this ain't good."

CHAPTER FOURTEEN

"Push, Carri, push!" Laine yelled in my ear. "You're almost there! Go! Go! Go!"

I felt as if I'd been pushing for hours. If Jack or Laine told me to push one more time, somebody besides me would need a doctor tonight.

At least Ella Rae wasn't trying to pull that rah-rah crap with me. The last time I had seen her, she was in the corner of the room gagging. She bugged out at the first sign of blood. I would've laughed about it if I weren't giving birth to what was surely an alien baby, ripping its way into the world. I gritted my teeth and pushed again. Sweat dripped into my eyes, and I gripped Jack's hand so tight I thought his bones would break. The contraction finally subsided and I flopped back down on the bed.

"Great job!" Laine, ever the cheerleader, patted my shoulder.

"Shut up, Laine, and get out of my face."

"I know you don't mean that." She smiled and wiped my forehead.

"Oh, yes, I do mean it." I caught my breath, waiting for the next contraction that was about forty-five seconds away. I tried not to watch the fetal monitor, whose waves alerted me when another contraction would begin. Why did they even have it pointed in my direction? I sure wasn't likely to miss it.

Why, oh, why had I wanted to experience natural child-birth? It was like saying you wanted to experience someone peeling your fingernails off or having a root canal without the gas. Doctor Davis should have told me I really wanted the epidural when I assured him repeatedly I didn't. This was excruciating. It was worse than any injury I had ever suffered on the softball field. Worse than torn ligaments and pulled muscles and a bloody nose. I could have all of those at the same time and not even touch this pain.

Surely something was wrong. This couldn't be normal. Jack kissed my hand.

"Don't kiss me again. Not *ever*!" I snatched my hand away. But then the contractions returned, and I grabbed his hand back as quickly as I'd discarded it. I pushed and pushed until I couldn't push any more, then fell back against the bed.

"You're making progress, Carrigan," Doctor Davis said. "Don't quit on me."

"I can't push again." I grabbed the front of Jack's shirt. My breath came in gasps. "They're coming too fast. I'm too tired. I can't take another one. Please don't make me push again. Make it go away."

He looked so pained and pale I felt sorry for him. He kept telling me I never had to do this again, that he never wanted to see me hurt this way again. That he'd get a vasectomy tomorrow. That was the best idea I'd heard in years. I even offered to perform it myself, only my version involved a rusty hatchet and some rubbing alcohol.

"It won't be long now, baby, I promise. Just try again, okay? Just a few more times—"

"Go to hell." I flung his hand away and turned to Laine, who was on my other side. "I know you have drugs in your purse," I said. "I know what they are. Give me something, anything, please!"

Laine looked dumbfounded. "Carri, I can't give you cancer drugs!"

Great. Here I was, stuck with Susie Sunshine. All she was missing were pompoms and a short skirt.

"Useless . . . Get out of my sight." I turned back to Jack. At least it gave me some small amount of satisfaction to see the pained look on his face. I wanted him to suffer. He had killed me!

"Carrigan," Doctor Davis said, "if you will give me one more hard push, I promise you I'll hand you a baby."

My eyes pled with Jack. "Please, just leave it in there. I can't," I said. "Too tired, I can't do it again."

"Look at me, baby," Jack said, wiping my face with his hands and kissing me. "You are the bravest, most beautiful girl I have ever known, and I love you so much. Please, just one more time and you can stop. I promise. Just one more time."

I looked into his eyes, so full of love and concern. He was

so good to me. Even when I didn't deserve it, he was good to me. But I still wanted to kill him.

"Once more and that's it." I ground the words out through gritted teeth. "That's it, you hear me?"

I looked at the monitor. The last wave of contractions was almost here. I took a deep breath and prepared to push. If it didn't happen this time, I would just go ahead and die on this table. I was remarkably all right with that.

I shut my eyes tight, locked my jaws together, and pushed. I felt the scream through my clenched teeth, felt the release, and then relief came at last as I collapsed on the bed.

I had done it. I opened my eyes and saw tears roll down Jack's face. I heard Laine gasp in awe and heard Ella Rae hit the floor when she fainted. Then I heard my baby cry.

"It's a girl!" Doctor Davis said. "A very mad little girl with a whole lot of red hair!"

"Is she all right?"

"She is perfect," Doctor Davis said. "Give me a couple of minutes and she's all yours."

I was crying, Jack was crying, Laine was crying, and Ella Rae was being helped into a chair by two nurses. We watched as they cleaned the baby, weighed her, and wrapped her up tight in blankets. Doctor Davis brought her to me and put her in my arms. "Congratulations, Mama and Daddy," he said. "She's an eight-pound beauty. You did good, Mama."

All I could do was stare at her. Perfect, indeed. A perfect little beauty with pouty pink lips and a tuft of red hair. I knew as soon as I touched her that my life would never be the same, and I didn't want it to be. This soft little helpless creature wiggling and squirming in my arms tugged at my heart in a way I had never felt before.

How could that happen in thirty seconds? Surely there was a word for this stronger than love. Holding her made me feel like I had come home after a very long trip that I hadn't really wanted to go on. I couldn't take my eyes off of her. I hadn't even known I wanted her, but her existence somehow soothed me. My life up until this very moment seemed like a series of hits and misses. Then someone had placed this gift in my arms that I didn't deserve, and now my life made complete sense. Just like that.

I'd heard the word *miracle* thrown around all my life. But tonight my infant girl changed my whole perspective on the world just by entering it. If that wasn't a miracle, I didn't know what was.

I held her up to Jack, and he carefully took her from my arms. I'd only seen Jack cry once in my life, when his grandfather died. Watching him hold our daughter for the first time was one of the sweetest moments of my life. Like me, he just stared at her.

Ella Rae finally hobbled over to us and rolled her eyes. "I am *so* embarrassed," she said.

Laine and I both laughed, finally breaking up the tear fest.

"In the immortal words of Tommy Weeks," Laine said, "it ain't a party till somebody hits the floor."

"I just couldn't take all that grunting and pushing business," Ella Rae said. "I'm glad that's over."

"The show was tough on you, huh?" I made a face. "You should've been in my seat."

"I was fine until that first . . . thing came out."

"What thing?"

"I don't know what it was," Ella Rae said disgustedly. "There was stuff coming out of you all night!"

I was horrified. "Tell me you didn't take pictures."

"Take pictures?" she said. "I couldn't even look."

"Thank God!" Ella Rae was the official photographer for the event, but I had told her repeatedly not to get anything that showed me in a less than flattering light. Meaning, don't snap pictures of my business.

"By the way, Carrigan," Laine said, "you had some pretty harsh words for me tonight. I was only trying to help."

"Seriously?" I said. "I expected you to start turning cartwheels any minute. You were like an NFL cheerleader. It was very annoying."

"I actually thought at one point you were gonna take a swing at me."

"Too much energy," I said, "or I would've."

"Look," Laine whispered. She pointed at Jack and the baby by the window. He was holding her close to his face and whispering. She looked as if she were watching him and understanding every word. Ella Rae, thankfully, had the presence of mind to snap a picture of it. Jack just kept on whispering.

"I told you what kind of man Jack Whitfield was, didn't I?" Laine said softly.

I smiled and wiped at the tears. "Yes, you did," I agreed. "You always did."

"Okay, okay," Ella Rae said, "that's enough of the *Little House on the Prairie* crap. Bring us the baby, Daddy!"

Jack walked over and handed her to Laine. "Hi, baby," she said. I had to look away. I was intensely aware of this moment between my daughter and my best friend.

"Her name is . . ." I faltered. "Jack, tell them. I can't do it without blubbering."

"Ladies, meet Ella Laine Whitfield," Jack said.

Their jaws dropped. "Are you serious?" Ella Rae asked.

Laine pursed her lips together in an effort not to cry.

"We'll call her Elle," I said.

"Hi, Baby Elle," Laine said. "I'm your Aunt Lainie." She kissed her face lightly. "You are such a pretty girl. I love you already. I have so much I want to tell you." She paused and kissed her again. "So much to say and not so much time."

That cut us all like a knife. I was physically exhausted from the birth, and I was emotionally and mentally exhausted by the explosion of feelings that flooded my heart and my mind. I was still in awe of the wonder of her birth just minutes ago. How she was just a promise, and suddenly she was real and breathing and mine.

Then I was crushed by the reminder of how fragile life is. When Laine told my child hello and good-bye in the same breath. This bubble we'd been living in was delicate and precious, but bubbles don't last forever.

"There are a lot of people outside waiting to meet you,

little girl," one of the nurses said. "There must be thirty people out there."

"Y'all better take her out there, Jack," I said. "The family will be dying to see her."

Laine gave the baby back to Jack, and he held her close to my face for a kiss. "Tell Mommy we'll be right back. We just gotta meet some people."

I kissed her and adjusted the blanket around her little face. "Don't stay out there too long," I said. "And don't let anybody hold her . . . She's . . . little, you know?"

Jack smiled. "Already turned Mama Bear?"

They slipped out the door to introduce my daughter to her family, to all the people who would love her and mold her and shape her into a woman one day. I could already imagine how loved she was going to be. Laine's heartbreaking and heartwarming words to my baby played over and over in my mind. *Not so much time.* I began to cry.

Doctor Davis stood by my bed and put his hand on my arm. "I know what you're thinking, but it's a happy time, Carrigan," he said. "Don't look down the road right now, just look at today. She's a beautiful, healthy baby. Concentrate on what you have."

"Thank you, for everything," I said.

"You're welcome." He patted my shoulder. "They will get you to a room shortly, and I'll be around in the morning to check on you."

I closed my eyes and tried to follow his advice. He was right. Of course there was so much to be thankful for. And I was thankful.

Much later that night I woke up and realized I had managed to hold on to that thought. I opened my eyes to see Jack sitting by the window holding Elle and telling her what a big world there was outside. He told her there were ponies to ride and wagons to pull and puppies to love. And then he said the most beautiful thing of all: "Daddy waited a long time for you, little girl." I drifted back to sleep happier and more at peace than I'd been in a very long time.

CHAPTER FIFTEEN

We brought baby Elle home two days later to a house full of people. I was a nervous wreck. I wanted everybody in the house to provide me their full medical history including a report on the last time they sneezed. I didn't say that, of course, but I had a buffet of assorted hand sanitizers available for all the germ-laden people salivating to hold my baby. You would think they were a horde of strangers fresh from the CDC instead of Elle's grandparents and family.

This new, strange, and overpowering need to protect had taken me by complete surprise. Every time someone passed her to another pair of hands, I envisioned them as a petri dish swimming with the most horrible diseases ever known, including the plague and something that made your head explode. I'd seen that one on a horror film when I was fourteen.

As I watched my daddy fumble with Elle's pacifier, I wondered if he'd been working in his garden this morning, if he'd used fertilizer, if he'd washed his hands afterward. Suddenly, Elle grew a third hand in my head. I took a deep breath.

"Hey," Laine said, "come see." She held her hand out to me.

I looked back at my daddy, who was now holding the pacifier by the bulb. I almost died. Luckily, Jack took it and said, "Here, let me try." I had given Jack the "don't you dare put your nasty fingers on her binky" speech last night at the hospital. Jack had been thoroughly briefed on the importance of clean hands.

"I don't know if I should leave," I said.

"Carrigan," she said, "come on. We're only going to the kitchen. She'll be ten feet away. If there's an outbreak of chicken pox, we'll have time to save her. Now, come on. Follow me."

Ella Rae was waiting in the kitchen and smiling at me when I walked in. She stepped away from the huge island and there sat a Hummingbird Cake under a glass dome. I squealed and threw my arms around Laine.

"Thank you, thank you, thank you!"

Laine laughed. "You are very welcome. I hope it's as good as you think it is."

"Oh, it will be," Ella Rae said. "She wouldn't let me cut it until you got here. I've been mad at her all day."

"Ella Rae," Laine said, "you didn't have a baby."

"If that's the ticket, I better eat two pieces of this one." Laine and I laughed.

"What are we waiting on, ladies?" I hurried to the cabinet to get a plate and grabbed a fork and knife on the way. I lifted the glass dome and closed my eyes. "Ahhhh . . ." I could smell that cream cheese frosting and the toasted pecans sprinkled on top. I couldn't wait to taste it and cut a large slice. The first bite was everything I knew it would be. Pineapple, banana, the faint taste of cinnamon and something . . . something I just could never put my finger on. But today I wasn't going to try. Today I was just going to enjoy this cake. Period.

I licked a sliver of icing off my finger. "Laine," I said, "you've outdone yourself this time."

"Mm-hmm," Ella Rae said as she enjoyed her first bite.

Laine smiled. "It's the exact same recipe," she said.

I shook my head. "No, this time it's better than ever. It must have more of the secret ingredient."

"Carrigan," she said, "about that secret—"

I put up my hand. "I get it. I'm not going to ask any more. I promise. I just want you to know, using more was the key. This is the best Hummingbird Cake you have ever made."

She smiled. "Maybe so."

We quickly fell into a routine at the Farm. Elle was a good baby during the day. She nursed, stayed awake for a little while, and then slept again. She had quickly become the light and the center of my life, and everybody else's life too. And I had stopped making every one boil themselves before they touched her.

Then six weeks later, things changed. Every night at two a.m. the den became the site of the Nightly Colic Festival, and the whole house got up for the party. They didn't really have another choice. I don't know where the child got her set of lungs, but they were strong, I assure you.

Everybody had their own version of what would work. Poppa Jack usually took the first swing, walking her around showing her pictures and telling her stories. Then Mrs. Diane would take her into the parlor and play the piano while Elle sat in the bouncy chair. Laine would join them and sing every children's song she could come up with. Ella Rae never took a turn, but sat miserably in a chair and marveled at the volume of Elle's screams. Jack thought taking her on the porch was the magic trick, and when I finally got to hold her, I rocked her and waited it out. Some nights they all tried to send me back to bed. Tonight I had taken them up on the offer.

I lay in bed thinking about how drastically my life had changed. Just a year ago I was running around, chasing my tail, looking for something I couldn't identify. I had been scared to death Jack would make a fool out of me before I could make one out of him. We'd never finished our conversation about what happened between us. But it didn't matter any more. After Laine got sick, I became intensely aware that the only day that mattered was this one, right here, right now.

Besides, even if he was guilty of everything I ever suspected, I had made a terrible and irrevocable choice during that time too. And I didn't ever want to think of it again. But that was easier said than done. I had tried many, many times to file it, tuck it away, bury it. But sooner or later, it would pop up again. And it wasn't just my indiscretion that weighed me down. I had a surplus of negative emotions swimming around inside me every day. Guilt. Regret. Sorrow. Anger. But there was nothing I could do about any of them right now. My focus had to stay on Laine, and most of the time it did. Thank God for this house full of unconditional love.

Being at the Farm was like being safely tucked away in our own little corner of the world, like being wrapped in a cocoon where nothing and no one could ever touch us. I rarely even made the trip into Bon Dieu Falls any more, and when I did it was brief and necessary. I didn't even go to my parents' house too much because they were in and out of here all the time too. All I needed was already here and nothing could hurt us, bother us, or threaten us. Of course, that was nothing more than a brittle illusion that I clung to like a life raft. I shuddered to think one day soon something bad was going to happen.

The Farm might have been a cocoon holding us safely and keeping the outside at bay, but that protection didn't apply to Laine. She was frail and in more pain now. She would have to stop and catch her breath if she climbed the stairs or walked the length of the porch. And it wasn't like she could hide it any more. She only talked about her medical issues with Debra and Mrs. Jeannette, so there was no use questioning her, but there was no way to ignore it either. She took her meds more often, she napped more often, and she ate less food. She'd lost interest in most everything except Elle and whatever she did in her bedroom when she disappeared for hours at a time.

One day Ella Rae and I confronted her and asked the

dreaded question: "Don't you want to go back to the hospital, at least for a checkup with Doctor Rougeau?"

"For what?" she said. "What's he gonna do? Take an X-ray and tell me I'm dying?"

⚜

Since last summer, when we found out I was pregnant, we had started taking pictures. Lots of them. It had been Laine's idea. She wanted the baby to have pictures of her, and she wanted me to pick out my favorites so we could use them at her funeral.

The funeral. Right. Discussing funeral plans was like planning a holiday. Food, decorations, guest list.

"Do not," Laine said, "I repeat, do not let anyone see me after I'm gone. The family, okay, but no one else. You got it? Slam that thing shut and leave it that way. I won't be there anyway. I'll be in heaven." I tried to find comfort in the idea of heaven and a loving God, but it was no good.

My mother always told me to pray—about the baby, about Laine's cancer. When Elle was born, I knew she was a blessing, a heaven-sent blessing. And I was thankful for her, but still I wanted nothing to do with God or prayer.

All my life I had been taught stuff like, "Everything happens for a reason," or "Something good always comes from something bad," or "God's timing is always perfect."

I accepted that, up to a point. After all, I had lost the grandparents I loved so much, I had lost aunts and uncles,

182

and I had grieved for each of them. But they had lived their lives. That was the way it was supposed to happen. Not like this. Not snatched out of the game in the fourth inning.

What possible reason could God have for taking Laine? She was a gift to everyone who knew her, not just to Ella Rae and me. The children she'd taught in the past still loved her. They'd run up to her to say hello everywhere we went. She was a huge part of our church, not a sporadic part of it like I was. She was kind and gentle and wise. So how could God justify this move? And how was I ever supposed to forgive him for it?

I was raised in the Deep South where God, family, and country were the other Holy Trinity right next to onions, bell peppers, and celery. My parents had taken me to church all my life, and after I grew up, I went on my own, even if it was hit and miss. But I was beginning to question all those things that had been drilled into me since I was small. Was life truly all a part of some grand design? Was God sitting up in the sky with a clipboard and a red pen keeping score and rolling dice? "You live, you die, and you I haven't decided on"? Or was it all just some huge. random crapshoot? I truly didn't know what I believed any more. Another manila folder in my rapidly growing filing cabinet.

I went back to sorting pictures and picked up one of Laine swinging around a column on the front porch. It had been taken last fall. I could see all the mums blooming in the background. She had a huge smile on her face and looked healthy. And happy. Really happy. It captured her perfectly. This was the picture we'd use as the centerpiece at the funeral. I'd have it enlarged and framed, and we would set it on the table beside her at church. Tears came freely now, spilling down my face. I didn't even really notice them and didn't bother to wipe them. They were nearly as natural as breathing these days, and I had accepted them as normal. I set the picture on my nightstand and flipped off the light, very aware of the significance of the decision I'd just made.

I woke up at ten a.m. I couldn't believe I had slept that long. I would've probably slept longer too, but my milk had soaked my shirt. Whoever the winner of the "I'm holding Elle" contest was today must've used frozen breast milk.

I went downstairs in search of my family and couldn't find a soul, not even Mamie. But I could hear laughter coming from the porch and followed the sound. I peered out the bay window. They had a regular living room set up outside. Elle's bassinet, Laine's chaise, and Mrs. Diane's settee from the sunporch were all on the big porch now. This porch was well shaded and the outdoor ceiling fans kept it cool. The tea service was beside the front door and was full of Mamie's pastries and her signature cinnamon rolls. I reached for one but thought better of it and put it back. I only had five more pounds of baby weight left to lose, and I was determined to get rid of it. I poured a cup of tea, skipped the sugar, and went outside.

"Good morning, Mommy," Mrs. Diane said and turned Elle around so I could see her.

"Good morning, my baby," I said, put my tea down, and took her from her grandmother. I still fell in love with her all over again every morning as soon as I saw her. I kissed her little pouty baby lips and nuzzled her neck. She smelled so good. How did I ever do something this right?

I walked to the end of the porch and into the morning sun, careful to shield her eyes from it. It was a beautiful morning, and the sky was a bright and brilliant blue. Elle scrunched her little body up and made those baby grunt sounds I loved so much. It was the middle of May, and the temperatures were still in the lower eighties. I loved this time of year, but I knew it wouldn't be long before the Louisiana humidity would make it impossible to sit out here with the baby. For the thousandth time in the last few months, I wished I could freeze the moment.

"Okay," Laine's voice said behind me. "You've said good morning to her. Bring her to me."

I kissed my baby again and walked back to the others. "Let's go see Lainie," I said. I looked down at Laine smiling and holding her thin arms out to cradle Elle. Dear God, she looked bad this morning. She was so thin, and the circles under her eyes were deeper and darker today. I placed Elle in her arms and sat on the chaise beside them.

"How are you this morning?" I said.

"I'm fine."

Always the same answer.

Her breathing became more labored every day, and this morning seemed to be a particular struggle. I suspected the cancer was in her lungs now. She had begun coughing a couple of weeks ago, especially at night. She had practically stopped eating anything at all too. Mamie gave her meal replacement shakes that were very high in calories and vitamins, but she rarely finished drinking one. She had promised us months before that when the cancer became too much for her, too painful, she would ask Debra to sedate her. But until then, if she could stand it, she wanted to be aware. She wanted to let nature do what nature did. We sat in silence for a while, enjoying the morning, the smell of freshly cut hay, the sound of birds singing, and Elle's baby sounds. An unflawed companionable silence where words weren't necessary. My heart was full. It was a beautiful morning, indeed.

Laine and Elle fell asleep, and I reached over to pick up the baby. Elle did her little baby scrunch again, arms over her head, legs doubled up beneath her, that made me feel like my baby had just accomplished some incredible feat, when in reality all she did was stretch. I was still sure my daughter scrunched better than any other baby in the world.

Laine stirred slightly. "Is she asleep?"

"She is," I said. "I didn't mean to wake you."

"No, it's fine. I need to talk to you and Ella Rae anyway."

Mrs. Diane got the hint and took Elle from me. "You girls stay on the porch and chat," she said. "My granddaughter and I have things to do, don't we, sweet girl?"

I kissed Elle's hand and sat back down on the edge of Laine's chaise. Ella Rae pulled her chair closer to us.

"Whatcha got, girl?"

Laine took a short breath and looked at both of us a moment before she spoke. "It can't be much longer now, right?" she said. "Maybe a week or two . . . if that."

Ella Rae began to cry, and I bit my lip until I was sure I tasted blood.

"It's okay, y'all," Laine said. "Really it is. It's kind of a relief. I'm tired . . . and I'm ready. Almost."

I didn't reply. Ella Rae grabbed Laine's hand but stared out across the field.

"We always knew this was coming," she said softly. "Please don't get all weird and nervous on me now. You both promised. Remember?"

I nodded my head and swallowed. She never failed to mention that stupid promise. Of course we knew it was coming. The knowledge permeated every hour of the day. But knowing it was coming did nothing to lessen the anxiety it brought or soften the blow it dealt.

"Answer me," Laine said.

"Yes." I choked on the words. "We knew it was coming. What can we do? What do you need?"

Laine tugged at the afghan in her lap and seemed to struggle for words. "Look," she said, "I don't know if this is right or wrong. And I don't even know if I should do this . . . but . . . I think I'd like to see Mitch. Do you think that would be possible?"

I couldn't have been more surprised. "I don't know, Laine," I said. "But we'll surely do what we can to find him."

Ella Rae dabbed at her eyes and turned around to face us. "He's in Dallas." Laine and I stared at her, and she shrugged her shoulders. "The Internet is a wonderful thing."

"When . . ."

"I started looking for him the day after you told us," Ella Rae said. "I kept it to myself because you said you didn't want to see him. But I kept thinking . . . maybe you'd change your mind."

"You sneak!" I said. "I didn't know you had it in you to keep a secret that long!"

Ella Rae smiled. "Me either."

"What did you find out?" Laine said. "Do you think he would come if I called him? Or maybe you could get an e-mail address?"

Ella Rae looked down at her feet. "There's more, Laine."

"What?" Laine said. "Is he okay?"

Ella Rae looked up, her eyes brimming. "No," she said. "I mean, yes, he's okay, but . . . I sorta . . . Well, I already talked to him."

"What?" She shrugged again. "Nobody said I couldn't call him. He wants to see you, Laine. He's wanted to for a long time. Even before I called."

Laine looked stunned. "Swear!"

"I swear," Ella Rae said. "He said he would be by the phone waiting for my call." She pulled a wrinkled piece of paper out of her pocket. "See? I keep his numbers with me all the time. Work, cell, home."

"But if he wanted to see me, why hasn't he tried in all these years?" Laine said. "I mean, Bon Dieu Falls isn't a huge place."

"He figured you were married now, with a house full of kids." Ella looked away again. "He didn't want to disrupt your life."

"And?" Laine said.

"What do you mean, 'and?'"

"I mean, what are you not telling me?"

"That's it." Ella Rae shifted in her chair. "He has no family left here, no ties, no way of knowing anything about you. That's it."

That wasn't it, though. I knew it and Laine knew it. Something about Ella Rae's tone and body language belied her words.

"Rae . . . ," Laine said, "don't make me beg . . . please."

Ella Rae sighed heavily and she took Laine's hand in hers. "Mitch and his wife divorced about a year and a half ago. He said the marriage had always been rocky, but he stayed for his son. And by the way, that is the only child he has. But he's always thought about you and wondered where you were and what you were doing. He never forgot you, Laine."

Ella Rae paused for a second, but Laine urged her on. "Come on, Rae . . . just say it, whatever it is."

"He came looking for you last year." Ella Rae started to cry in earnest then. "It was the same time you'd gotten sick and we were all at the hospital. He couldn't find anyone he knew around here until he ran into Jeff Nealy at the post office. Jeff told him what had happened."

Laine's lip trembled, and I took her other hand in mine.

"He was crushed, Laine," Ella Rae said. "I could hear it in his voice. He even went to the hospital and sat in the lobby for two days. He saw Carrigan and Jack in the parking lot one day but couldn't make himself ask."

Laine started to cry, too, and I got mad, as usual. What a Greek tragedy this had turned into.

"In the end, he thought it would be worse on you if he showed up then, so he went back to Dallas." Ella Rae was sobbing now. "I'm so sorry. Please don't be mad at me. You said you didn't want to see him . . . but then when I talked to him . . . I didn't know what to do."

Laine shushed her. "Ella Rae, I'm not mad at you. You respected my wishes." She dabbed at her tears. "This is just all . . . such a shock. So . . . so . . ."

"Unbelievable." I handed Laine the box of tissues from the wicker table beside us.

"Yes," she said, "the perfect word."

"I wanted to tell you," Ella Rae said, "but he begged me not to. Not until you asked for him. He texts me every day and asks how you are. I'm so sorry, Laine."

Laine closed her eyes tightly and digested that information. "There is nothing to be sorry about."

This had to be gut wrenching for Laine. Just the "what might have been" part of it was breaking my own heart. She was getting screwed out of a life, and now she'd gotten screwed out of ever having the one man she ever loved. I wanted to scream, for her and for me. At that moment, I was intensely aware of all the things I didn't deserve that had landed in my lap.

Laine gathered her composure and looked over at me. "How do I look?"

I blinked. "The truth or a lie?"

"Truth," she said, "always."

I shot the arrow. "You are still beautiful," I said. "And you look like you may be fighting a really hard battle right now."

Ella Rae stood up. "He knows the score, Laine," she said. "He understands what's going on."

"Laine," I said, "you really are still beautiful."

Ella Rae got her phone from her pocket. "The text has been written for weeks," she said. "All I have to do is hit Send."

Laine drew in a breath as deeply as she could. "Send it."

CHAPTER SIXTEEN

"Hold still," I said.

"I'm trying to," Laine said, "but you're pulling my hair."

"Because you won't sit still."

"Why won't you let me look in the mirror?"

"Because I'm not finished," I said. For the tenth time. "And just so you know, your hair is gorgeous. Looks just like it always did."

"And I kept it too." She winked.

I smiled but didn't answer. We had never exactly seen eye to eye on the chemo thing, so I didn't comment on remarks like that. No way was I going to stir any pots today. Mitch Montgomery answered Ella Rae's text message in less than thirty seconds. Now, two days later, he was on the road, due to arrive within the hour. The mood in Laine's bedroom this morning was euphoric. We'd even gotten her to eat a few bites of scrambled eggs at breakfast and drink half her juice. That itself was a cause for celebration.

My mother picked Elle up earlier and took enough frozen milk to last the whole day. We ran everybody else out of the house so Laine and Mitch could be alone. But Ella Rae and I were staying, just in case she needed us. We'd decided to make a day of it on the sunporch.

Ella Rae held up two shirts. "Purple or blue?"

"Purple," Laine and I said in unison.

Ella Rae pulled a chair up in front of Laine. "I'm gonna start your makeup," she said. "Don't whine."

"I'm not gonna whine," Laine whined.

"See!" Ella Rae said. "You have done this our whole lives. Somebody comes at you with a powder puff and you automatically start."

"Fine," Laine said. "I won't talk at all."

"That would be great."

"Did you hear that, Carrigan?" Laine said.

"You just talked," Ella Rae said. "Now close your mouth and let me work."

Fifteen minutes later, I pronounced her perfect. "You may turn around now." I spun her around in the swivel chair to face the mirror.

"Wow," she said. "I don't even look sick any more! My eye circles are gone too! I look amazing."

I turned so she wouldn't see my expression. She did look amazing. Her hair was still thick and beautiful. And Ella Rae had done a masterful job camouflaging her hollow cheek bones and the dark circles under her eyes. But she was so thin it startled me. Debra had begun helping her bathe a few weeks ago as well as dress in the mornings and undress at night. I hadn't seen her without clothes on until this morning. Her bones protruded under her skin so that she resembled a refugee from a concentration camp. "You look beautiful," I said.

"You do," Ella Rae said. "Now, come on, it's getting close. Let's get you dressed."

I had made a flying trip to Shreveport and bought three different outfits for her. I knew she'd want jeans, so I got different styles in each pair and shirts and summer cardigans in every color I could find. She chose a pair of jeans with rhinestone pockets to go with the lavender top and a purple cardigan. She'd always worn a size eight. I had bought a size two and they were a little loose. But she looked pretty, and more importantly, she felt pretty, and that made all the difference.

Poppa Jack's dogs started barking. I glanced at my watch. Mitch was right on time. We walked Laine into the living room and settled her on the sofa. I fluffed her hair around her, gave her a quick hug, and met Ella Rae at the door to greet Mitch Montgomery.

"Hey," Laine said, "thank you both. For everything. I don't know what I'd do without you."

"Well, lucky for you, you never have to find out."

Ella Rae and I walked out on the porch and waited as Mitch walked up the driveway. He was taller than I remembered, and his hair was short now but still curly. He was a very handsome man. He stepped onto the porch and extended his hand.

"Carrigan," he said, "you look exactly the same."

"Thank you. I only wish that were true." I smiled at him and took his hand. "I'm glad you're here, Mitch."

He looked over at Ella Rae. "May I hug you?" Ella Rae opened her arms to him.

"I can never thank you enough for calling me." His voice was thick with emotion. "I'll never be able to repay you."

"I just wish it could've been sooner," Ella Rae said. "She's awfully weak."

He looked worn and worried. "I have a lot of regrets," he said. "If I could go back and do things differently—"

"Stop," I said. "We all have things we'd like to take back or do over, I assure you. It doesn't matter. You're here now." I couldn't believe I had said that to Mitch Montgomery. Just a few months earlier I had wanted to strangle him with my bare hands in front of God and everybody. But he was here to make our girl happy. If only for a little while. And that was good enough for me.

"She's in the front room on the sofa," Ella Rae said. "Go on in."

Ella Rae and I sat on the porch swing when he went inside. Before long, we could hear muffled crying from both of them. It was sweet and awful and heartbreaking all at once. I was dying to look in the window.

Ella Rae must've read my mind because she was suddenly racing to the window. "I can't help it," she said. "I have to see!" She peered into the window and said, "Awww . . . Carri, come look."

They were wrapped in an embrace; Laine was practically in his lap. I couldn't see her face, but his was twisted in tears and regret. It's funny how you can read things on people's faces when you've been through it too. You can see the pain, the sorrow, the regret, and you can recognize it easily because you've seen it in your own mirror. My heart ached for him. Years ago he did the right thing and gave up the person he loved to be with the ones who needed him. I had to respect him for that. He loved Laine, which was evident. Maybe he'd gone about it all wrong. Maybe it hadn't started under stellar circumstances, but I was absolutely not sitting in a place to judge anybody's decisions.

Mitch and I were a lot alike. He'd ended up in the arms of the love of his life and so had I. Only I had gotten the fairy tale and he'd gotten the Greek tragedy. Life could be both beautiful and cruel.

"Come on." I caught Ella Rae's hand. "This isn't our moment."

We walked back to the porch swing, her hand still in mine. I was so grateful Mitch had come. It was comforting to see Laine actually excited this morning. She had . . . I looked down. "What is wrong with your hands, Ella Rae?"

"What do you mean?" she asked.

"It's like holding sandpaper," I said. "What have you done?"

She rubbed them together and made a face. "They do feel rough."

"Use some lotion. They feel positively reptilian," I said, "and don't touch me with them again."

Jack walked up the steps about the same time Ella Rae began rubbing her hands all over my face.

"Stop it, sandpaper girl," I said, trying to slap her hands off of me.

"What are y'all doing?" Jack asked and stopped in front of us.

"Feel her hands, Jack," I said. "Touch him, Rae."

She moved her hands up and down Jack's arms.

"What's wrong with you?" he asked. "You been using sandpaper on your hands?"

"See," I said.

Jack walked up the steps and headed toward the door, but Ella Rae and I both shouted, "No!"

"What?"

"Laine and Mitch are inside. You can't go in."

"I'm thirsty," he said. "Can I go through the sunporch?"

"No!"

"Well, crap," he said, "what am I supposed to drink?"

Ella Rae pointed at my chest. "Drink from the fountain of homogenized," she said.

I slapped her hand as Jack laughed.

"Go drink out of the hose," I said.

He grimaced. "Maybe the boys have something in the barn." He started back down the steps. "You look good today, Mama." He gestured toward the house. "Let me know how that goes."

I smiled. "Hurry home," I said.

"I will," he told me.

"Now," I said and folded my arms, "if you're gonna sit here, don't touch me with those Brillo pads."

She laughed. "Fine," she said and tucked her hands under her thighs. "Carri," she said, "do you ever wonder what it will be like . . . later, I mean."

I knew exactly what she meant. "After she's gone . . ."

"Yes."

"I think about it all the time," I said. "I try not to, but I do. Do you think about it?"

She nodded her head. "All the time."

"It's strange to think about the future without her, isn't it?" I said.

"I don't even know *how* to think about it without her."

"It's like it upsets the balance, tips the scales or something," I said. "Who's gonna keep the score at ball games? Who's gonna put together our electronics? Who's gonna tell me my jeans are too tight?"

"Who's gonna make the Hummingbird Cake?" Ella Rae continued. "Who's gonna make me behave like a lady?" She smiled. "Who's gonna be the responsible one now?"

We both laughed at ourselves and our ridiculous questions, but we laughed to keep from crying. The truth was, Laine's absence was going to leave a huge hole in our lives. What would happen when a third of our lifetime trio was gone? We'd starred in the "Carri, Laine, and Rae Show" for so long, I wasn't sure Ella Rae or I would have an identity without Laine. Life would go on, but life as we knew it would not.

Several years ago we'd lost our classmate Ricky Cahill

when he was killed in an automobile accident. We'd gone to school with him all our lives. We were all in our early twenties at the time. We weren't really close friends, but in a small town, you show up at wakes and you pay your respects.

Ricky was a friendly guy, outgoing and good-looking. I remembered being at his wake and thinking how awful and tragic it was. I also remembered something Laine said that night sitting on the church pew beside me. "I know this is sad," she said, "and I'm sad too, especially for his family. But I keep hearing people say, 'Isn't it tragic because he had his whole life in front of him.' But what difference does that make? It's not how long you live; it's what you leave behind. Ricky was a great guy. Everybody loved him. That's an amazing way to be remembered."

It's not how long you live; it's what you leave behind. Those words brought me some measure of comfort on this day. Laine would leave this world having made a difference. I knew it because of the students who came out to the Farm. I knew it because of the mailbox that was stuffed with cards. Her life, brief as it would be, had touched countless others. I was both proud of that and grateful for that.

I also knew Laine wasn't afraid to die, and that helped me too. While my own faith had been shaken by her illness, hers had been bolstered. She spoke of heaven as if she'd seen it already. She could see her daddy again, her grandparents, a cousin she'd lost early in her life. Even pets.

She reminded me constantly that as soon as she closed her eyes, she'd be in the presence of God. "I don't want an open casket. People would look at me and see a shell and feel sorry for me. But I'll already be in paradise." She had the faith of a child, and I wished I had half of it.

"Do you think she'll save us a seat?" Ella Rae asked suddenly.

It took me a moment or two to realize what she meant.

"In . . . heaven?" Ella Rae said. "You know, I'm just saying . . ."

"Oh, sure she will, Rae," I said. "Because she so loves to do that." I put on my best Laine imitation: "If y'all could get your butts anywhere on time, I wouldn't have to save seats every time we attend a function."

Ella Rae laughed. "I do remember that. She said it at church!"

"On the front pew."

"Do you ever wonder what she does in her room all the time?" Ella Rae said.

"I know," I said. "It's driving me crazy! But every time I ask her, she just says she's working on a project."

"I went in her room the other night to get her a sweater and tried to snoop around a little," Ella Rae said. "Then Debra walked in. I was so busted."

I suddenly felt my boobies begin to sting and I knew it was meal time for my sweet Elle. I needed to pump.

"Oh no," I said, "I forgot to get my breast pump upstairs."

Ella Rae made a face while I held my hands against my chest. "Do you have any idea how disgusting that is?"

"It's not disgusting," I said. "It's natural."

"It's appalling."

"What do you think they're there for, Ella Rae?" I said. "And when did you find out what *appalling* meant?"

"I read sometimes." She narrowed her eyes. "And I think they are decorative. You know, like Christmas ornaments."

I shook my head. "I have to get my pump. This stuff is liquid gold. I can't waste it." I pressed my hands tighter against my chest.

"Don't you have maxi pads in there?"

"What?"

"Didn't you stick those maxi pads in your bra?" Ella repeated. "You always do."

"Ella Rae, they are not maxi pads," I said. "They are breast pads."

"Thick, white, poofy. Same thing."

I shook my head. "I cannot *wait* for you to have a baby."

"I hope you don't think I'm gonna feed it with my boobies," she said. "Besides, that's why doctors make dry-up shots and Walmart makes bottles. Now keep those things away from me."

"You are crazy," I said. "Run look in the window and tell me what they're doing. Maybe they won't notice us."

Ella Rae crept over to the window and gestured for me to come as well.

They were still on the sofa, but lying down now. Mitch had pulled her against him, and I was pretty sure Laine was asleep. Mitch was gently stroking her hair and looking down at her. He'd stop briefly to wipe his tears and then begin to stroke her hair again. He glanced up and saw us and silently mouthed the words, *Thank you.*

I grabbed Ella Rae's hand, and I didn't even mind the sandpaper this time. We'd just witnessed an extraordinarily sweet moment. The last few months had been full of them. I was grateful for them all. Laine would die in peace with everything and everybody now. What a rare and incredible blessing.

Chapter Seventeen

Mitch stayed with us for the next five days. He met Mrs. Jeannette, Michael, and his wife and girls. Ella Rae filled them in about Mitch. I don't know if they were shocked by his presence, but they accepted him immediately and thanked him profusely for coming.

He made friends with Jack and Tommy too. They tried to make him feel as at home as possible, offering to take him places and show him things, but he didn't take them up on it too often. He stayed by Laine's side most of those five days. Laine became more and more emaciated, but I'd never seen her smile so much.

I had grown to like Mitch and had come to understand his decision to leave Laine years ago. I had assured him an explanation wasn't necessary, but he insisted on sharing the story with Ella Rae and me. It was during these days I began to realize there was just no easy way to understand anyone's choices until you've walked in their shoes.

On the fourth night after Mitch's arrival, it started raining and hadn't stopped. The forecast called for seven straight days of it. The thunder was constant and maddening. I hadn't slept over an hour at a time since Laine had said, "It can't be much longer now." Sweet baby Elle had gotten over her bout with colic and was sleeping peacefully in her bassinet beside our bed. Jack was snoring lightly when I slipped out of the bedroom.

I tiptoed down the stairs and into Laine's bedroom. Mrs. Jeannette was asleep on the sofa beside the bed. Laine was sleeping soundly, the only noise the steady hum of the oxygen machine. I watched her for a minute or so, until I felt satisfied, then left the room.

I let myself out the front door quietly and stepped onto the porch. This had become my nightly ritual, slipping out to the porch to wrestle my demons. But tonight I had company.

"Hey," Ella Rae said.

I looked over to see Ella on the porch swing and Mitch in a rocker.

"So I'm not the only one?"

"I haven't slept in days," Ella Rae said.

Mitch smiled a little. "It's been years for me."

I sat down in the other rocking chair and tucked my feet under me. "Jack and Elle are having no trouble."

"Neither is Tommy," Ella Rae said. "I'm glad that job is done and he's home for a while. Things are sure gonna be strange around here when it's ov—" She stopped abruptly, caught herself like the day I said Laine would take the Hummingbird Cake recipe to her grave. And she felt the same way I had.

"It's okay, Ella Rae," I said. "We just can't pretend any more."

Her eyes filled with tears. "Every day I feel like we could've done more. Do you feel like that too?"

"All the time," I said. "I still think about the chemo."

Mitch cleared his throat. "Surely the two of you can have no guilt. I left the woman I loved. I sent her on her way, knowing she loved me too. You two are already grieving, I'm the bad guy here."

"Don't say that, Mitch," Ella Rae said. "You love her too."

"A lot of good that did her." He shook his head. "I have so many regrets, and all of them have to do with Laine. I know you don't need to hear this, but I need to say it. Will you indulge me?"

Ella Rae and I nodded.

Mitch didn't speak immediately. I'm not sure he could. We sat in silence until he was ready.

"I didn't have a pleasant childhood," he began. "My parents fought my entire life. About everything. My dad drank. A lot. So did Mom. My childhood memories consist of screaming matches between them and not much else. I was relieved when they sent me to live here with my grandparents because it was the only stability I ever knew. Even though it was tough on a new kid in high school here."

He chuckled a little. "I wasn't athletic, wasn't a hunter, didn't fish. I liked to read. Still do. And please don't take this the wrong way, because it isn't meant to be a reflection on anyone, but Laine was one of the only people in high school who acknowledged my existence. I always remembered that."

"It wasn't you," I said. "It was softball. It was all-consuming."

"I know. I've seen you both play. Pretty impressive." He

smiled. "Anyway, when I was a freshman at ULM, I met Sydney. She was a nice enough girl and we began dating. It was going pretty well for a few months until one night when we were at a restaurant and I saw a girl from my English class. I don't even remember her name. We talked about class, she introduced us to her boyfriend, normal stuff. When they left, Sydney accused me of flirting with the girl and humiliating her in public. I didn't even know how to respond. And it gets better. When we got in my car, she started slapping me and scratching me with her nails. I never said another word. I drove her straight to her dorm and didn't call her again. I had lived through that in my life already. She called me every day, she camped outside my apartment, she left notes all over my car, she keyed my car, smashed a window in my apartment. You get the picture."

"I know women like that," I said.

"My way of responding was not to respond," Mitch continued. "I thought it had worked. For a couple of weeks, I heard nothing from her. Then one day she showed up outside my history class, crying, apologizing, begging me to talk to her. We went outside and she told me she was pregnant. I didn't believe her. I assumed it was another attempt to make me stay with her. She showed me a—what do you call those pictures of babies?"

"Sonogram," Ella Rae said.

"Yes, a sonogram," Mitch said. "She said it was why she'd been so crazy lately. I was eighteen. It made sense to me. And one thing I knew from an early age, I would never let a child of mine go through what I'd been through. I thought it was the best thing to do for the child, so I asked her to marry me. That day. She said yes. Worst mistake of my life. No, second worst."

He fell silent again for a little while.

"You don't owe us any of this, Mitch," I said. "It's okay if you want to stop now."

"But I do owe you this, Carrigan," he said. "I owe you both."

"No," Ella Rae said, "we don't need—"

"Let me finish," Mitch said. "We got married the next weekend. She moved into my apartment, and for a month or two, I thought it might work out. I didn't love her, but as long as she wasn't destroying something, I thought I would learn to. Well, I was wrong. She began accusing me of cheating on her at least once a week, always followed by breaking plates, throwing things all over the apartment. And she never missed an opportunity to claw my face.

"I swear, I never touched her, never cursed her, never raised a hand to her. And I didn't tell her this, but before our son was born, I had already been to a lawyer and had divorce papers drawn up. But I wasn't going to leave her before she delivered. Finally our son, Adam, arrived. Let me say, regardless of the relationship you have with the other parent, you fall in love when you look at your child."

"Yes, you do," I said.

Mitch smiled back. "So for him, I tried one more time. This time it was worse. She'd gained quite a bit of weight during the pregnancy and it only escalated her jealousy. She began to accuse me of seeing our next-door neighbor, who happened to be a pianist at a local church. I came home from work one night to find her beating on the poor woman's door and screaming things you wouldn't hear in a locker room."

He paused and took a breath. "That was the last straw. I filed for divorce the next day. Sydney still tried everything she could to get me to come back, and then she'd go off the deep end again. Finally I got a restraining order against her and told her I would take our son away from her if she ever pulled another crazy stunt. A few months later, I ran into Laine. She was . . . and is the love of my life."

He stopped and wiped his eyes. "I don't know how much she's told you," he said. "But we were in love. Those months were the happiest of my life. She loved Adam. And he loved her. She was a better mother to him on the weekends I had him than Sydney ever was.

"One day I told her I was going to petition the court for custody. And that's when things began to change. Laine couldn't bear the thought of taking a child away from his mother. She started encouraging me to mend my fences with Sydney, at least while Adam was young. She didn't want him bouncing between us. And she reminded me of what I had been through as a child.

"In the end, I chose my son. Sydney agreed to counseling, and finally got proper treatment for a bipolar disorder. And that helped tremendously. But I could never look at her without thinking she was the reason I had lost Laine. And Sydney knew that. Last year she asked me to leave. It was a relief for us both, and Adam finally has two fully functioning parents."

"I am so sorry, Mitch," I said. "You didn't deserve any of this."

"What I didn't deserve was Laine," he said. "The day I went back to Sydney, Laine told me if we were meant to be, then love would always find a way. And love finally did. Thank you for calling me, thank you . . ."

Mitch began to weep openly, and Ella Rae got up and embraced him. I clenched my teeth as hard as I could and turned my head away.

"Let's go inside, Mitch," Ella Rae said. "This is too much for you tonight. You need to get some sleep."

Mitch regained his composure. "Thank you both," he repeated, "for everything."

I squeezed his hand.

Ella Rae stayed inside too and left me alone with my thoughts. And they weren't good ones. Listening to Mitch describe Sydney, I couldn't help but think how close I had come to becoming someone like her. All crazy and mean and unpredictable. At least Sydney had an excuse, a real illness. I was just hateful. I had done something awful for no other reason than to hurt Jack. And the craziest thing about that? I still had no idea if Jack had done anything at all to warrant it.

Maybe this was just who I was. Laine had sacrificed everything for a child she barely knew. I had hurt three people for nothing as noble as love . . . but just because I was feeling hurt and rejected. I was so sick of myself.

I jumped from the rocker and ran upstairs to our room, not bothering to be careful or quiet. Being with Elle made me sane again. I watched her sleep and felt the calmness creep back into my body. I curled up on the edge of the bed and kept one hand on the bassinet.

I glanced at the bedside clock. Three a.m. Maybe sleep would come for a little while at least, but it took its own sweet time showing up.

At exactly seven a.m. there was a light knock at my door. I sat up straight and was instantly wide-awake. I looked in the bassinet. Jack must've taken Elle down already. I opened the door and found Ella Rae standing there.

"Debra says Laine wants to talk to us."

I didn't care for the look on her face. "Why?"

"I don't know," Ella Rae said. "It doesn't feel right, though."

We went downstairs and into Laine's room. She was in her bed, slightly elevated and . . . glistening. Laine's word for sweating. The thought almost made me smile.

"Not feeling too good this morning?" I asked.

"Not so much." Her voice was just a decibel above a whisper.

It was the first time since her diagnosis that she had ever acknowledged that. I glanced over at Ella Rae. The statement wasn't lost on her either.

"What can we do?"

"Mitch is packing," she said. "I've asked him to leave."

"Why?" Ella Rae said. "Don't you want to spend . . ." Her voice trailed off.

"Whatever time I have left with him?" she asked. "No . . . I don't. I don't want him to see the rest of this." She gestured around the room. "The end of this."

"But he wants to be here."

"No," Laine said, "that's enough. I can't let him watch. It'll hurt him too much." She struggled a bit for another breath before she continued. "It doesn't matter how much time we had . . . or didn't have. Never did."

I didn't understand the Laine Logic behind that, but it wasn't the first time I didn't understand the way she thought. I didn't want her to waste any more energy. Every sentence was a battle.

"Stop talking, Laine," I said. "It's okay if you want him to go. Ella Rae just wanted to be sure." Laine's eyes were closed, and I looked at Ella Rae and silently put my finger over my lips so she wouldn't ask her anything else about Mitch.

"I need to say this," Laine said. "I need you both to hear this . . . Mitch was the only man I ever loved. When he left me years ago, the last thing he said to me was 'I love you and I'll see you again. I promise.' He said it to me again this morning." She paused. Catching her breath was harder this time.

"Laine, you don't have to explain it," I said. "Please stop talking. Save your strength."

She smiled a little but still didn't open her eyes. "Save it for what, Carri?" She continued her monologue. "The next time Mitch sees me . . . I'll be whole again . . . and not like this. Maybe we didn't have the perfect love story. But we had the perfect love. Because it endured, and it remembered, and it forgave." She paused again. "Not everybody gets a gift like that. God has been so good to me and I am so thankful." Her voice broke and tears escaped from her closed eyes.

"It was a beautiful love story," I said. By now tears were

streaming down my face. "Please don't talk any more, Laine, okay?"

She smiled slightly and nodded. "I love you both, so much. Stay while I sleep?"

"We love you too," I said. "Of course we'll stay."

Ella Rae couldn't answer at all.

Debra had given her a pretty strong shot for pain, and I could tell it was already working. A few minutes later, Laine was asleep. I adjusted her oxygen and continued to look at her.

"This ain't good, Carrigan," Ella Rae said.

"I know." For the last couple of days, every time she went to sleep, I was afraid she wouldn't wake up. This morning I was horrified.

"We can't leave her today." Ella Rae reached for a tissue. "At all."

"I know," I said. I took my cell phone from my pocket and texted Jack, asking him to come to the bedroom. He was beside me in an instant.

"Hey, baby," he said softly and knelt on one knee by the chair. "What can I do?"

"Will you take the baby to Mama? There's milk in the freezer. Take plenty. I don't know when."

"I'll go right now." He kissed my cheek. "Are you all right?"

"Probably not."

"I'll be right back," he promised. "I love you." He looked at Laine for a moment and turned to leave.

Ella Rae's face was ashen and frightened. "Is this the day?" she asked quietly.

"I don't know," I whispered.

I could feel an uncomfortable pressure in my chest, like the one I'd had the day at the hospital when Doctor Rougeau was telling us Laine was going to die. I tugged the collar of my T-shirt away from my neck and tried to breathe steadily. I couldn't afford the luxury of a panic attack right now. I had to be here. I had to stay present. I had promised I wouldn't leave her, no matter what. I had promised, promised, promised.

Debra came back into the room and put her hand on my shoulder, startling me.

"I'm sorry," she said.

"What's happening here, Debra?"

Debra sighed. "No one can predict—"

I cut her off. "Please don't lie to me or speak in medical terms. I can take it. Just tell me."

"I put a catheter in last night, but there's not much output. Her blood pressure is dropping and her color isn't good."

"And all that means?" Ella Rae asked.

"All that means she's getting close to letting go."

Neither of us replied, but we both waited for her to answer the unspoken question.

Debra lowered her lids, then looked up again. She put her hand on my shoulder once more and gently squeezed it. "Hours . . . maybe a day at the most. I could be wrong, but . . ." Her voice trailed off.

Ella Rae began to cry quietly, and I felt the familiar anger in the pit of my stomach.

"I'm so sorry," Debra said. "I'll be right outside. If she's in pain when she wakes up, let me know."

We sat on either side of her bed for the next half hour, each of us holding her hand and lost in our own thoughts. We didn't speak at all.

I didn't know Mrs. Jeannette was in the room until she patted my shoulder. I got out of the chair so she could sit down.

"It's so hard . . ."

"I know," I said. "Would you like for me to stay?"

"No, sweetheart," Mrs. Jeannette said. "Michael is on his way. We'd like to sit with her alone for a while. I know this is the end, and I know what she wants."

She took my seat and reached for Laine's hand. "Good morning, baby."

Laine moved her legs a bit. "Hey, Mama."

I motioned to Ella Rae, and we left Mrs. Jeannette alone to tell her daughter good-bye.

During Laine's last stay in the hospital back in December, she had shooed Ella Rae and me home so she could talk to her mother and Michael regarding her wishes when this time came. One thing she'd been adamant about—she did not want her mother to watch her die.

Mrs. Jeannette had been alone with Laine's father when he'd suffered the heart attack that killed him. It had devastated her. Laine didn't want her to watch it happen to someone else she loved. She wanted Ella Rae and me with her because it would be easier on her mother.

Mrs. Jeannette balked at the idea immediately, but after

Laine got pretty emotional about it, she finally relented. Laine assured her that every word they wanted or needed to say would be said before she left this earth.

※

Time seemed to stand still that day. Every hour felt like it packed ninety minutes into it instead of sixty. Everybody and everything moved in super slow motion. Word got around quickly in Bon Dieu Falls. People were in and out of the house all day long. Tommy and his family, my family, the pastor at our church, a few of Laine's co-workers and a principal she'd been close to came to say good-bye to her.

Kids she had taught left cards and letters, and one of them brought her a picture of her cousin who had died recently in a wreck. I flipped it over. She had written, "Please look for my cousin Blake when you get there." That had nearly killed me. Then one of the Thompson boys who was in her class the past year was openly weeping, and that totally broke my heart. Others had come to sit with Mrs. Jeannette, offer their support, bring food, hold a hand, and anything else we needed. Small towns.

Around six p.m., the thunderstorms began to close in, with pounding rain and high winds. Mrs. Jeannette had left Laine's room for the last time. At the first loud clap of thunder, I looked across Laine's bed at Ella Rae. Laine had always loved thunderstorms, and I wished she were awake to hear this one. Suddenly I remembered my grandmother saying that during thunderstorms, the heavens were opening up so the angels could come to earth and pick up a soul. It wasn't a comforting thought.

By nine p.m., the almost constant thunder was grinding on my nerves, and any other sound in the house nearly made me jump out of my skin. The grandfather clock in the corner of Laine's room got louder and louder with each tick until I wanted to punch the glass out. "Hickory, Dickory, Dock" played over and over in my mind like a broken record. And I could've sworn the room was getting smaller and smaller. I unconsciously moved my feet back and forth against the rug and tried to concentrate on keeping my breathing even.

An hour earlier I asked Jack to go to my parents' house to check on Elle, and he still wasn't back. I was worried about him driving in this weather, worried about my baby—although I knew she was in excellent hands—and worried about Ella Rae, whose tears had never stopped flowing today. It seemed I was back to square one, with no tears left to cry. I felt defeated and powerless. I wanted to stomp the floor, throw things, and slam doors. I knew that was stupid and childish, but I felt stupid and childish. All my life I had defined things by competition. It was the only way I knew how to measure anything. If you couldn't do something like dribble behind your back, lay down a perfect bunt, or outmaneuver a chick trying to take your man, you just hammered and hammered and hammered until you got it right.

I couldn't fix this. Ever. I had no control over this situation with Laine. I'd never had any control of it. She'd orchestrated everything about her death right down to this minute. This was the first time in my life there was literally nothing left to do except sit by this bed and wait for her to die. It was hot in here, hot enough that I was sweating, although Ella Rae had a light sweater on. Every time I looked at Laine, it seemed like her color was worse, a strange grayish color that no human ever needed to be.

Why didn't God just take her if he wanted her? What was his deal? Is this how he got his kicks? I didn't want to look at her again, but every time I looked away, the room was tinier. I tried to breathe in deep, but the air never seemed to reach the bottom of my chest.

I didn't want to do this any more. I wanted to run out of this room and down the road and never look back. I wanted to go back to a time where my most difficult decision of the day was which jeans made my butt look better. I wanted my life to be fun again, and I wanted this awful, horrible nightmare to end. I didn't want to be around death and dying and tears and pain. Not another second.

The thought made me so ashamed of myself, I buried my face in my hands. How could I be wishing anything for myself while Laine was lying in bed with oxygen crammed up her nose, an IV shoved in her arm, and her skin a pasty grayish white? She was dying. Dying! And I felt anxious?

I hated myself at that moment and wanted to claw my own skin, again, like I had from Day One. She loved me, and I didn't deserve that. How could she possibly love me? How could anyone? I was selfish and hateful and mean. I didn't deserve anything, not Jack, and not the baby. And my baby certainly didn't deserve me.

I stood up, suddenly unable to stay in this death chamber another second. I felt like someone was holding a pillow across my face and I had the urge to swing wildly until I connected with whatever held me captive. But there was nothing and no one to swing at. I had to get out of here. Now. I wanted to run, and so I did. I knew I was failing her with every step I took, but I couldn't help it. Besides, I failed everybody.

"Carrigan," Ella Rae said, "what are you doing? Where are you going? You can't leave."

"I . . . I'll be right back." I groped the door handle that seemed stuck and unyielding. "I just have to . . . I'm gonna . . . I'll be back."

"Carrigan, you can't go too far."

"I *know*!" I snapped. "I said I'd be back."

Her brows creased in question, but she didn't answer, tucked Laine's hand back into hers, and lay down on her recliner. Ella Rae was dependable. Unlike me.

I slipped quickly out of the bedroom door and past Debra, sitting in her ever-present chair doing cross-stitch or needlepoint or some such crap. Did she ever move? She was always here, with some kind of needle, one for Laine or one for fabric. Her eyes met mine briefly, but I didn't hang around long enough to talk. God, what a depressing life. Always living in somebody else's tragedy. How could she live like this? How could anybody?

I could feel her eyes on me as I picked up speed, but I didn't care. Let her think whatever she wanted to think. I ran into the living room, where Tommy was asleep on the sofa. I could hear low voices from the kitchen and changed direction again. Dear God, was there not a place where I could be alone? I ran out the front door and right into Jack's chest.

"Carrigan, what is it?" He grabbed me by the shoulders. "Laine?"

"No." I pulled away from him. "She's breathing . . . dying . . . then breathing. I can't stay here." I backed away from him off the porch.

He took a step toward me.

"Don't!" I shouted. "Stay away from me." I ran toward the barn, lightning all over the sky and rain stinging me everywhere it touched. I expected to see angels arriving with Laine's chariot any second.

Jack was close on my heels. "Carrigan! What are you doing?"

I ran in one direction and then the other, zigzagging, trying to bypass his touch, but he caught me when I flung the barn door open.

"Carrigan," he said, "what's the matter?"

I backed away from him. "What's the matter?"

"I mean, what happened?"

I spun around so I didn't have to look at him. I was so ashamed of the things I had been thinking, of what I was still thinking. I was so ashamed of the things I had done. I was sure he could read them all over my face if he looked at me. Then he'd know for sure what kind of person I was.

"Tell me."

I shook my head. "I can't."

"Yes, you can."

"I was just sitting there . . . waiting," I stammered. "Just waiting, and I started thinking . . . I can't . . ." I shook my head and squeezed my eyes shut.

He laid his hand on my shoulder. "Carrigan, this is me you're talking to."

That sentence broke the dam. I began to cry. I sobbed the way I had in the rose garden the day Doctor Rougeau had told us Laine was going to die so you better get used to it because we sure can't stop it, thank you very much. I cried from the pit of my soul. Why? Why Laine? Dear God, why did it have to be Laine? When I caught my breath, I bawled, yelled, and roared everything I had kept trapped inside me the past year. The words tumbled out of me on top of each other, sometimes coherent, sometimes not. I was powerless to stop them.

"I'm so mad at her!" I marveled at how good it felt to scream. "Why didn't she just take the treatment? Maybe it would've made a difference. She didn't know. She just quit! Who just quits?" I kicked dirt and threw whatever I could get my hands on. "She didn't even *try*. It makes no sense. Her God gives out miracles every day. Surely he would've given her one . . . surely. But no. She just lay there." I gestured to the house. "She just lay there and withered up, and now she's gonna die. I'm so mad at her! She didn't care about us. It was all about her and how she wanted to do this. Screw Carrigan and Ella Rae. They'll get over it. Well, I won't get over it. Ever!"

I kicked a water bucket and scared the horses. "Nobody just

quits. Nobody. I can't even . . ." I plopped down on a bale of hay, put my hands over my face, and then jerked them away again.

Jack moved toward me, but I put my hand out to stop him. "No," I said. "No, there's more. Don't you touch me. There's more. Did you hear all the stuff I just said? About my best friend? The one who is dying while I am out here screaming about how mad I am? How selfish is that? Who does that, Jack?"

A new flood of self-loathing spilled over me. "I am an awful, horrible person. You don't know it, but I am. I really am. You can say it. I don't deserve her. I don't deserve you. And Elle? She *surely* doesn't deserve me. I'm not fit to be a mother. Any one of these cows is a better mother than I am. Would you want me to be your mother? Of course not. A mother is supposed to be stable. I feel crazy. Crazy! I am not a good person, Jack. You just don't know everything about me. I'm not a good person at all."

I jumped up again to throw something, but this time he caught me in his arms and held me there. I twisted and turned to remove myself from his grip, but he wouldn't let me go, so I stopped fighting, slumped against him, and began to cry again.

Jack held me against him while I wailed into his chest. "Just get it out."

I let myself go limp in his arms. I was exhausted, so tired of being strong. I couldn't hold up another second.

Finally there were no tears left to cry. "I'm sorry," I said.

"Sorry for what?"

"For everything," I said. I felt too guilty even to look up at him.

He pushed me away from him gently and curled his finger under my chin. "Carrigan, I'm gonna tell you something," he said slowly, "and I want you to listen to me very carefully, okay?"

I shook my head and swiped at the tears.

He cradled my face in his hands and said, "I don't know another person who loves people any deeper than you do." He paused and searched my face. "So I don't wanna hear what a bad person you are. You are the mother of my child, and I wouldn't want anybody else on earth to have that job. And I hope she turns out just like you. Full of grit and spirit and life."

He sat on a bale of hay and pulled me down into his lap. "I wish Laine would've tried the treatment too," he said. "But, Carri, it doesn't matter how I feel or how you feel. She's the one in the bed. You can't want something *for* somebody. You forget she doesn't have the will or the fight in her that you have. She can't pick up that pitchfork and take on the world. Not five years ago or ten years ago. You can't expect her to now."

I didn't answer him, but I knew he was right. Laine wasn't physically strong, in any sense of the word. She was delicate and gentle and fragile. She always had been. We were as different as daylight and dark.

"Besides," he said, "you aren't really mad at her about the chemo. You're mad at her for dying."

I looked at him. His words punched me in the gut and nearly sucked the air out of me. It sounded like such an . . . insult. "That's not her fault."

"Exactly."

I let that sink in a moment. How could you be mad at

someone for dying? Laine couldn't help it. She hadn't chosen it. She'd done nothing to give herself cancer. The truth was the harsh and high dose of chemotherapy needed to treat her type of cancer would have made her a lot sicker, a lot faster. Laine wasn't physically strong. She never had been. It would have been awful for her. I didn't really blame her for not taking it. It was purely for selfish purposes I had insisted she should. I was horrified of losing her. Jack was right. I was mad at Laine because she was leaving me. Not for a little vacation or a week on the beach. She wasn't coming back. She was such a huge and important part of my life, and her absence would leave a hole impossible to fill. How would Ella Rae and I live without our other piece? The puzzle would be forever broken, and it was Ella Rae and I who'd have to stare at the pieces forever.

We were going to Ireland one day. We were going to Hawaii one day. We were supposed to build houses together and have babies together and have lives together. She was supposed to be here for those things, and now we had to do them all without her.

I was scared to death. But that wasn't her fault. She'd never leave us by choice. Never. She'd actually given us a gift by not drinking their poison. Until this week had come, most of our days had been really happy ones, filled with laughter and joy. Not marred by vomit festivals or a mouth full of ulcers or a myriad of other side effects. She had known what she was doing all along. Little by little, I felt the anger begin to fade, and I began to feel a tiny bud of gratitude for the insight she'd shown. I clung to that bud and to Jack.

Jack tugged on my thick braid of hair. "You're so tired, baby," he said. "You haven't slept in days. You pick at your food. I'm surprised this didn't happen sooner."

I relaxed against him. Just his presence calmed me, but his words tonight had begun to cure me. The heaviness I had carried inside me for so long felt different now, lighter. I'd become so accustomed to it, I barely noticed it any more. The anger had become as much a part of me as my arms and legs. Maybe it would never go away entirely, but tonight I even felt physically lighter. I felt my spirit filling up again like water pouring into a reservoir. I held him close to me. "You are such a good man and I love you."

"You are a remarkable woman and I love you too," he said.

I caught his hand and headed toward the door. I could help her do this now. I could help her finish it.

CHAPTER EIGHTEEN

Ella Rae was waiting when I got back to Laine's room. "Are you all right?"

"I'm fine," I said. "How is she?"

Ella Rae shook her head. "Not sleeping well."

I got into my recliner and reached for Laine's hand.

"Move over," Jack said.

"Jack," I said, "you are going to be so uncomfortable. You don't have to—"

"I been uncomfortable before."

I moved over in the chair and Jack eased his six-foot-plus frame down behind me. I was grateful he was here. I looked at Laine and my heart softened. I could see her through different eyes now. I wasn't mad at her any more. Of course she would never leave us if she had a choice. She went along with every stupid idea I had ever come up with. She fought for my marriage when I hadn't. She pushed and pulled and pleaded for Ella Rae and me to be better people. She had my back so many times, I'd never remember them all, and now she was leaving me. She loved me and I was losing her, and it was that I had been mad about all along.

I still had no idea how it would feel when she was gone, but I felt surrounded by a very unfamiliar and welcome peace. I closed my eyes and let it wash over me. What a sweet relief it was to put an end to the constant turmoil that had boiled inside me the past year. I pulled Jack's arm closer around me and held Laine's hand a little tighter.

"Close your eyes and try to rest," Jack whispered.

I squeezed his hand but didn't answer. I brushed a strand of hair away from Laine's face and smiled. She had been so happy the past few days while Mitch had been here. She was clearly and absolutely in love with him. I still couldn't believe we hadn't picked up on it. Guys asked her out all the time. Sometimes she would go. But after a couple of dates, she never went out with them again. Ella Rae and I said her standards were too high. She said we had none. But never once did I think her lack of dating had anything to do with a love affair that never really ended. A love affair so fierce and consuming that anything else paled in comparison. A perfect love, indeed.

Those last five days had a different effect on Mitch. I had walked him to his car when he left this morning and held him while he cried—deep, gut-wrenching sobs that echoed the anguish in his heart. He would apologize to me for a while, and then thank me for a while.

My heart had ached for him all day. What a terrible situation this was for him. Trapped in a loveless marriage, trying to do the right thing, and when he finally became free, he found the love of his life dying. He was just as hurt as Ella Rae and I were, perhaps even more so. His pain was laced with regret and guilt. He begged me to persuade Laine to let him stay. I told him I would try, but I knew it was futile. Laine had made up her mind, and as we'd all learned in the last few months, when she decided on a course, she didn't change it.

Jack was right. I was tired, mentally, physically, and emotionally. Still, sleep wouldn't come. I laid my head on the cool leather of the recliner and watched Laine sleep. I thought about grammar school and how Ella Rae was forever beating the crap out of somebody who picked on Laine because she was clumsy and wore glasses. I thought about junior high and high school, our first real dates, which we'd all gone on together. I thought about summer camps, football games, bike rides, shopping trips, and proms. I almost laughed out loud remembering the weekend Jack and I got married and Laine had spent the entire three days in a panic because she was worried about the fallout. I thought about the nights, not so long ago, we'd ride around all night long listening to music.

Laine would preach the whole night about how pointless it was to ride around while we could sit in a house and listen to a new CD. It was safer, she argued. It was boring, we said. She'd roll her eyes and complain, tell us we were killing her, she never got any rest, and she wanted to go home. She reminded us she was the only one with a real job and she needed real sleep. But bamboo under her fingernails couldn't have made her exit that vehicle with us still in it. The girl wouldn't step on a spider but would fight a grizzly bear for me and Ella Rae . . .

I must've fallen asleep at some point because I woke with a start, as if something had jerked me awake. I glanced at the clock. It was two twelve a.m. Ella Rae was asleep, still holding Laine's hand. Jack was asleep beside me. In fact, the only sound at all was the hum of Laine's oxygen . . . and the grandfather clock. I looked at Laine. She was awake and smiling at me, very slightly, but she was smiling. She stared into my eyes so intently I realized she must've willed me awake.

"Hey," I whispered. "Do you need anything?"

She didn't nod or answer, she just kept looking at me with that faint, faraway smile. I laid my head back down and stayed locked in her gaze. When I think back on that moment, I am sure I saw a multitude of emotions in her eyes, peace, gratitude, love, even joy. Then she took a deep breath, exhaled, and didn't breathe again. I stared at her chest, waiting for the rise and fall that never came. And just like that, she was gone. I looked at her in awe of what I'd just witnessed. She had slipped out of this world and into the next without crash carts, without bells and whistles, and without white coats. Just like she'd wanted. Just like she'd planned all along.

Even as hot tears poured silently down my face, I felt an overwhelming sense of gratitude. I held her hand against my cheek for a minute or maybe an hour, I don't know. I never wanted to move from that chair. As long as Laine was in this bed, we could still see her, talk to her, touch her, even if she were dying. But I knew when I woke the others her life would truly be over.

I wanted it to be our secret. I whispered, "I love you" over and over again during that treasured time I shared with her. Finally I realized that her spirit was gone. The angels had taken her home. I felt it as sure as I could feel the sun on my face or the wind in my hair. Laine wasn't here any more. She'd slipped away from us as quiet as a whisper. Reluctantly, I laid her hand gently across her chest and sat up.

My voice was shaky when I finally spoke. "Ella Rae, you need to wake up."

She bolted upright in her chair, Laine's hand still tucked in her own. She knew as soon as she looked at me. She still hadn't looked at Laine, but she knew it just the same. She began to cry. "I wasn't ready," she said. "I wasn't ready yet."

Jack stood up and pulled me close to him. "I'm so sorry." He kissed the top of my head.

I nodded against his chest, my tears still falling. I wasn't frantic, as I had imagined I would be when this moment came. I could still feel the peace that had wrapped itself around me earlier, even more so now that she was gone.

She hadn't struggled or fought or resisted. She just . . . didn't breathe again. Relief washed over me. I welcomed the feeling. I had been amazed by her life and was now amazed by her death.

I glanced at Ella Rae. "Please get Tommy, Jack," I said.

Ella Rae was struggling. I moved out of Jack's arms and held her close to me. She was inconsolable. "I knew she was going to die, but I wasn't ready. I didn't want her to die."

Ella Rae laid her head on Laine's chest and sobbed. I placed my hand on her back, helpless to do much else, and let her cry. Sweet Rae. Ready to defend either of us at the drop of a hat, a tiny little thing that would take on anybody who threatened Laine or me. But if she loved you, she was gentle as a lamb.

Tommy came in quickly and took Ella Rae into his arms. "It's okay, baby," he soothed. "It's gonna be okay."

"I wasn't ready," she said again and again. "I didn't want her to die."

Tommy, in his Southern boy logic that I had always loved and admired, told her, "It don't matter what you wanted, baby, this world didn't want her any more. Shhh . . . baby, it's gonna be okay."

Debra came in and removed the oxygen from Laine's nose and gently took the IV from her hand. She folded Laine's hands in her lap and started to pull the sheet over her.

"Wait," I said. "Please, can you just not do that yet?"

Debra stepped away from the bed. "Of course," she said and turned to leave the room. When she got to the doorway, she stopped and looked at us. "I have had the privilege of working with many families," she said, "but I have never seen so much love and support from people who weren't blood relatives. It's been an honor, and I am so sorry for your loss. She was a treasure." She closed the door gently behind her.

Jack leaned over the bed and kissed Laine on her forehead. "Good-bye, sweet girl." He blinked back tears and patted her hand.

Watching that broke my heart. I knew how much he loved

her and respected her. She had adored him. And she had believed in us. Always.

Ella Rae had calmed down somewhat and I put my arms around her. I knew a multitude of people loved Laine. But nobody else felt exactly the same way I did except Ella Rae. We held each other for a long time and cried without saying a word. Then we stood by Laine's bedside for the last time.

Finally I pulled her away. "Come on, Rae, we have a celebration to plan."

CHAPTER NINETEEN

The funeral director ushered us into the viewing room and then left us to view Laine's body alone.

"What?"

"Oh . . . my . . ." Ella Rae said.

"She looks like a hooker!" I said, as shocked as I'd been in my life.

"Oh . . . my . . ." Ella Rae shouted this time before I put my hand over her mouth.

"Shut up, Rae, he's gonna hear you!" I scolded her.

"He NEEDS to hear me," she said. "Who's the makeup artist around here? The bouncer at Sugar & Spice? That is *ho* red lipstick."

"Keep your voice down and give me something," I said.

"Like what?" Ella Rae asked. "A washtub and some bleach?"

"Help me, Ella Rae," I said. "Just reach in your suit purse and get me something! Mrs. Jeannette and Michael will be here any minute!"

She pulled out a toothbrush.

"Really?" I asked.

She dug some more and came up with makeup remover wipes.

"Thank God!" I said and began scrubbing Laine's lips. "Help me."

She wiped at the bright-blue eye shadow. "What is this stuff, all-weather stain?" Ella Rae asked.

"This is awful," I said.

"I need paint thinner!" Ella Rae said. "I'm gonna have to put my foot against her chest. I need traction."

"Don't you dare!" I said and methodically rubbed back and forth across Laine's painted lips.

"This is spray paint," Ella Rae said. "It has to be. It won't budge. I can't rub any harder, Carri. I'll make her bleed."

I stopped scrubbing and looked at her. "Are you serious?"

"I'm 'bout to break her skin," she said. "I can't rub any harder."

"Um, Ella Rae, you can't make her bleed. She's . . . dead."

"Well, that doesn't mean she won't bleed, does it?" she asked.

"Her heart isn't pumping," I said.

"So?" Ella Rae said.

"You know you are responsible for the blonde joke movement, don't you?" I began scrubbing again, this time making progress.

"Whatever," she said.

"There," I said, effectively removing the red paint. I

reached into my purse and pulled out my coral lipstick and carefully applied it to Laine's lips. Carefully, until Ella Rae's elbow bumped my hand and I dropped it. It left a thin coral line down the front of Laine's pale-pink dress.

"Ella Rae!" I said.

"Ella Rae?" she said. "You're the one who dropped it!"

"Give me something," I said.

She pulled out a laundry stick.

I paused and looked at her. "Where do you get all this crap?" I asked.

"Well . . . I got that at Wal-Mart, if you must know. What's so wrong with having a laundry stick in your purse?" she asked.

"Nothing's *wrong* with it," I answered, shrugging my shoulders. "It's just if I asked you for two bricks and a water hose, you'd pull it out of your purse. It's strange, that's all."

She put a hand on her hip. "At least I don't put maxi pads on my tatas."

"They are NOT . . . ," I started but realized this nonsense would rage on for hours if I allowed it to. "Never mind, just help me. Please!"

Finally we got the stain out of her dress, a subtle light-brown shadow on her lids, and her lips covered in coral. She looked like Laine again. But now . . . we really looked at her.

She looked peaceful, I could agree with that. But this mahogany box with its ornate handles and satin pillow held the truth inside it. Our friend wasn't asleep, and she wasn't going to sit up and tell us to stop bickering. She was gone. Forever gone. She wasn't coming back. It was over.

I clasped Ella Rae's hand in mine. She had begun to cry, of course, but my tears had dried up. Just when I needed them most. I stared at the dressed-up shell before me, all that was left of a once beautiful girl with green eyes and rich, chocolate-brown hair. So this was where it ended. In a wooden box, in a dreary room haunted with thousands of tears from others who had stood where I was standing now. At that moment, I felt as dead as she was.

Laine had been adamant about closing her casket. She only wanted four people to see her in this coffin: Ella Rae, Mrs. Jeannette, Michael, and me. She'd barely agreed to that because she knew we'd need to see her, to tell her good-bye. She wanted people to remember her like she'd been, not "all dressed up and sleeping in a box." When the lid closed on this casket, it wouldn't be opened again.

I had been calm since she'd passed. Serene, almost. I was still in awe about watching her leave this world, how gentle it had been, how comforting it had been. But now, looking at her, it became too real. A slight panic or at least a heightened awareness had started to sink in. My emotional paralysis was waning. Laine *died*. She *died*. There would be a wake, then a funeral, and we would *bury* her. Then we'd all go home, but Laine would stay at the cemetery.

And somewhere in the midst of all of that, I had to stand up in church, in front of everybody I knew, and explain to them who Laine Elizabeth Landry was. I didn't mind speaking in front of people, but I was horrified at summing up Laine's life in twenty minutes or less. How could I ever make these people understand? I had lived who she was. Ella Rae had lived who she was. I couldn't do her life justice by telling someone about it. For weeks I had attempted to put something on paper for this occasion. But nothing ever sounded right, and it still didn't. So the day before I was to deliver her eulogy, I still had no idea what I was going to say.

"Mrs. Jeannette and Michael are here," Ella Rae whispered.

I leaned over and kissed Laine's cheek, told her I loved her, and squeezed her cold hand.

"You'll always be with us," Ella Rae said to her. "Always."

We walked away and met Mrs. Jeannette and Michael at the entrance of the room.

"Does my baby look pretty?" Mrs. Jeannette's voice sounded broken and small.

"She does."

She hugged Ella Rae and me tightly. "I will never be able to thank you girls enough for what you did," she said. "And, Carrigan, Jack and the Whitfields... How can I ever repay..."

"There's no need for that," I told her. "They wanted to do it, and Laine would have done it for any of us. You know that."

She shook her head. "They just went above and beyond, and I am eternally grateful."

"They loved her." I glanced back at the coffin. "Everybody did."

"Yes, they did."

"Take your time here," I told her. "We'll see you at the church."

Ella Rae and I hugged Michael and left the room so they could be alone with Laine.

❧

Two hours later, Ella Rae and I sat outside our church in the back parking lot and waited for the wake to begin. They had brought Laine's body from the funeral home and were setting the casket up inside the church. We had watched somberly as they'd wheeled it through the door in the misty rain. The weather report had been right on the money. Apparently the proverbial black cloud really did exist.

People had already started to arrive even though the wake didn't officially start until five p.m. But they streamed into the Fellowship Hall anyway, bringing food. That was a huge Southern tradition. I didn't know how they did things in the rest of the country, but in the South when somebody died, you cooked for three days. I watched them trail in, one after the other, and knew somewhere in all those containers there lurked pecan pies, fried chicken, rice and gravy, cornbread, every fresh vegetable and dessert imaginable, and a whole lot of sweet tea.

I also knew Mrs. Birdie Jordan would show up with chicken and dumplings. She had to be about a hundred and thirty years old by now, but she still brought chicken and dumplings to every wake in the area. Chickens she killed herself. Isn't that awful? But as bad as I felt for the chicken being chased by an old lady with a hatchet, my stomach rumbled just the same. I couldn't remember when I'd eaten a full meal. I had gone to my parents' house this morning to nurse Elle and leave more bottles, and grabbed a piece of toast. At least, I thought it had been this morning. That could've been sometime last week. My days had started tumbling on top of each other.

Mrs. Jeannette asked Ella Rae and me to stand in the receiving line with her and Michael at the wake. That was also known as stand beside the coffin and say "thank you for coming" all night. But I was grateful for that. I didn't want to miss seeing a single person who came to tell Laine good-bye.

Mitch drove up as we were walking in the back door of the church, and we waited for him under the porch. He'd been at the Farm since early this morning. Ella Rae and I had spoken with him earlier and he seemed to be doing pretty well, under the circumstances. Mrs. Jeannette had asked him to stand with us tonight, but he'd declined. I think he felt like it would somehow take the attention off Laine if everyone wondered who he was and why he was there. But we'd made him promise to come early. He walked through the back door of the church with us.

"Mrs. Whitfield?" a voice said.

I looked around for Jack's mother. But the only person I saw was the funeral director.

"He's talking to you, stupid!" Ella Rae said.

"Oh," I said. "Yes, I'm Mrs. Whitfield." If I lived to be a hundred, I'd never get used to that.

"Mrs. Landry asked that you all join her in the front of the church."

"Thank you." We walked toward the sanctuary.

"He was creepy," Ella Rae said.

"No, he wasn't," I told her.

"Yes, he was," Ella Rae said.

We had enlarged and framed Laine's picture, and Jack was placing it on the table beside the casket. It was stunning. We'd chosen an antique gold frame that complimented the colors in the picture beautifully. She looked amazing in the photograph, happy, healthy, and full of life. It was just what I'd wanted. Everyone thought it was perfect. Ella Rae and I were going to give it to Mrs. Jeannette after the services tomorrow.

"Mrs. Landry," the funeral director said, "it's five o'clock. Time to open the doors."

Ella Rae looked at me with wide eyes as the funeral director walked away. "See?" she whispered. "Creepy!"

I shook my head and smiled. It would be a long night in more ways than one. "Come on," I said. I took Ella Rae's hand. "Let's go get in our places."

We stood beside Mrs. Jeannette and Michael and waited for the doors to open so our town could pay their respects and say good-bye to Laine. I looked at the front pew and touched Ella Rae's arm. "Look," I said.

Jack, Tommy, and Mitch were sitting together. We both smiled. All our handsome men were on the front pew of the First Baptist Church of Bon Dieu Falls. Laine would've been ecstatic.

The doors opened at five, and from that moment until ten we greeted, spoke to, and thanked people. Everyone had a story they wanted to share or a memory they passed along to us. I was amazed at the number of people who had shown up, and even more so at the things they said.

Mrs. Leta Gray, an elderly woman who lived in town, hugged me as if she'd never let go. "Laine used to pick up my medicine for me and my husband at the drugstore," she said. "That sweet girl would drop it off at my house and share a cola with me. I sure do miss that."

Mrs. Jessie Rodgers told us how she had feared she'd have to give up her beloved rat terrier because her social security check had been cut and she couldn't afford to keep him any more. Laine heard her granddaughter talking about it at school. "Do you know that lovely girl started bringing me a sack of dog food every Friday? When she got sick, she left instructions at the bank for one of those Thompson boys to pick up some money and bring it to me. She had such a big heart."

Kristie Williams cried as she told me about how hard her son had worked to make the basketball team, and when he did, she couldn't afford the tennis shoes he needed. Laine had shown up at her house one afternoon a few days later and said, "These were delivered to the school today by mistake. We called the company, but they told us to go ahead and keep them. You think they'll fit Derek? We hated to throw them away."

She couldn't believe it. She prayed for days for a way to get those shoes for Derek, but she didn't realize an angel would deliver them. She found out later that Laine had asked Derek's coach for his shoe size and directions to the store in Shreveport that sold them.

On and on they went, the stories of Laine's compassion for children who had less than ideal lives at home. How she would stay after school to listen to them when no one else would. She was an encouragement to her co-workers. She brought food to the janitors, and she held the hand of a sexually abused child while the child told her mother her husband was a monster.

Ella Rae and I knew none of this.

I could've listened for days and never gotten tired of it, never ceased to be amazed by it. But by ten p.m., I was almost too exhausted to stand. My breasts ached, my feet hurt, and my stomach was growling loud enough for everybody in the church to hear it. Jack had come around three different times to urge Ella Rae and me to go to the Fellowship Hall and eat, but we didn't want to leave. Now the line had become smaller, and I was about to excuse myself to Mrs. Jeannette, when Ella Rae said, "Twelve o'clock."

I looked down the aisle and saw Lexi Carter moving toward us. For a moment, a tug of long-forgotten angst stirred inside me, but only fleetingly. She looked old and worn and tired. For some reason, I immediately felt sorry for her, although I had no idea where that had come from. She walked up to us and offered her hand.

"When I heard about Laine, I had to come and pay my respects," she said. "Laine was a really good person." She looked at Ella Rae, then at me. "And I wanted to tell you . . . I was sorry . . . about many things. I didn't mean to cause any . . . Well, I just need you to know I'm sorry."

I took her hand. "Thank you for coming, Lexi," I said, and I meant it. "And thank you for your words." I thought for a moment, then added, "You should say hello to Jack before you go."

She smiled. "I will, Carrigan," she said. "And congratulations on the new baby. I know you'll be great parents." She spotted Jack and said, "I'll just go say hello. And I really am so sorry about Laine."

Ella Rae had watched it all without opening her mouth. I was more shocked about that than Lexi Carter's heartfelt apology.

It couldn't last forever, of course. "What the hell?"

"Shut up, Rae," I said. "You can't curse in church."

"Like God can't hear me when I'm outside?" she said. "Why did you just send Lexi to see Jack? And by the way, he is freaking out. Look at him."

Poor Jack. He looked very uncomfortable. He glanced up at me and I smiled at him. *It's okay*, I mouthed.

"You are a better woman than I am," Ella Rae said.

"She's . . . pitiful," I said. "I mean, look at her. And I'm *not* trying to be funny here. She looks broken. Life hasn't been good to her."

"Maybe she hasn't been good to life," Ella Rae said.

I looked at her to see if she was being callous. But I could tell by her face it was just an observation. An astute one, at that. Ella Rae may have seemed shallow sometimes, but she was more perceptive than people knew. I think she liked to keep it that way.

I shrugged. "Whatever . . . it is it doesn't matter. Not any more."

Jack appeared and looked intently into my eyes. "You okay?"

"You mean . . . Lexi?" I asked. "Yeah, it's fine."

He slid his arm around my waist and kissed the top of my head. "You need to eat."

Mrs. Jeannette thanked us profusely for helping her receive. Ella Rae and I held her in our arms for a long time without saying a word. There was really nothing left to say.

Tommy joined us outside. I stopped at the door of the Fellowship Hall. "I can't talk to another person tonight," I told Jack. "I just can't."

I was so tired, I felt strange. Everything and everyone seemed surreal. I felt "floaty." That was Laine's word for how she felt right before she went to sleep at night. It described this sensation perfectly. Then just for kicks, at some point during the evening, I had found my tear ducts again. My emotions were running rampant. I was crying, I was laughing, I was fine, then I was crying, then laughing, then fine again. I couldn't take another emotionally charged conversation tonight, with anyone.

"I don't want to talk to anybody either," Ella Rae said.

Jack ushered us around to the side of the Fellowship Hall where there was a small garden with a beautiful fountain and white concrete benches. Brides about to get married inside the church took pictures here. I had an album full from this very spot.

"Sit," he said. "We'll be right back."

He didn't get an argument from either of us. We sat on the benches under the overhang and waited in silence. The rain had turned to a fine mist. I don't know what was more depressing, the torrential downpours of the last few days or this thick, watery air that distorted the world.

A few minutes later, Jack and Tommy showed up with plates piled high with food and a gallon of tea.

"We didn't know what you wanted, so we got a little bit of all of it." Tommy handed us two plastic forks.

I thought I wouldn't be able to eat, but I was wrong. Ella Rae and I dug in like we'd been in the desert starving, sharing plates and drinking out of the gallon jug. The food was delicious, just as I had known it would be. And Birdie Jordan's chicken and dumplings were superb. I just couldn't think too much about the death of the chicken while I ate them.

I hadn't realized Jack and Tommy were watching us until Tommy said, "Y'all eat like men."

"What do you mean?" Ella Rae asked, then took a gulp out of the jug of tea.

"That's what I mean," Tommy said.

"Do you see a glass?" Ella Rae said.

"I could get y'all some."

"No need." I took a gulp.

"No use, Tommy." Jack shook his head. "They have their own way of doing things and their own language. They always have."

Twenty minutes later we were both so stuffed we could

hardly move. The only thing missing from our buffet tonight was a Hummingbird Cake . . .

It was getting close to midnight, and the crowd had thinned considerably. People would sit up in the Fellowship Hall all night because that's what we do in the South. I've never thought to ask why. But the church doors would be locked at midnight and not opened again until eight in the morning.

"Jack," I said, "will you do something for us?"

"You know I will."

"Will you go over to our house and get Ella Rae and me some blankets and pillows?" A new wave of tears came over me. "We can't leave her by herself, Jack. We just can't."

"We promised her we never would," Ella Rae said.

He didn't answer at first, and I knew he was about to protest. He wanted me to go home and sleep all night.

"Please," I said, "we'll never be able to do another thing for her."

"All right," he agreed, "but if you stay, we stay in the Fellowship Hall tonight."

"Agreed," Tommy said.

"Okay," I said. "Please call Mama and check on Elle."

"Already have and I will again," he said. "We'll be right back."

Just before midnight, we made our way back to the sanctuary. The funeral director was escorting the last of the guests out. Jack and Tommy arrived with our things and prepared a makeshift bed on either end of the center pew for us.

Jack kissed me lightly. "Come get us if you need anything. Reverend Martin gave me a key, we'll check on y'all through the night. I know you need to stay, Carri, but please try to sleep, baby. You're so tired."

"I will."

Ella Rae and I lay on opposite ends of the pew and stared at the mahogany box and the smiling girl in the giant picture on the easel.

"She was so pretty," Ella Rae said.

"She really was."

It was comforting to lie here. I couldn't believe we'd ever considered going home tonight. This was where we were supposed to be. One last sleepover. When I closed my eyes, I fell into a deep and dreamless sleep.

CHAPTER TWENTY

"Wake up, Carri." I could hear Ella Rae, but I couldn't seem to open my eyes. "Wake up!"

I opened my eyes and had no idea where I was.

"Church," Ella Rae said.

"Yes." I remembered and sat up.

"We need to go," Ella Rae said. "And if I look as bad as you do, we need to go now."

"Am I a train wreck?"

"The poster child for the walk of shame."

I tried unsuccessfully to smooth the wrinkles out of my black dress. A strand of hair was wrapped around my pearls and keeping me from turning my head. I had apparently slept on top of one of my heels because it was folded in half. I laughed in spite of the situation. After all, it was the first time I had ever spent the night on a church pew guarding a coffin. Maybe this was the way you were supposed to look the next morning.

Ella Rae rolled up the blanket and threw the pillow on top.

"Laine wouldn't like the way you folded that blanket." I grinned.

She smiled back at me. "You're also the poster child for OCD. I wonder how I stayed so normal hanging out with you two all my life?"

"You just wish you were normal," I said. "What do you think was the weirdest thing she did? The pantry with the cans alphabetized?"

"I was thinking more like that weird thing she did with her dishes," Ella Rae answered. "You know, blue plate, green plate, yellow plate."

We laughed for a minute and looked at Laine's picture.

"Come on," Ella Rae said. "I don't want to leave her either, but we're gonna look pretty stupid dragging her around behind us."

"Wouldn't be the first time we've looked stupid."

"Won't be the last either," she said.

The side door to the sanctuary opened, and Jack and Tommy appeared. Jack grinned at me. "Looks like you slept," he said.

"That obvious, is it?" I said. "What about you?"

"We didn't sleep at all," he said. "Around two a.m. Mitch joined us. He had left the wake around ten and headed out to the Farm, but ended up driving around a couple of hours, then coming back to the church." He pointed to the blankets and pillows. "Y'all ready to go?"

"We better," I said, "before we get caught looking this way."

As we drove home Jack continued talking about Mitch. "I think he is going to have a tough time dealing with Laine's death. Maybe even more so than you and Ella Rae. His guilt is going to eat him alive if he lets it," he said. "And I know how that feels."

I touched his hand. "What do you mean?"

"Pull over," he said.

"What?"

"Just pull off the road for a minute." I drove into the parking lot at the softball field and stopped the car.

"Look at me," Jack said.

I turned to face him and he caught both of my hands in his.

"I know this is a terrible time to do this, but I have something I need to say to you."

He took a second before he started to talk. His face was a combination of guilt and pain. "Whatever it is, I don't care," I said. "Jack, really. It doesn't—"

"Just listen. Please. I was a fool, Carrigan," he said. "Our life together was good. It was better than good. It was exactly what I wanted. But I heard you say something . . . and then Lexi came back to town . . ."

Last night's goodwill for Lexi Carter disappeared, and I felt my well-established anger rise up again. But I didn't say anything. Wherever this discussion was headed, I had to let it happen.

"She said she was in town and wanted to say hello, wanted me to meet her for lunch, but I said no," he said. "I never loved

Lexi, Carrigan. I want you to know that. I liked her and we had fun together, but I never loved her. And she knew it. I was always honest with her about it."

He looked at me and waited for me to respond. When I didn't, he continued.

"We talked on the phone a long time that day, mostly about her life since she left here, which hasn't been good." He cleared his throat. "And eventually the subject turned to you and me. I told her things were great, and they were. I told her the truth. She said she'd heard some things about you she thought I should know. And I know I should've cut her off then. But I didn't."

I was getting increasingly angry, but I wanted to know the rest. "Go on."

"She said a friend of hers had told her you were getting restless in our marriage," he explained. "She said you were making comments at the diner about how bored you were all day and how you needed something more. I didn't believe her, Carrigan." He paused and looked out the window. "But I started paying better attention after that."

I don't know what kept me calm in the car that day. Maybe it was because it was the day of Laine's funeral. Maybe I had matured over the course of the year. Or maybe I was just curious. But whatever it was, I never spoke until he was finished.

"A few days after I talked to her," Jack said, "I overheard a conversation you were having with Ella Rae. You told her you were sorry you hadn't gone to college and were sorry you'd given up your softball scholarship." He looked at me. "I felt like a piece of crap. I had taken all that away from you."

I felt my heart soften a little.

"It wasn't just the scholarship," he said. "There were other things too. You'd stopped coming to the Farm to work. You'd pretty much stopped going out there altogether. Then one night I asked you about starting a family. Do you remember what you said?"

I did remember, but I didn't answer.

"You said, 'I don't want a baby right now. Maybe never. I haven't even had *my* childhood yet.' You have no idea how that made me feel. You weren't happy, and I knew it. That made me feel lower than a snake. Not only had I stolen your teenage years, I was trying to take the next decade too."

"Jack," I said. "Please—"

He clenched his jaw. "Let me finish. Lexi showed up at the barn one evening. Said she hadn't seen Mama and Daddy and wanted to visit before she went back to New Orleans, but they had gone to Dallas for the weekend. I should've known she was lying, because neither of them ever cared for Lexi too much. So we sat in my office in the barn and talked. That's all. She told me about her prescription pain pill addiction, how she was going to check into rehab, the whole nine yards. I believed her. Hell, I felt sorry for her."

I was waiting for the other shoe to drop, and I knew it was coming. It was going to explain a whole lot of questions I'd wrestled with for a long time. But to be honest, I was terrified of what I was about to find out.

"We talked till about eight o'clock that night," he said, "at least that's the last time I remembered looking at my watch. You were in Natchitoches at a tournament, so I knew you wouldn't be at home wondering where I was. Lexi had never caused any trouble after your birthday party years ago, and I had no reason to believe she was there to start any that night. Besides, she was on her way out of town."

I wished he would just say it, just blurt out whatever it was. This was driving me insane. "Please, Jack," I said, "just tell me."

He took a deep breath. "Sometime before midnight, I woke up in the barn with my shirt on the floor by my desk and my belt unbuckled. And I didn't remember a thing after eight o'clock."

I was instantly infuriated. Confess or don't confess, but don't ever lie to me. "Are you kidding me? That's all I get? You're going to sit here and lie to me on the day of Laine's funeral? So, you slept with Lexi. I figured you had. I knew something wasn't right—"

"Carrigan, stop," he said. "It isn't what you think."

"Not what I think? What a coincidence! That's the same thing Laine used to say." I tried to get out of the car, but he caught my arm.

"Carrigan, stop!" he said. "Nothing happened."

I jerked my arm away.

"Nothing happened."

"Don't lie to me!"

"She put something in my beer, Carrigan," he said. "Some

252

kind of drug. I passed out at my desk. When I woke up, she was gone. There was a note on my desk that said, 'I knew it would be just like old times.' I couldn't remember what happened. The last thing I remembered was looking at my watch at eight o'clock. After that . . . everything's a blank."

I tried to process this information, but was overcome with questions. "I don't understand, Jack. What happened? Did you have sex with her? I mean, if you did . . . I can take it . . . Just tell me what happened."

"She was trying to extort money, blackmail me, shake me down, Carrigan. Whatever you want to call it," Jack said. "She was trying to make me believe we had slept together, then she left town again. Two months later, she called and told me she was pregnant."

"What?"

"It was a lie, Carrigan. All of it. She needed money. She got herself mixed up with some pretty bad folks in New Orleans. Started using drugs and God only knows what else. She owed a lot of money to some pretty seedy characters, and she and her boyfriend came up with a scheme to get it out of me."

I sat in the car, my hands on the steering wheel, and stared at the rain. This was plain crazy. This kind of stuff didn't happen in Bon Dieu Falls. It happened on soap operas. Yet I knew Jack was honest to a fault. "You'll forgive me if I find this a little hard to digest."

"I know," Jack said.

"Did you sleep with her?"

"No!" Jack said. "But I couldn't remember anything. I

made it home that night before you did. The next day I found it difficult to even look at you because I didn't know exactly what I had done. All I had was Lexi's note . . . and what I thought was a hangover. I couldn't tell you. I wanted to, but I couldn't. It became easier not to talk to you at all. Then when she called and said she was pregnant . . . well . . . That's when it really got bad. I tried to stay away from you as much as I could. I knew what it was doing to you, but I thought in the long run . . . you'd be better off without me."

What a mistake that had been. "When did you find out she wasn't pregnant?"

"She was pregnant," he said. "But it had nothing to do with me. The child belonged to the man she was living with in New Orleans. She was already pregnant the night she came to the barn."

I thought about how distraught Lexi had been last night. How much she apologized. I thought it was a little odd then, but now I understood. "How did you find out she was lying?"

"She finally told me," he said. "I told her if the child was mine, I would take care of him financially. But I wanted a paternity test. She agreed to that. Six months later . . . the day before we found out about Laine, she called me. The baby was stillborn. And she told me the truth on the phone that day. I was furious, but relieved. That's what I was going to talk to you about the day of our picnic. We never got around to having the conversation."

It was a good thing I couldn't get my hands on her. "Why isn't Lexi in jail? Or at least in trouble? Why is she back in Bon Dieu Falls again?"

"She's going to rehab tomorrow," Jack said. "That was the deal she cut with the DA. She testified against her boyfriend in a drug case that had nothing to do with this. He got a twenty-year sentence. She was here because . . . I asked her to come before she left for rehab. I wanted you to hear it from her . . . just in case you didn't believe me. It wasn't the ideal time . . . but I had to do this today. I haven't decided whether or not to press charges against her. I wanted to see what you thought."

I began to cry, and when Jack tried to console me, I pushed him away. At that moment, I hated Lexi Carter more than I ever had, and it had nothing to do with Jack. Not only did I want to press charges, I wanted her to go to prison for the rest of her life. She was responsible for what I had done. I never would have been in the emotional place I had been if it weren't for her. I never would have cheated on him. It was her fault. She'd been a thorn in my side for years, and she was still poking and prodding and sticking me. Her actions were not only criminal, they were deplorable. I was about to tell Jack I wanted him to press charges when I heard it.

"You are responsible for what you do. No matter what you go through, no matter what happens to you, no matter how much someone hurt you, the choices you make are ultimately your own." It was Laine's voice. I heard it as clear as a bell.

It was true. I had made my own choices, no matter what the catalyst had been. I made the decision to cross the line. Nobody held a gun to my head. I made a conscious decision to sleep with a man who wasn't my husband. Lexi hadn't made me do anything. I did it out of selfishness and out of self-pity.

I did it for revenge. I did it because Jack wasn't paying attention to me, and I was too immature to see how he must have been hurting.

Me, me, me. It was always about me. Maybe before Laine's death I could've justified blaming Lexi. But now . . . things were different.

I was different.

"I have to tell you something," I said, still crying and so, so ashamed. "I did something, something so wrong and so—"

"Stop." He gathered me into his arms. "I already know. I've known for a long time."

I was stunned. I stared at him, trying to make sure we were on the same page, and I knew from the look on his face, we were. He had known all along. Of course he did. Jack always knew everything.

"I pushed you into his arms." Jack's face twisted in pain. "I should have told you from the start what had happened. It's not your fault. Stop punishing yourself."

I threw my arms around his neck and cried. "I'm so sorry, I'm so, so sorry."

He pushed me away from him and put his hands on either side of my face. "I love you," he said. "I've never loved anyone but you. I didn't tell you I knew about him for you to be ashamed. I told you so everything would be on the table. And now it is. I watched a man I barely know cry last night, and I listened to him spill his guts because he'll never get a chance to fix his mistakes. But we can fix ours. And that's all they were . . . mistakes. We got a second chance here. Not everybody does."

I clung to his words. He was right. We got a second chance. I wondered how many people, including Laine and Mitch Montgomery, never would.

"We will talk about it more," Jack said. "I will tell you every detail, everything you want to know. But for now, I needed to tell you the bulk of it. Do you want to talk to Lexi tonight?"

"No," I said. I didn't exactly feel a vast amount of generosity for her, but maybe something akin to compassion began to stir inside me. I thought about my sweet baby Elle, how much joy and happiness she'd brought me. Then I thought about Lexi's stillborn baby, how sad and apologetic she had been last night, her addiction, and how . . . worn . . . she had looked. Lexi was living in her own private hell. There was no need for me to help her move in.

"I'm so sorry I lost my faith in you," he said. "If I'd told you . . ."

"It was not your fault. I know how I am, how I was . . ." I hesitated. "And let me say this and we won't have to talk about it any more today or tomorrow or until we want to. I never wanted out of this marriage. Maybe I was just bored that day when I said something about it. And honestly, maybe I should've played softball in college. I have thought about it, but it didn't mean I didn't want to stay married. And the baby thing . . . I never knew how much I wanted her until I held her in my arms. Does anybody? You didn't steal my youth or keep me from anything. You gave me the world. You gave me everything. If I had it to do all over again, I would still marry you. At age seventeen." I grabbed his hand and held it against my face. "And him . . . I am so sorry, so sorry. He meant nothing to me. I swear." I felt fresh tears sting my eyes. "Nothing."

"I know," he said. "It tore me up when I found out. But I thought maybe it was the best thing for you. He was your age, played on your circuit. I thought you could find happiness with him. I was a fool."

"I never wanted another man and I never will."

We sat in the car and held each other for a long time. I felt a lightness around me that morning that I hadn't felt in a very long time. I hadn't realized what a heavy burden it was to carry guilt around—until it wasn't there any more. Yes, there was more to say, but for us, there was time to say it. Thank God, there was time to say it.

Jack pressed his mouth against my ear. "Let's go see our daughter."

"Yes," I whispered.

As we got to the Farm I saw my mother's car, and I knew my baby was inside. I took the steps two at a time, even in my unfamiliar heels.

Mama was holding Elle and Mrs. Diane was showing her a new rag doll. I rushed straight to them.

"Hi, my baby!" I said and took her from my mother. Elle felt so warm and smelled so good. Just having her in my arms was like tonic for my soul. I held her little body against me. I closed my eyes and drank her in, her coos, her nuzzles, her soft baby skin that smelled like lotion and everything in the world that was sweet. Just seeing her made the world seem right again. I didn't even realize I was crying until my mother reached over and wiped a tear away.

"I'm sorry," I said. "I don't even know where these tears come from any more. You know I'm not much of a crier, at least I never was one before."

"You've never lost Laine before," my mother said. "It hurts."

"How long will it feel like this?" I was crying indeed now and gave Elle to Mrs. Diane. I didn't want to hold her and sob.

"Sweetheart, there's no time limit on grief," Mama told me. "It would be nice if it had an expiration date, but it doesn't. There are many days I want to pick up the phone and call your grandmother, and she's been gone for years."

I could remember times my mother had said, "I wish I could talk to Mama today," then go on about her day. She still grieved my grandparents. I had been crushed when Papaw died and then again a few years later when Mamaw passed. But Laine was young and that made it different. I had operated under the assumption my grief was greater because Laine still had things to do in her life. But it wasn't true. Perhaps Laine's age made it more tragic, but my grief was no greater than my mother's. It wasn't a person's age that made death sad. It was the size of absence it caused in the ones left behind.

My mother and my grandmother were together every day. Mama felt her absence more than the rest of us did, the way Ella Rae and I would feel Laine's.

I suddenly felt sorry for my mother and hugged her tight. "I'm so sorry about Mamaw."

"Oh, sweetheart," she said, "it's all right. All these things you feel are normal. That's the bad thing about grieving anyone or anything. You have to go through it, not around it."

I cried in my mother's arms and was still amazed how her voice could soothe me. No wonder she missed my grandmother so much.

"Carrigan," Mrs. Diane said, "I hate to ask right now, but it's mealtime for Elle. Do you want me to give her a bottle, or would you rather do it?"

"No," I said. "I want to nurse her. I want to hold her before I have to get ready to . . . go back."

She gave Elle to me, and I took her into the nursery where we could be alone. I had missed my baby so much. Jack came into the nursery and sat on the daybed.

"Is she hungry?"

"She's starving!" I said. "Like a little pig."

He watched as I nursed our daughter for a few minutes. "Are we good, Carrigan?"

"We're better than good," I said. "We're the best we've ever been."

CHAPTER TWENTY-ONE

The church was already near capacity when Jack and I arrived at noon. After last night's testaments, I don't know why that surprised me. I had thought I'd be back soon enough that Ella Rae and I could spend a few minutes alone with Laine . . . for the last time. But Ella Rae wasn't even back yet.

Jack and I made our way through the back entrance of the church and I headed straight to Laine's casket. Strange as it sounds, it made me feel better to stand next to it, to keep my hand on it. I sighed and rubbed the cool mahogany with my hands. It was so smooth. I wanted to make Creepy Guy open the coffin, just to look at her again, but I knew that was out of the question. I briefly toyed with the idea of popping the top myself. Laine would probably sit up and slap me. I bent down and put my face against the cool wood.

"I'm back," I whispered. "Rae's on her way."

The mahogany felt so good against my face. I stayed in that position and talked to Laine. I wasn't crying and I wasn't upset.

I just wanted to talk to her. I told her that everything between Jack and me was going to be okay. I told her about how sweet Elle had been that morning and how I wished she'd been there to see her. I told her how upset Mitch had been last night and to send him some comfort if she found a way. I stroked the mahogany with my hand and whispered all the things I wanted her to know. Jack was standing near talking to someone I couldn't see. His hand was on my waist, but his attention was on his companion. I could've stayed there all day, having a sweet, private, last conversation with my girl. I felt Jack move his hand away, and presently Ella Rae appeared. She put her head down on the casket too and draped an arm around my shoulder.

"Hey," she said.

"Hey."

"What are you doing?"

"Just talking to Laine."

We stared at each other for a moment.

"I thought you were crying."

"Why?"

"Because you're laid out over this coffin. Duh," Ella Rae said.

"I was just talking to her and the wood felt good against my face."

"It's a bunch of people who think you are crying," she said. "I thought you were crying, and now I bet they think we're both crying."

It never occurred to me people would wonder what I was doing.

"This wood does feel good," Ella Rae observed and began stroking the top of the coffin with her free hand. "It's very cool to the touch."

I made a face. "It's very cool to the touch?" I asked. "I have never heard you say anything like that in your life."

"What's wrong with that?"

"There's nothing wrong with it," I said. "You just don't speak like that. She speaks like that."

Ella Rae rolled her eyes. "Whatever. Anyway, people think you are upset."

"I'm not upset."

"About anything?"

"Well, other than Laine being dead and all," I said. "Maybe we should get up now."

We started to move, but she stopped me. "Wait."

"What is it now?" I asked.

"Do you think we should . . . cry?" she said. "I mean, should we be upset? We can't just act like we were taking a nap."

"I can't cry right now. I'm not upset," I said.

"Let's just stay like this until the funeral is over," she said.

"Perfect," I said. "We can ride the coffin out of here like a mechanical bull."

"Yes," Ella Rae said, "and the band can play something out of *Urban Cowboy.*"

"It's a choir, not a band, barhopper," I said. "This is called a church."

"Oh yeah," she said. "I knew I made the wrong turn."

Call it ridiculous, call it childish or irreverent, but we began to laugh. Really laugh. And it felt good. Looking back, I'm sure it was because of anxiety, nerves, or sheer mental and physical exhaustion, but there was no stopping it.

Within a minute or two the giggles took over completely. "Creepy Guy would try to move us," I said.

"Oh, I am sure," Rae said. "He would appear out of nowhere, just like a vampire, swoop down, and catch us both around the neck. Then he'd say, 'Hey baby, how 'bout a little formaldehyde on the rocks at my place?'"

My entire body shook with laughter. "Stop!" I said. "Stop it now."

"Ladies." Jack appeared behind us with an arm around us both. "I don't know what's going on, but most everyone in this church has become distraught watching the two of you. Now . . . I know you're laughing . . ."

"What gave us away, Jack?" Ella Rae said. "It was her, wasn't it? She's so uncool in these situations!"

"These situations?" I said. "When's the last time you laid on a casket, Rae?"

"I was in Caskets R Us just yesterday, smarty pants," she said. "I'm their new spokesperson. I laid on every casket in the house. I personally like the newer models because—"

"Okay, okay," Jack said. "Here's what we're about to do. I'm going to stand up with my arms around both of you, and you two are going to put your heads as deep into my chest as you can get them, and we'll walk out the back. Got it?"

"Did you wear deodorant?" Ella Rae asked.

"What the hell is wrong with y'all?" he asked. "Now behave and hold on."

We walked out the back with our heads buried in Jack's suit jacket until he pushed us into the ladies' room. Thankfully, no one else was in it, because he came in too.

"What was that?" he demanded when we were safely behind the locked door.

Ella Rae sat down on the toilet and laughed so hard she had to hold on to the wall. I sat on the floor and held my sides, shaking all over.

Jack shook his head. "The only sane one in the bunch is gone."

That was the funniest line of the day. We were nearly screaming with laughter now.

"Dead puppies, dead puppies, dead puppies," Ella Rae began to chant. That had been Laine's favorite mantra when she'd contracted the inappropriate giggles.

"And I don't want to know what that means," Jack said. "For God's sake, try to get it together in the next five minutes." He closed the door behind him.

After the laughter finally subsided, Ella Rae looked at me and smiled. "I can't tell you how much I needed that."

I shook my head. "I know, me too. And, girl . . . do I have a story for you."

"Tell!" she said.

"Not today," I said. "Today belongs to Laine."

"This funeral is gonna suck, Carrigan," she said. "I wish we could skip over it, and then again, I want it to last for three days."

"Me too."

"I wish we could go back and do every bit of it again."

"Even the crappy parts," I said, "and even if I knew it would end all over again just like this."

"We didn't let her leave here without . . . without . . . ," Ella Rae said.

"We left nothing unspoken," I said. "We turned over every stone. We shook every tree. We said it all."

Ella Rae shook her head. "I know you are right. I just can't remember saying it all. I would think of things I wanted to tell her when I was in bed at night, and then I couldn't remember what they were the next day."

"We told her everything," I said. "I promise you we did."

She stood up and smoothed her dress. "Let's go," she said. "I'm ready now."

I took the hand she extended and got up off the floor. "I'm ready too."

Mrs. Jeannette asked Ella Rae and me to sit on the front pew with the family. "You girls were her sisters," she said. "Where else would you be?" Jack, Mitch, and Tommy were on the pew behind us. Jack leaned up right before the service began and gave me a hug. "You'll do her proud, Carri. You always have." I hoped he was right. I had finally come up with what I wanted to say in the eulogy, then completely changed my mind. Twice. I hoped I could convey what was in my heart.

As soon as the music began, Ella Rae began to cry. I tried to think about something else, anything else. I didn't want to start the waterworks before I had to speak. I thought about

Elle. I thought about football. I thought about frog hunting. Nothing worked. I dabbed at my tears with a dainty hankie that had belonged to Laine.

"Friends, family, and loved ones, we are here to celebrate the life of Laine Elizabeth Landry," Reverend Martin said. "Let us open with a word of prayer."

I stared at my shoes while Reverend Martin prayed. I stared at their heels, the way they were made, the way the straps looked, the point of the toes. I did everything I could to avoid listening short of putting my fingers in my ears. I finally heard him say, "Amen" and I looked up again. It was going to be a long hour or so.

"Laine came to see me last year, a few weeks after she'd been released from the hospital. She wanted to write the opening remarks for her funeral and asked me if I could help her with that. While this may seem a bit unorthodox to some, I intend to follow her wishes."

I glanced over at Ella Rae, and she shrugged slightly. Laine continued to surprise us.

Reverend Martin began to read. "My name was Laine Elizabeth Landry. I was a daughter and a friend and a teacher and an aunt. Those were the most important things in my life and the things I hope to be remembered for. I am survived by the most wonderful mother a girl could ask for, Jeannette Landry, who gave me a treasured childhood and wings to fly when it was over. I love you, Mama. I had one brother, Michael, whose strength I always relied on and envied. I love you, Mike; you and Belinda take care of my nieces. I had two sisters, Carrigan Whitfield and Ella Rae Weeks, who were, indeed, my sisters in every sense of the word. They showed me what unconditional love was time and time again. I am also survived by four nieces and a niece by proxy. It's a beautiful world, girls, but it's a tough world too. Ask for help when you need to, be good to your parents, and find true friends who will love you through it all. Remember, it isn't always blood that makes a family. I asked Michelle Lange to sing this song for all of you, my family. I loved you all very much. Thank you for everything. And don't worry . . . I will save you all a seat."

Ella Rae was openly sobbing by now. So were Mrs. Jeannette, Michael, and most everyone in the church. I was hanging on by a thread. I was pretty sure I would make it without dissolving into a puddle. But then the music started. I recognized the chords immediately, and so did Ella Rae. She buried her face in my shoulder, and I put my arm around her as Michelle began to sing a song we'd loved since junior high. It was a ballad about life and love and loss and fit the occasion perfectly.

Laine had known all along what music would be played today, what would be said today. She had only pretended to make us plan her funeral so we'd get used to the idea of having one. And stop being so frightened by the word. All this time, I thought I was the sly one of our trio, and it turned out to be Laine. She'd punked us. I wanted to laugh, but my tears were falling too fast, so I put my head against Ella Rae's and cried instead. The music finally ended and Reverend Martin stepped back to the podium. He began speaking of heaven and how Laine was there, healthy again, whole again, visiting with her daddy and other loved ones who had gone before her. He spoke of green valleys and golden streets, of mansions and angels. I heard bits and pieces, ignoring what I could and feeling much like I had in Doctor Rougeau's office the day this nightmare had first begun. I didn't want to hear anything about heaven, especially the part where Laine was there now. Heaven was no comfort to me. Laine was gone and God took her. I was going to need a signed letter from him to explain this.

The sound of my name jerked me back into the world. Reverend Martin had just announced I would deliver the eulogy. I squeezed Ella Rae's hand and walked to the podium on automatic pilot. I still had no idea what would come out of my mouth.

I looked around at the packed house, then at Jack and Ella Rae. Then from somewhere inside, I found my voice. "When Laine asked me to do this, my first reaction was to tell her 'No, I can't and I won't.' But she wore me down. I knew there was no possible way for me to tell you who Laine Landry was. I knew I could never make anyone understand what we had *all* lost.

"Then, in the last two days—no, really in the last few months—I realized I didn't have to tell you who she was and what we lost, because you all told us. It was obvious in the visits to the Farm by her students, past and present. It was obvious by the flowers that arrived continuously. It was obvious in the phone calls and the cards and the food and the words you shared with us . . . especially in the last few days. You told us things about her that we never knew. The lives she touched weren't exclusive to Ella Rae and me, although we probably thought they were."

I looked at Ella Rae, my sweet friend, still crying but smiling now too. "We lived in our bubble . . . and we really, really loved our bubble. But she lived out here . . . with all of you. So I want to say thank you. Thank you for sharing those things with us that we never knew anything about. Thank you for loving our friend. And thank you for allowing her to love you, because she really did."

I paused for a second, trying to decide which direction I should take. "I suppose my real job is to stand here and tell you some crazy stories about Laine, but I probably can't without incriminating Ella Rae and myself." A ripple of laughter ran through the crowd.

"So I'm just going to tell you the truth, and the truth is . . . my heart hurts. It hurts for myself and for Ella Rae and for Laine's family. I want my friend back. I want to see her walk across the street to my house and keep score at a ball game and ride her bike and play with my baby. And it kills me to think my daughter will never know this wonderful, beautiful soul who watched her come into this world. She was wise beyond her years and a true and trusted friend. Poppa Jack once said to me, 'Laine is a fighter in her own way.' I thought he was crazy, because I only knew her to be just the opposite, kind and calm and gentle. But I have come to realize he was right. She was a fighter. She fought me, all the time. She fought *for* me all the time. She fought for Ella Rae and for her students and anywhere she saw injustice. And she fought cancer too. She rose above all it stripped her of, and she won that battle. Because it may have taken her body, and it may have taken her from us, but it never took her spirit, and it will never take her memory."

I stepped down from the podium and kissed Laine's coffin for the last time. I managed to make it back to Ella Rae's arms before the dam broke.

Chapter Twenty-Two

I gathered the shawl closer around Elle's shoulders and pointed at her daddy turning into the driveway.

"Who's that?" I asked her as she spotted Jack's truck.

She began flailing her little arms and legs as she recognized him. It was her normal reaction whenever she saw him. She was only seven months old, but she was very bright, even if I do have to say so myself.

Jack was wearing a huge grin as he stepped out of the truck, which was his normal reaction when he saw Elle. I was surprised he didn't flail his arms and legs as well. He took the steps two at a time, planted a quick kiss on my lips, and scooped Elle out of my arms. She immediately began patting his face with her hands.

"What did my two favorite girls do today while Daddy was at work?"

She responded by placing both her hands in his mouth and squealing.

I shook my head and smiled. Elle was becoming a poster child for a daddy's girl.

We'd been back in our own house for months now, since the week after Laine died. I hated to leave the Farm, but we needed to be back in our own places and back in the real world. Our protective bubble was no more. Laine's passing had forced us all to step back into reality and leave our magical realm where each moment was full of laughter and love.

Those days had often contradicted the impending doom that lay ahead. Even though we had all clung to a desperate hope for a miracle that never came, they remained some of the most treasured times of my life. Those days had also changed me. No, change was not a large enough word. This last year had transformed me. Every moment of every day was no longer about me and my wants and needs. I never realized how selfish I was until the year Laine was dying. Oh, I would do anything for Laine or Ella Rae, even before then. But I always examined every angle of a situation to assess what I could get out of it. What was in it for me? My thought process had certainly changed the past year. For the first time in my life, I felt like a grown-up.

I looked at Jack and Elle and felt the familiar tug on my heart. I loved them both so much. I wondered for the millionth time how I had ever entertained the thought of leaving Jack. Laine had told me time after time after time how much Jack loved me. I know now that it was because she recognized what loving someone from afar looked like. She was, in many ways, the wisest person I had ever known. I had been too full of pride and arrogance to see my husband was hurting. All I knew was he wasn't paying attention to me. Laine always knew it wasn't another woman. Laine . . .

"You coming inside, Mommy?" Jack asked. "It's getting cool out here."

"In a few minutes, okay?"

"Sure, baby." He kissed me again. "Take your time." He took Elle inside and left me in the porch swing.

Sweet Jack. He'd been so good to me since Laine died. We didn't talk too much about the Lexi drama. I had asked a few questions, but a very few. He answered them truthfully and thoroughly, and I was satisfied. He never asked me anything about Romeo, although I had assured him I would tell him whatever he wanted to know. Mostly we felt an abundance of gratitude. Things could've turned out so much different. Laine and Mitch taught us that.

Jack was unbelievably patient when I ranted and raved about God and his logic. He was always attentive and understanding when I got in these occasional blue moods, like the one I was in today. I think the general consensus was that I needed to take a little something like Prozac until I could get past the first few months. But I knew it wasn't depression. It wasn't even sadness. I knew Laine was happy where she was and that part didn't sadden me at all. It was more like I was on a quest for an answer. Why did Laine die? What possible good could come from it? Would I ever make peace with it? I needed resolution. I needed it to make sense. But the more I groped for an answer, the more the answer eluded me. So frustrating.

I gazed across the street at her house and pictured her in the yard, spraying a speck of dirt off her bike, watering flowers, waving to me. I still had a hard time imagining anyone there but her. Mrs. Jeannette had mentioned putting Laine's house on the market a few weeks ago, and I had become so frantic that Jack bought it. He walked in one evening after work, gave me a kiss, and handed me the deed. The relief had been tremendous, and I had thanked him constantly for days. I still had no idea what we'd do with it, but for now, just owning it was enough.

Ella Rae and I sometimes walked over and sat in the empty living room. I didn't know if that was a good thing or a bad thing, but it was certainly an emotional thing. I don't think a day had passed since Laine died that Ella Rae didn't sob at least once. I fretted and paced and the questions continued to hound me, but I didn't cry. In fact, I hadn't cried since the day of the funeral.

I laid my head on the pillow of the porch swing. I still went about my life. I loved my baby and my husband and I put one foot in front of the other. I did what I was supposed to do. Yet when people offered condolences, I could hardly stand it.

Especially the ones who said, "Some things just can't be explained," or "God's timing is perfect." What the hell did that even mean? I knew they meant well, but in reality I wanted to slap them all. Why say anything to me at all if you're only going to frustrate me more? Of course, that was wrong too. They were just trying to help.

I supposed this was just what happened when you were

grieving. The mood swings, I mean. Some days, every memory was funny and heartwarming and comforting. Other days, like today, I was mad and discouraged and confused and the memories I clung to were unclear and unfocused. I was horrified that one day they would fade altogether. On days like today, her absence enveloped my world and all that was in it. I hated these days. They usually began with me telling God about all the people in the world who didn't deserve to take another breath. Pedophiles, serial killers, and people who were mean to animals still walked around laughing and talking and living, yet he took Laine? It made no sense to me. Where was the logic in that? If I lived to be one hundred, I would never understand it and God still wasn't talking. I started to wonder if he was even there at all. I needed an explanation, something tangible to make her death reasonable. I needed somebody to say to me, "Laine died so global warming would subside," or "Laine died so there would be peace in the Middle East," or even, "Laine died so teenagers would no longer suffer from acne."

Something. Anything. I had to have some answers, but I had no idea where to start. Church left me even more confused and sad. I couldn't sit there without thinking of that awful mahogany box that was now covered in dirt. And I certainly couldn't linger on that thought for long. Mama had sent Reverend Martin over a few times, even though she'd denied doing it, but he'd only made me feel guilty when he said I should never question God. I had toyed with the idea of consulting a medium, but Ella Rae nearly fainted at the thought. Such a Baptist.

So I mostly just sat in this swing and pondered. I'd even grown to hate the word *ponder*. Sometimes I looked up at the night sky and asked Laine if she was there. If she was in the paradise she was so certain about. But like God, she didn't answer.

Enough. I got up and peered through the window to my living room. Jack and Elle were sitting on the floor playing, and once again, I physically felt my love for both of them. The questions about Laine would still be here tomorrow. I went inside to join my family.

⚘

The next morning was cold and rainy, and I loved snuggling in bed with Jack on days like this. Elle would sleep for twelve straight hours, usually from eight p.m. to eight a.m. Everyone told me what a blessing that was and spoke of horror stories about their children and their sleeping habits. Charlotte Freeman said neither of her kids had ever slept through the night and they were three and four. I couldn't imagine. Elle's nocturnal habits left an awful lot of time for her father and me to reconnect and, boy, did we reconnect. Jack was trying his best to reconnect this morning, but I slapped his hand when he slipped it under the covers.

"No," I said, laughing, "she'll be awake in five minutes!"

"All I need is three," he said, nuzzling my neck.

"Then, *hell* no." I laughed again and scooted away from him. As if on cue, Elle began moving in her bed beside us. "See?" I said.

"I'm gonna have to have a talk with this girl," Jack said and leaned over me to pick her up.

"About guys like you," I said. "Ugh . . . you're squashing me."

"Good morning, little one," he said to Elle as she rubbed her sleepy eyes and smiled.

She squealed appropriately and flailed her legs.

Jack got up and changed her diaper, then got back in bed, depositing Elle between us. She laughed and cooed and smiled and then demanded her breakfast. She was such a happy baby. I loved mornings like this. My blue moods never made an appearance during these moments.

"Are you going to work?" I asked, hoping he'd say no.

"Nah," he answered. "Not much going on, and it's cold and rainy and I'd rather spend today here."

"Yay!" I said to Elle. "Daddy's hanging with us today!"

Jack began rubbing my thigh. "How much longer until she takes a nap?" he asked and winked at me.

"You are awful!" I accused, but his hand sure felt good on my thigh. I bit my lip. "After lunch."

A knock on the front door interrupted our fun. "I'll go," Jack said.

Elle had finished nursing, and I was buttoning my shirt when Jack came back into the bedroom with a huge box in his arms and a strange expression on his face.

"What's that?"

"I don't know," he said. "It's addressed to you and Ella Rae . . . from Laine."

I stared at him. "What do you mean?"

He put the box on the chaise and gestured toward it. "See for yourself."

I picked Elle up and walked over to look. Jack was right. It was addressed to Ella Rae and me, at my street number. It was Laine's impeccable handwriting. The return address read, *Laine E. Landry, Heaven.* I continued to stare at it, but I didn't touch it. "What is this?"

Jack put his arm around me. "I don't know, sweetheart," he said. "The UPS man brought it, not the Archangel Michael. Are you all right?"

I didn't answer and just continued to look at the box with curiosity. Of course I knew the Archangel Michael didn't bring it, just as I knew it hadn't come from heaven as the return address suggested. But where had it come from? And where had it been? Who had sent it? What was in it?

Jack took Elle from me. "Listen," he said, "Elle's already had breakfast. We have three or four hours of cushion. I'll get her dressed and take her out to the Farm with me. Why don't you call Ella Rae and open the box together?"

I shook my head and sat on the chaise beside the box. "Okay," I said. I reached for the phone and called Ella Rae. She promised to arrive in fifteen minutes.

Jack and Elle hadn't been gone long when Ella Rae busted through the front door. "Where is it?"

I pointed to the box. "There."

She folded her arms and stood beside it, inspecting it without touching. "What's in it?

"I don't know, Ella Rae," I said. "I obviously haven't opened it."

"You have no clue what's inside it?"

"Do you see an X-ray machine?"

"You are such a smart ass," she said.

"And you're a dumb ass," I said. "You see the box is still taped shut."

She poked at the box with a pen from Jack's desk.

I stared at her wondering once again what it was like to live in her world. "Laine ain't in the box, Rae," I said.

"Yes, I know," she said. "Open it."

"You open it."

"It's addressed to you."

"It's addressed to both of us."

"But it's got your street number on it," she explained. "She must've wanted you to open it. If she'd wanted me to open it, then it would've had my street number on it, but the UPS man doesn't come to my part of town until after lunch. Especially on rainy days . . . but sometimes he comes around noon if—"

"Oh, shut up, Ella Rae," I said as our conversation took a familiar turn to the ridiculous. "Go get me a knife from the kitchen."

She ran out of the bedroom and was back a few seconds later with the largest knife in my house.

I took it from her. "We aren't skinning a hog, Rae," I said.

"It was the first one I saw."

We stood in front of the box and looked at each other for a moment.

"This is so stupid," I said finally. "I don't know what we think is in there." I began cutting the tape from the top as Ella Rae peered over to get the first look. When I pulled the top apart, at least six or seven spring snakes flew out of it in every direction. We screamed in unison and jumped up and down.

I picked up one of the snakes and flung it across the room in a fit of hysterical laughter.

"Almost gave me a heart attack!" I said, my hand on my chest. My heart beat wildly.

"Why did she do that?" Ella Rae said. "If she wasn't dead, I'd kill her!"

Inside the box was a big white sheet of poster board. She'd written, "Gotcha! LOL! LOL! LOL!" in big purple letters with smiley faces all over.

I wiped at the laughter tears and looked back into the box. There was a huge leather-bound book on top. It appeared to be some sort of journal. I took it out of the box carefully and laid it on the bed. Two more just like it were underneath. I opened the first one. I read the inscription aloud. "For Carrigan, with your fiery spirit and huge personality, you took me places I never could have gone without you. When you ask why, and I know you will, pick up this gift. I love you always and I'll see you again. Laine."

I looked at Ella Rae, who was, of course, crying, and handed her the next journal. She opened it, wiped her eyes, and read hers aloud too. "For Ella Rae, with your childlike innocence and mean right hook, you showed me what it was like to love someone so much, you'd fight for them. Literally.

When you cry, and I know you will, pick up this gift. I love you and I'll see you again. Laine."

We both began to flip through the pages, filled with pictures from grammar school until our time at the Farm, just months ago. Laine had filled both books with ticket stubs, napkins, notes, matchbooks, a program from a school play, a piece of the uniforms we'd worn when we'd won the state softball championship. Pieces of our lives were scattered across every page, and she'd written something under every memento. We sat on the bed and compared our books, relived moments, laughed, and remembered. I was amazed. The book was huge and it was full.

"This is what she did in her room all that time," I said.

"You're right," Ella Rae agreed. "I am sure it is."

We both sat in silence on my bed and continued looking at our books, comparing things, laughing at things, marveling in the amount of time Laine had obviously spent putting these together. Trying to guess where the box had come from. Who had sent it, where had it been? We must've sat there an hour and a half just remembering. Everything she'd attached to the book had a story with it. When I finally reached the last page, there was Laine's perfect penmanship again, this time a letter, or a long note, I guess you'd say. This one I read in silence.

An American writer, Rita Mae Brown wrote, "I still miss those I loved who are no longer with me, but I find I am grateful for having loved them. The gratitude has finally conquered the loss." I know you are struggling with my death. But it's been six months, and that's long enough to bang your head against the wall.

Please don't even try to deny that. I've seen you do it a thousand times when you can't rationalize something. Not everything makes sense. You go round and round and round until it makes you nuts. Stop! To use a phrase you have always despised, "it is what it is." I want you to remember me, but I don't want you to get lost in remembering.

Feed a stray dog when you get lonesome for me. Check on some of the older ladies in town who have no help when you get lonesome for me. Or better yet, go to church. I bet you haven't been twice since the funeral. I'm not in the casket, Carrigan, and I'm not at the cemetery . . . I never was. Now, go live, and stop obsessing on this.

I'm so proud of you, of the mother you are and the wife you have become. (And oh, about Jack . . . I hate to say I told you so . . . but . . . I told you so!) By the way, how'd you like the song at the funeral? Okay, that was a cheap shot, but it was our song. I had to.

Take care of your family. Take care of Rae and Tommy, and take care of yourself. I love you.

Always, Laine

I swept my fingers across the written words. I opened my mouth to read them to Ella Rae and then stopped. I wouldn't share them yet. I knew I would one day, but not today. Today I wanted to keep them to myself and read them over and over

and over. Besides, Ella Rae was reading her own note, and
smiling . . . and crying.

I flipped the book over to the back and was surprised to
find something inscribed into the leather. It was a recipe . . .
for Hummingbird Cake. I quickly scanned the ingredients,
hoping to find the ever elusive spice I was sure she had pro-
tected even until her death. But it was all ordinary items.
Flour. Sugar. Salt. Pineapple. Bananas. But then I saw it,
at the bottom of the book, an asterisk. It read, "The secret
to Hummingbird Cake is I only made it for people I loved.
Perhaps yours tasted the best because I loved you and Ella Rae
most of all."

In a moment that stunned, I realized that the journal in
my lap had done more than give me mementos of our adored
Laine and our cherished time together. I felt . . . untroubled . . .
maybe for the first time in *years*. Had God just answered a
thousand questions? I was unexpectedly filled with an abundance of gratitude for having known Laine at all. I had been
most fortunate to have her in my life—not everyone had
a Laine—and so much more. I looked around me, at my
home, the pictures of my family, of Jack, of my baby. I looked
at Ella Rae sitting beside me quietly thumbing through her
own journal. To say God had blessed me would forever be an
understatement.

Laine had been our voice of reason. She'd been our calm
during a storm. She'd been our conscience and constant companion . . . and now she'd become our comforter. Memories
that had been foggy in my mind were suddenly as real as the

journal I was holding, and they flooded my soul like the tears that were *finally* flowing freely once again from my eyes. It was the sweetest release I had ever felt. I grabbed Ella Rae's sandpaper hand and kissed it. I could *hear* Laine's laughter. I could *see* her face. I could *feel* her around us. I realized that day, sitting on my bed with Ella Rae, that even though Laine wasn't across the street, or sitting beside us, her spirit surrounded us and it always would. Laine lived on every day. She was just somewhere else.

And the peace and acceptance that had eluded me for months was delivered to me in a box from heaven.

$\mathcal{E}$PILOGUE

Some things never change; such is life in a small town.

Otis is still on the street corner by the post office when I go into town, nursing his ever-present forty-ounce beer. I still have to steer Elle away from Miss Lucy at the ballpark for fear she'll swat at her. Bethany Wilkes is dressed impeccably every time I see her, even if her clothes are several sizes larger now. I'm guessing that bakery thing worked out after all.

Lexi Carter relapsed after her first stint in rehab. But then she went back, and this time it took. Afterward, she went to college, got a degree in social work, and now works for the rehab center where she finally got clean. I haven't talked to her in years, but I know she speaks to Jack on the phone every now and then. I don't mind at all. The truth is, on some level I am thankful to Lexi. She has gotten me out of my own way.

Ella Rae and I found a wonderful way to share Laine's enthusiasm for helping other people. We started the Laine Landry Foundation that assists older residents of Bon Dieu

Falls with things like transportation and groceries and medicine. Several of Laine's former students volunteer and provide much needed help like mowing lawns for the elderly, planting flowers in their yards, tending their gardens, and shopping for them. The Foundation is completely privately funded, and we have transformed the annual Crawfish Boil into our big fund-raiser for the year. The support has been overwhelming.

Laine's house has become our office and also a place for those older folks to gather. Mrs. Jeannette cooks for them several times a week while they play cards, watch movies, or just visit. Mamie even comes by some mornings to leave her famous cinnamon rolls.

The older folks are a complete joy to be around, and now, at age five, Elle thinks she has a dozen sets of grandparents, white and black alike, because they all dote on her. They teach her all sorts of things from the proper way to shoot marbles to the fine art of cursing.

A week ago at home, she picked up a coffee cup and threw it back down. "Dammit, that's hot!" she said. Thank you, Mr. Henry.

I thought Jack would pop trying to hide his laughter. I explained to her gently that wasn't language we used. She seemed very unconcerned. Clearly we have a ways to go with this little redhead.

Mitch never remarried but seems to be happier nowadays. He left Dallas and moved to Natchitoches, closer to home. He owns a financial advisory firm and takes care of the money for the Foundation. His heart is in the project, he's a whiz at his job, and he has really helped us grow.

I have met his son a few times and he seems like a great young man, with his father's curly hair and good looks. Ella Rae and I have both tried to introduce Mitch to some friends of ours, but he keeps saying, "Not yet." Perhaps Laine was right, if you love someone right the first time, once is enough.

Ella Rae and Tommy had a little boy last year, Thomas James Weeks, Jr. or T.J. as we call him. He is adorable and looks just like his mother, with blond hair and brown eyes. Ella Rae quit drinking the day she found out she was pregnant and hasn't had a drop since. She says T.J. is more fun than alcohol. She is my cochairman at the Foundation, so we are still together every day.

Ella Rae single-handedly oversees the annual Laine Landry Memorial Softball Tournament. Every year the tournament continues to grow and prosper, providing scholarships to two graduating seniors. Last year we were able to give each recipient five thousand dollars, and this year we are on track to give even more.

Jack and I are stronger than ever. It's hard to believe we just celebrated our eighteenth anniversary. He took me to the Farm . . . for a picnic. The days behind us are just that, behind us. I sometimes feel sorry for couples who have never gone through anything, who never have their limits tested. There's no doubt in my mind we can weather any storm life throws our way.

We'll be adding another member of the family soon, another

girl. Jack says we're stopping after this one. I think he fears he'll drown in the hormones around here after a while. Elle is very excited about a little sister. She is totally convinced T.J. is her little brother, so there is no need for her father and me to give her one. She wants to name the baby "Bubbles" and is very adamant about it. While we have yet to decide on a proper name, I fear "Bubbles" may stick. Thank God she's into bubbles these days. A year ago we might have had to call her Sponge Bob.

Oh, and the third journal in the box from heaven? It was for Elle. A handwritten guide for every year from Elle's first through her twenty-first birthday, things Laine wanted her to know, to see, to do. Every year on her birthday, Elle gets a card from her and a charm for the bracelet she got on her first birthday. I still have no idea where they come from, who sends them, how they remember. But Elle gets ridiculously excited when she receives them and talks about her "Laine Book" all the time. It's her favorite bedtime book.

Sometimes she asks me, "Mommy, can Laine see us? Is she watching us?"

I tell her, without a doubt in my mind, "Yes, sweetheart, she watches us all."

$\mathcal{D}$ISCUSSION $\mathcal{Q}$UESTIONS

1. Do you think Carrigan grew as a person during the course of Laine's illness? If so, how?
2. Do you feel the town of Bon Dieu Falls was a character in the book?
3. Do you agree with Laine's decision not to take chemotherapy?
4. In the end, do you feel like Carrigan's relationship with another man actually strengthened her relationship with Jack?
5. Do you think Ella Rae was actually much wiser than she exhibited?
6. Were you surprised at the hospitality of Jack's family to take Laine in during her illness? Do you find that a "Southern" thing?
7. Do you think Jack and Carrigan stayed together after the book ended?
8. Do you think food actually tastes better if you prepare it for those you love?

$\mathscr{A}$CKNOWLEDGMENTS

It is a dangerous thing to believe when you accomplish some-thing, you've done it by yourself. I wouldn't be the person I am without constant love and support from my family and friends.

Clay, Lea, Brady, and Camille . . . no matter what I do in my own life, I never feel accomplished until I look at all of you. You are the most important things. Always.

JW . . . we are peas in a pod. I remember when PapPaw died and I said, "No one will ever love me like that again." And you said, "Somebody already does." Your love for me has always been unconditional and except for our daughter and grandchildren, that is the best gift I have ever received.

Mama & Daddy, thank you for teaching me how to love and accept people. I don't know anyone else with the heart of Christ like both of you have. I am so thankful to be your baby.

Steve, Candy, Kristen, Adam, Indy, Logan in Spirit, Joshua, Stacy, Carrie, Blake, Luke, Allie, Becky, Heather, Joe,

Seth, Baby Kate, Zach, and Conan . . . the happiest times in my life are when all of us are together.

Kay, I seriously won the sister-in-law lottery with you. I know over the years you have HAD to look at me and shake your head sometimes, but the only thing I ever found at your house was acceptance. I love you and appreciate you. Keep my boy, Tom, away from anything sharp.

Greg, I have learned so much from listening to the way you think and watching how you live. I am grateful for the lessons. Thank you for the blanket of calm you sometimes spread over my angst.

Emily Jo. . . . unlike the previously mentioned folks . . . you didn't HAVE to love me. You chose to. I will be eternally grateful for that.

Michelle, thank you for bringing style & grace to my life, which comes to you so effortlessly.

Janelle, Em & I love you. You have the strength of Hercules and a heart of gold.

Joann, I have just these words for you. Thank you. . . . for both of them. They were so very loved.

Cindy, you have been my friend for as far back as I can remember. Our lives have mirrored themselves in hundreds of ways. Even when we're far apart, I know you're just a phone call away. You'll never know how much that means to me.

Darlene, thank you for being my friend and for being my computer-smart friend. You've saved me more than once.

Davis . . . you are a gem. I appreciate your love and loyalty. Back at you, brother.

And Scott, the smartest man I have ever known, thank you for being my perspective guru. I always leave our conversations thinking, *he made perfect sense.* You are a true friend.

ABOUT THE AUTHOR

Celeste Fletcher McHale lives on her family farm in Central Louisiana, where she enjoys raising a variety of animals. Her hobbies include writing, football, baseball, and spending much time with her grandchildren.